A VOTE OF CONFIDENCE

 This Large Print Book carries the
Seal of Approval of N.A.V.H.

THE SISTERS OF BETHLEHEM SPRINGS, BOOK 1

A VOTE OF CONFIDENCE

ROBIN LEE HATCHER

THORNDIKE PRESS

A part of Gale, Cengage Learning

GALE
CENGAGE Learning™

Detroit • New York • San Francisco • New Haven, Conn • Waterville, Maine • London

GALE
CENGAGE Learning™

Copyright © 2009 by RobinSong, Inc.
All Scripture quotations, unless otherwise indicted, are taken from the Holy Bible, King James Version.
Thorndike Press, a part of Gale, Cengage Learning.

Thorndike Press® Large Print Christian Fiction.
The text of this Large Print edition is unabridged.
Other aspects of the book may vary from the original edition.
Set in 16 pt. Plantin.
Printed on permanent paper.

LIBRARY OF CONGRESS CATALOGING-IN-PUBLICATION DATA

Hatcher, Robin Lee.
  A vote of confidence / by Robin Lee Hatcher.
    p. cm. — (Thorndike Press large print Christian fiction)
  (The sisters of Bethlehem Springs ; 1)
  ISBN-13: 978-1-4104-1858-6 (alk. paper)
  ISBN-10: 1-4104-1858-8 (alk. paper)
  1. Frontier and pioneer life—Idaho—Fiction. 2. Idaho—History—20th century—Fiction. 3. Large type books. I. Title.
  PS3558.A73574V68 2009b
  813'.54—dc22   2009017236

Published in 2009 by arrangement with The Zondervan Corporation, LLC.

ACKNOWLEDGMENTS

With much appreciation to all the people at Zondervan who work so hard to bring my books to readers. Without my publisher, editors, designers, and marketing and publicity people, these stories would be nothing more than entertainment for myself.

Many waters cannot quench love,
neither can the floods drown it.
Song of Solomon 8:7

ONE

Idaho, May 1915

The Torpedo Runabout cut the corner from Shenandoah Street onto Wallula Street, driving over two of the boarding house's rose bushes in the process. The automobile then weaved dangerously close to Guinevere Arlington's white picket fence.

With a gasp, Gwen jumped up from the porch swing.

In the nick of time, the Model T Ford veered away from her fence, avoiding disaster.

"Hello, ladies." The driver tipped his hat to Gwen and her sister as if nothing was amiss.

"And there goes our next mayor." Cleo shook her head and cast a look of despair at Gwen. "Ten o'clock in the morning and drunk as a skunk. Can you imagine him holding the reins of government?"

"No, I can't." Gwen sank onto the porch

swing again. "Hiram Tattersall is a fool, not to mention his penchant for strong spirits."

Cleo crossed one booted foot over another as she leaned against the porch railing. "Why don't you run for office, Gwennie? Not a reason in the world you couldn't do it."

"Me?" Gwen looked at her twin in disbelief.

"Of course you. There's nothing in the law that says a woman can't be the mayor of our fair town. You're a nicer person than Mayor Hopkins, the old coot —"

"Cleo. Don't be unkind."

"I'm sorry. I know he's sick or we wouldn't be having this special election. But he hasn't done a single, solitary thing of worth while he's been mayor, and everybody knows Tattersall will be an even worse mayor than Hopkins."

"I have no qualifications for political office."

"And Tattersall does? You'd do a better job than Hopkins and Tattersall put together. Folks like you." Cleo winked. "Especially the men, pretty as you are."

Gwen wasn't amused. "If I were to run, I wouldn't want to be elected for my appearance."

"So don't let that be why. You got that

fancy education burning to be put to use. Why not let folks see you're as full of information as a mail-order catalog?"

It was a ridiculous idea. Gwen had no intention of running for mayor. She was content giving piano lessons to the children of Bethlehem Springs and writing her columns for the local newspaper.

Cleo drank the last of her iced tea, set the glass on the porch floor, and pushed off from the railing. "I'd best get back to the ranch. I've got a load of chores still to be done." She slapped her floppy-brimmed hat onto her head, covering her mop of short, strawberry-blonde curls. "You'd be doing this town a favor if you were its mayor. We could use a little forward thinking, if you ask me."

Gwen smiled as she rose from the swing. "Darling Cleo, I could never be as forward thinking as you."

"Ha!"

Gwen followed her sister off the porch and around to the back of the house where Cleo's pinto was tethered to a post. Cleo stopped long enough to give Gwen a hug and a kiss on the cheek, then untied her horse, grasped the saddle horn, and swung into the seat. "You think about it, Gwennie. I'm telling you. It's the right thing to do.

You pray and see if the Lord doesn't agree with me." With a tug on the brim of her hat, she twirled her horse away and cantered down the street.

Gwen shook her head. Cleo could come up with the most outlandish ideas. Imagine: Gwen Arlington, mayor of Bethlehem Springs. It was preposterous. Not that she didn't believe women should serve in public office. She did, and she was glad she lived in a state where women had the right to vote. But she had no political ambitions.

With a sigh, she returned to the front porch and settled onto the cushioned seat of the swing, giving a little push with her feet to start it in motion.

The air smelled of fresh-turned earth, green grass, and flowers in bloom. The mountains of southern Idaho were enjoying warm weather, although snow could be seen on the highest peaks to the north and east of Bethlehem Springs.

Gwen loved this small town. She loved her neighbors, the children who came for lessons, the women in her church sewing circle. She loved the long, narrow valley, the river that flowed through it, and the tree-covered mountains that overlooked it all. She loved the sense of the old West and the new century that surrounded her, horses and automobiles, outhouses and indoor plumbing, wood-burning stoves and electric lights.

Her mother, Elizabeth Arlington, hadn't felt the same about Idaho. She despised everything about it, so much so that after four years of marriage, she'd left her husband and returned to her parents' home in Hoboken, New Jersey, taking two-year-old Gwen with her.

"Be thankful, Guinevere," her mother said on many an occasion over the years, "that your father allowed you to come with me. We're alike, you and I. We need society and fine culture. Think of the advantages you've had that poor Cleopatra has gone without. The opera and the theater. Fine schooling. You would never be suited to live in that backwater town where your father chose to settle."

But her mother was wrong. Bethlehem Springs did suit Gwen — a truth she discovered soon after her arrival in Idaho seven years before. At the age of twenty-one, and with the reluctant blessing of her mother, she had come to Idaho to meet the father and sister she couldn't remember. She hadn't intended to stay, but in a few short weeks she'd fallen in love with the area. Her heart felt at home here as it never had in

New Jersey.

A frown puckered her forehead. What would happen to Bethlehem Springs if Hiram Tattersall became its mayor? He wouldn't try to better their schools or improve roads or help those who had lost jobs due to mine closings. And if the governor of the state succeeded in passing Prohibition in Idaho, as many thought he would, Tattersall wouldn't enforce it in Bethlehem Springs. She was convinced of that.

I would do a better job than he would.

But of course she had no intention of running for mayor.

No intention whatsoever.

Morgan McKinley wanted nothing more than to punch that artificial smile off Harrison Carter's face.

"You'll have to wait until after the election, Mr. McKinley. I'm sorry. The new mayor and the county commissioners must be in agreement on these matters."

Before Morgan did something he would regret — something that would get him tossed into the jail one floor below — he bid a hasty farewell and left the commissioner's chambers. When he exited the municipal building, he paused on the sidewalk long enough to draw a calming breath.

14

Harrison Carter had delayed this decision for personal reasons, not for anything to do with an election. Several times over the past year, the commissioner had offered to buy the land where New Hope was being built. If he thought these delays would change Morgan's mind about selling, he was in for a big disappointment.

With a grunt of frustration, he turned and headed for his automobile, parked on the west side of the sandstone building. Fagan Doyle, Morgan's business manager and good friend, leaned against the back of the car, his pipe clenched between his teeth.

"Well?" Fagan cocked an eyebrow.

Morgan shook his head.

"Then I'll be asking what it is you mean to do about it?"

"I don't know yet."

Morgan got behind the wheel of the Model T while Fagan moved to the crank. Once the engine started, Fagan slid into the passenger seat and closed the door. Morgan turned the automobile around and followed Main Street out to the main road, thankful his friend didn't ask more questions. He needed to think.

Occasional complications and delays were expected when a man undertook a large building project, but this felt different. Morgan had half expected Harrison to ask for money under the table, but that hadn't happened. Just as well since Morgan wasn't the sort who bribed public officials. Nor allowed himself to be blackmailed by them. Not under any circumstance.

Twenty minutes later, the touring car arrived on the grounds of what would one day be a unique resort — the New Hope Health Spa. The main lodge had taken shape at the upper end of the compound. Morgan no longer needed to study the architectural renderings to imagine what it would look like when finished.

He wished his mother had lived to see it. This spa had been her dream before it became his.

Before the automobile rolled to a stop, the site foreman, Christopher Vance, ran toward them. "Morgan, we've got a problem."

Another one? "What is it?"

"The dam on Crow's Creek. It's leaking. I'm not sure it'll hold. I've got a crew up there now working on it."

Morgan's gaze shifted toward the narrow road at the east end of the compound. About a mile up they'd built the dam that would provide and control the cold water used in conjunction with the natural hot water from the springs.

16

"I'd better see it for myself. Hop in," he said to the foreman, "and we'll drive up there."

If that dam broke, a good portion of the resort compound could end up covered in several inches of water. Not the end of the world, but it would stop construction until things dried out. Another delay.

"Somebody did this, Morgan," Christopher said. "It's no accident."

He frowned at his foreman. "Are you sure?"

"Sure enough."

Why would anyone want to sabotage the dam? It was deep into his property, and he hadn't diverted water that was needed by anyone else. No farmers or ranchers were dependent upon the flow of Crow's Creek. He'd made sure of that.

Could Harrison Carter be behind it?

On her way to the *Daily Herald* with her latest article, Gwen stopped by the mercantile to inquire about Helen Humphrey. The poor woman had suffered with severe back pain for more than two months, and nothing she'd tried had relieved it.

"The doctors say rest is the only thing that'll help," Bert Humphrey told Gwen. "And even then they're not sure she'll ever be without pain. Maybe the health spa that fellow's building will do her some good. Nothing else has. Not that we could afford it. Something that fancy's bound to cost more than we could come up with."

"I'm so sorry to hear you don't have better news, Mr. Humphrey. But, no matter what it costs, do you really believe taking the waters would help her? I'm afraid I'm somewhat skeptical."

"I don't know. I'd try just about anything at this point."

Gwen offered a sympathetic smile. "Please tell Helen I'll make some of my chicken and dumplings and bring it over."

He swept a hand over his balding head. "She hasn't had much appetite, but I know we'll be glad for it, all the same."

"I'll keep her in my prayers."

"We'd appreciate it."

Gwen bid the proprietor a good day, then left the store. As she walked along Wallula Street toward the newspaper office, her thoughts remained on the resort. There were varying feelings in Bethlehem Springs about the construction of the spa ten miles to the north. Many people thought it would be good for the town; quite a few local men were already employed as carpenters and general laborers. Other townsfolk thought the resort would change Bethlehem Springs for the worse, bringing in too many outsiders. Of course, there were a few in town who thought the spa would fail, so what did it matter?

Gwen didn't know what to believe. She'd never frequented a spa, although she had gone with Cleo a few times to sit in one of the natural hot springs on their father's ranch. Enjoyable, to be sure, but was it a cure for physical ailments? For all she knew, McKinley was a snake oil salesman of the worst kind, offering a cure to the hopeless — a cure that didn't exist.

There was also the matter of McKinley being a newcomer to the area. No local had heard of him until he arrived in the area a year ago. And although the wealthy Easterner had purchased the old Hampstead home on Skyview Street, it sat empty. Folks said the new owner was at the resort site every day of the week, coming into town only long enough to send a telegram, pick up his mail, and purchase supplies. Not once had he spent the night in town.

"The time I met him, he was genial enough," Nathan Patterson, owner and editor of the *Daily Herald,* had said once. "A newspaper friend of mine from Boston says the McKinley family is among the wealthiest in America. Doesn't it seem odd that he would end up here, of all places?"

"Thinks himself too good for the likes of us, I gather." That had been Edna Updike's opinion — something Gwen's neighbor never hesitated to share. "He doesn't even go to church. A heathen, no doubt."

"Not much mail ever," Dedrik Finster, the postmaster, had said in Gwen's presence just a week ago. "He is mystery, *ja?*"

Arriving at the newspaper office, Gwen shook off thoughts of the resort and the mysterious Morgan McKinley. "Hello, Mr. Patterson," she said as she stepped through the doorway.

"Ah, there you are, Miss Arlington. I was wondering when you would have your column for me. What's your story about this time?"

"The expansion of educational opportunities for women in the past fifty years and the importance of women taking advantage of them. Did you know, Mr. Patterson, that there were only five women lawyers or notaries in 1870 but almost fifteen thousand by 1910?"

Nathan shook his head. "Not sure I think women should be lawyers."

"Why not? A woman doesn't have an inferior mind. She is as able to grasp the

20

written law as any man. Deborah was a judge in Israel, if you'll recall. And if a woman is widowed, isn't it better that she have an education and a profession that will allow her to support herself and her children rather than to be dependent upon the generosity of relatives or her church?"

"Well, of course. But —"

"But not in a man's profession?" She offered a smile, taking the bite out of her question.

"You have me there, Miss Arlington." He chuckled. "There is certainly nothing inferior about *your* mind."

"Thank you." She held out the carefully penned pages.

Nathan took them. As he glanced down at some other papers on his desk, he muttered, "Wish I could say the same for our one and only candidate for mayor. Tattersall." He growled in disgust. "I can't figure why no one else has stepped forward to run against him. The election will be here before we know it."

Cleo's words echoed in Gwen's thoughts: *"Why don't you run for office, Gwennie?"* She ignored the shiver of excitement that raced up her spine and posed her sister's question to the newspaperman. "Why don't you run for office, Mr. Patterson?"

21

"Politics wouldn't suit me. I'm better reporting the news than making it."

"Not a reason in the world you couldn't do it," Cleo's voice whispered in her head.

Gwen glanced at the pages in the editor's hands. She'd written the article to encourage women to step forward, to better themselves, to make a difference in the society in which they lived. Was it possible God had been speaking to her even as she wrote those words to other women?

Softly, she said, "My sister thinks *I* should run." Nathan stared at her.

"It's a silly notion, of course." Her heart hammered and her pulse raced. "I told Cleo it was."

Wordlessly, he leaned back in his chair, rubbing his chin with his right hand. "Silly?" A long pause, then, "I'm not so sure it is."

"You're not?" Her throat felt parched.

"Isn't a woman mayor a little like a woman judge?" He shot up from his chair, knuckles resting on the top of the desk. "Do it, Miss Arlington. Run for mayor. The newspaper will put its support behind your candidacy."

"But Mr. Patterson, I've never held public office before. Why would you support me?"

"My gut tells me you would do what needs to be done. You're articulate and well educated. You obviously aren't afraid to speak out when you see a problem the community needs to address. You've done so often enough in your columns."

She wished she hadn't spoken. She wished she'd kept her thoughts to herself.

"Do it, Miss Arlington. The town will be grateful. And I must admit it would give me plenty of interesting things to write about in the coming weeks. Never been a woman mayor that I know of." He jotted a note on a slip of paper. "I'll have to look that up. Wouldn't it be something if we were the first?"

"I haven't said I'll do it yet."

"Think about what it'll be like here if Tattersall's elected."

Gwen took a step back from his desk. "I . . . I'll want to pray about it and . . . and talk to my father."

"Of course. Of course. You do that. But I'm telling you, Miss Arlington, you should do this."

Fortunately, Christopher Vance's worst fears weren't realized. The damage appeared less serious than first perceived. By late afternoon, the crew of men had stabilized the dam on Crow's Creek. More permanent repairs would be undertaken in the morning.

Later that evening, after the camp cook had served dinner and the men were settling in for the night, Morgan walked up the draw at the north end of the compound and sat on a log where he was afforded a view of the resort site. Behind him and across from him, ponderosa and lodgepole pines blanketed the steep mountainsides. Wondrous. Awesome. God's handiwork revealed for all to see. Morgan had traveled many places around the world, seen many beautiful things, but few had come close to stirring his heart the way this place did.

His gaze was drawn to the lodge. Four stories tall, the exterior was made of logs, giving it a rugged, western look. But the interior would be anything but austere. The plans called for fine wall coverings, elegant carpets, original artwork to satisfy the senses, and large, comfortable guest rooms. The kitchen would have all the latest innovations, a place where the resort's chef would create meals for lodgers that were both healthy and delicious.

On the opposite side of the clearing from the lodge, work had begun on the bathhouse and the two pools that would be fed by the natural hot springs on the property. The bathhouse was fashioned after some of the European spas Morgan had visited with his mother — private bathing rooms with large, porcelain tubs and two steam rooms, one for men and one for women. But there would be one major difference between New Hope and those European resorts. Morgan's spa would be a place for prayer as well as for relaxation, a place for both spiritual and physical healing. In fact, he was sitting near where the resort's Danielle McKinley Prayer Chapel would stand.

"What good is physical health," his mother had often said to him, "if one's soul is sick?"

God, I believe You gave the vision for this place to my mother. Help me make it become all that You desire.

On the heels of his prayer, he thought of Harrison Carter. Why was the man set against him, against this resort? Was it all because Morgan had refused to sell the land? Surely Carter saw how the resort would benefit Bethlehem Springs. The railroad. Telephone lines and electrical power. All of which would benefit the people who lived here. Morgan knew he'd find a way to get what he needed, but it would be difficult if the town and county tied up the lands where the railroad needed to come through.

"If I had a hand in making the laws, things would be easier for honest businessmen."

If I had a hand in making the laws . . .
He stiffened.
If I had a hand in making the laws.
No, that couldn't be the answer.
And yet . . .
If I had a hand in making the laws.
Bethlehem Springs was gearing up for a mayoral election. From what little he'd heard, there was only one candidate — and not one people were happy about. Morgan was a citizen of the town. He must be eligible to declare for office.
"The new mayor and the county commissioners must be in agreement on these matters."
What better way to make certain the new mayor supported Morgan's plans than for Morgan to be the mayor. Still, that was a bit drastic. There had to be a better way. Besides, he had no desire to run for office. God had brought him to Idaho for a different purpose. He didn't have time to devote to the day-to-day administration of a town like Bethlehem Springs. Governmental bodies were a necessary evil, but not one he need be part of.
And yet . . .
He cast a glance toward the sky. "Father, is this what You're telling me to do?"

Two

The horse and buggy moved at a nice clip along the road toward the Arlington ranch. Gwen had removed her hat as soon as she was away from town, and now she enjoyed the warmth of late-morning sunshine on the top of her head and the breeze tugging at her hair.

She hadn't slept well last night. Because of her sister and Nathan Patterson, she'd had too much to think and pray about. Could she do it? Should she do it? Or did even considering it mean she was delusional?

Mayor Guinevere Arlington. It did have a nice ring to it.

Laughter bubbled up in her throat and spilled into the fresh mountain air. Oh, she must be crazy.

At a comfortable pace, it took Gwen nearly an hour to reach her father's ranch. From November through February, her visits were rare because of snow. She didn't own a sleigh, so she had to depend on the generosity of her neighbors during winter weather. But the rest of the year, she tried to visit the ranch every Thursday. She loved the drive that took her north through a narrow canyon, across the river on a wooden bridge, and into the dense forest until the road broke through into a long, wide valley where cattle and horses grazed in belly-high grass. Even more, she loved the time spent with Cleo and their father.

Griff Arlington was a tall man, lean and whipcord strong, with an easygoing smile and a quick mind. At fifty-one, his features had been leathered by years spent in the sun and wind, and his once golden blond hair — so like Gwen's own — had turned white. He was a man with a gift for storytelling, and since the day Gwen arrived in Bethlehem Springs seven years before, he had entertained her with countless tales of Indians and cattle drives, forest fires and drifters, even about how he met and fell in love with her mother. She never tired of listening to his stories.

But above all that, Griff Arlington was a man of wisdom. He didn't make rash decisions. He had the ability to look at something from all sides and only then choose the side he would take.

Today she felt in great need of that wisdom.

The bridge that would carry her across the river had just come into view when the putter of a motorcar's engine reached her ears. The gelding pulling the buggy snorted and tossed his head. Knowing the animal's fear of automobiles — thankfully there weren't many of them in the area — Gwen drew back on the reins, slowing the horse to a walk.

"Easy, Shakespeare."

The automobile rounded a bend a moment later — a black Ford touring car with a gentleman behind the wheel.

Shakespeare tossed his head and nickered a complaint, and Gwen tightened her grip on the reins. "Easy, boy." She wondered if she was about to see the elusive Mr. Mc-Kinley. That is, she might see him if she could get her horse to stop dancing in the traces. "Calm down, Shakespeare. It's okay."

The motorcar slowed when the driver saw her, but before the car rolled to a stop, the engine backfired. Shakespeare reared and started to bolt. Thankfully, Gwen had twisted the reins around her hands, prepared for this very thing. She pressed her shoes into the footboard of the buggy and pulled back for all she was worth.

"Whoa, boy. Easy there. Whoa."

Shakespeare stopped before they reached the bridge, but the horse wasn't appeased. He continued to fight her firm hands on the reins.

"Are you all right, miss?"

She glanced to her left and saw the driver of the automobile as he shot past her to take ahold of the reins up close to the bit. "What are you doing, sir?"

"I saw your horse was frightened by the backfire and about to run off with you." The man looked Shakespeare in the eye, saying softly, "Easy there. Easy."

"There was no need for your aid, sir. I had him under control." Why was it men thought women needed to be rescued? Gwen found it an irritating trait, to say the least. "Please let go of the reins, so I may be on my way."

He didn't oblige immediately. "I'm sorry about the noise startling your horse. It was entirely my fault."

"I doubt that you intentionally caused your automobile to backfire, sir. As I understand it, all motorcars do so on occasion."

"True enough." He released his hold on the reins as he removed his hat with his other hand. "Morgan McKinley, at your service. I'm glad you weren't injured. I wouldn't have been able to forgive myself if you had been."

Injured? She'd had her horse under control in a matter of seconds. He seemed to think his presence of much greater importance than it was.

Perhaps sensing her irritation, Morgan McKinley took a step away from her horse.

She gave him a nod, then clucked her tongue. "Walk on, Shakespeare."

"Good day, miss," the man said as the buggy pulled past him.

Gwen resisted the impulse to look over her shoulder. Instead she slapped the reins against the gelding's rump, urging him into a trot, and the air was soon filled with the *clip-clop-clip-clop* sound of hooves upon wood as horse and buggy crossed the bridge. It wasn't until after they were on solid ground again and had entered the forest that she heard the faint sound of the automobile's engine start up.

Morgan wasn't sure if he should be amused or insulted by the young woman's dismissal. Not that it mattered, but he would like to understand why she'd been so cool to him. He'd apologized, hadn't he? And even she'd admitted that the backfire wasn't his fault.

So why was she so rude when he'd come to her aid?

Perhaps he shouldn't be surprised. He'd known more than his fair share of beautiful women — women in New York City, Boston, Atlanta, London, Berlin, Paris, Rome — who thought the world revolved around them. And if there was one word to describe the woman he'd just encountered on this road, it would be *beautiful.* Who was she? She might at least have given him her name after he'd introduced himself.

He gave his head a shake. He had no time in his life to think about this woman or any other. An hour ago, he'd reached his decision. He was on his way to the municipal building to declare himself a candidate for mayor. His mind had swirled throughout the night and morning hours, going over the pros and cons of serving in public office. He'd done his best to resist what he felt his heart nudging him to do, but finally he'd had to give in to it.

Now that his decision was made, he planned to approach the election with the same determination he gave his business dealings. If he won, he could bring about the changes necessary for Bethlehem Springs to enjoy new prosperity. With the passage of the right laws and with the right leadership in government, more business-men could be drawn to the area. Morgan's one regret was that being mayor would take him away from the resort a great deal of the time, and the resort was why he'd come to Bethlehem Springs.

His gaze wandered to the opposite side of the river, his brain shifting gears to calculate the expense, the time, and the labor involved in laying track for the train that would — if all went according to plan — one day bring guests through Bethlehem Springs and up to the New Hope Health Spa.

He frowned, wondering again why the commissioners seemed determined to block progress. Everything Morgan planned to do could only help Bethlehem Springs. Guests of the resort would have to travel through town first, meaning more business in the restaurants, the hotel, the general store. Having rail service would benefit the towns-folk as well as people traveling to New Hope. The electrical power and telephone services needed by the resort meant Beth-lehem Springs would profit from them as well. Why couldn't the commissioners see that? Hadn't Harrison Carter told the rest of the council that without his spa — and his money — the railroad would never com-mit to building a spur up to Bethlehem

Springs?

Frustration began to churn in his chest. He drew a deep breath and released it while reminding himself that if this resort were truly God's will then nothing could thwart it. He needed to keep the faith.

"I met Mr. McKinley on the road," Gwen told Cleo as they sat on the front porch of the ranch house. "His motorcar frightened Shakespeare, so he stopped to render me aid." Aid she hadn't needed in the slightest.

"What's he like? No one around these parts seems to know much about him."

Gwen pictured him in her mind. Tall, ink-black hair, clean-shaven, well-dressed. "I hardly gave him notice. Once Shakespeare quieted, I was on my way again."

"Is he handsome?"

"I suppose some would think him so." She frowned. "But I suspect he thinks rather highly of himself." Arrogant male. "He doesn't need my admiration too."

"Gracious, Gwennie. What did he say to you?"

She shook her head. "Nothing. He merely introduced himself."

"Hmm." Her sister took a sip of tea from the cup she held in her hand. "Well, I hope I get to meet him for myself. You've got me curious now."

"Do you have romance on your mind, Cleo? Maybe you hope to catch yourself a rich husband."

"Me and some Eastern dude? I don't reckon we'd be a good match at all."

"Why not?"

Cleo ran her fingers through her hair, tousling her curls, then made a sweeping motion toward her trousers and boots. "Can you imagine me living anywhere but on a ranch?"

"I could help you with your hair and clothes."

Her smile faded. "Gwennie, that's real sweet of you. But when I meet the man that's meant for me, I'll know him. I reckon if God had wanted me to change, I would have done it by now. I sure won't change to hide the real me any more than you would. Anyways, I want a man who'll one day make my heart leap like a jackrabbit." She sighed. "I want a man whose heart will leap for me first, just the way I am."

"Oh, Cleo. Any man whose heart doesn't leap for you is a fool."

Her sister laughed again. "Right you are."

Gwen didn't laugh. She meant it.

Cleo Arlington had one of the most loving hearts in the world, but because she wasn't pretty in the conventional sense of the word, and because she dressed in pants instead of dresses and could ride and rope with the best of them, men didn't notice her as a woman.

Gwen, on the other hand, had been told countless times that she was beautiful, but no one seemed to believe she had a brain in her head. Years before, she'd narrowly escaped marriage to a man who saw her as decorative — someone pleasant to look at across the table at dinner but not someone to be heard. As an unmarried woman, she had the right to make her own decisions, the right to control her own money and her own property, the right to live as it suited her. She meant to keep it that way.

So there they sat, two spinsters — one by choice and one by circumstance — twenty-eight years of age and past their prime. Fraternal twins, as different from the other as night to day, but whose bond of love was unbreakable.

"Here comes Dad," Cleo said, drawing Gwen from her thoughts.

Their father rode his horse to the hitching post in front of the house. "This is a surprise, Gwen. We didn't think we'd see you until tomorrow. I thought you gave lessons on Wednesdays." He looked at Cleo. "This is Wednesday, isn't it?"

"Yes, Dad. But Gwennie needs some advice from the two of us so she'll give her piano lessons tomorrow. We were waiting for you to come in for lunch so she could tell us both at the same time."

"Well, then. I'd best wash up so she can speak her piece."

Griff dismounted, looped the horse's reins around the post, and strode to a water pump near the corner of the house. With a few push-pulls of the handle, water gushed from the spigot. Griff tossed his hat onto the ground before leaning over and splashing his face.

Gwen sometimes wondered what sort of woman she would be today if she'd been raised on this ranch instead of in the home of her grandparents. Would she ride, rope, and wear trousers like her sister? Would she herd cattle with her father? Or would she still prefer books, music, and needlepoint?

God alone knew the answer to those questions, for it was He who had shaped her. As the psalm said, God's eyes had seen her substance when she was made in secret.

Her father grabbed a towel off the clothesline and dried his face and the back of his neck as he returned to the porch. Once there, he settled onto one of the wooden chairs. "I'm all ears."

"Me too," her sister chimed in.

"It's about" – she drew a deep breath — "running for mayor. Hiram Tattersall is still the only candidate to replace Mayor Hopkins. Cleo suggested that I should run for the office, and I haven't been able to forget her words. I . . . I'm thinking I should do it." She looked from her father to Cleo and back again. "What do you think?"

"Yes!" Cleo clapped her hands. "Do it, Gwennie!"

Calmly, her father asked, "Do you want to be mayor?"

"Don't you think I can do the job?"

"That's not what I said. I'm asking if you *want* to be the mayor."

She hesitated a moment, then nodded. "Yesterday, when Cleo suggested it, I thought she was crazy. But then Mr. Patterson at the newspaper said he would support me if I declared my candidacy, and the more I considered the possibility and the more I prayed about it, the more I realized I'd like to do this. I think I could be a good mayor."

"What would you like to accomplish if you were elected?"

She pictured Hiram Tattersall as he'd driven over her neighbor's flowers. "First of all, I would make certain we enforced the laws against public drunkenness."

"And then?"

"Then I'd like to find ways to better our school and to bring in new businesses now that the mines aren't operating like they used to. We have too many who are unemployed. Men who want to work but who don't have any place to do so. After that? Well, I'd just have to see."

At last her father smiled. "I have no doubt you will see and do what needs to be done."

"You do?" Relief rushed through her. "You think I would make a good mayor?"

"Of course I do. You're smart as a whip, Gwen. You can do anything you set your mind to. Of course, I may be a bit prejudiced, being your dad."

Cleo slapped her thighs with the palms of her hands. "You bet we're prejudiced, but we're right too. Gwennie, I'll help every way I can. Maybe I could be in charge of your campaign. You do it. You hurry back to town and file those papers or whatever you need to do to become our next mayor."

Gwen didn't care if they were prejudiced. Their support meant everything to her.

"All right. I will. I'll do it today."

THREE

"Well, I'll be." Jackson Jones, the Bethlehem Springs city clerk, peered at Gwen over the tops of his wire-rimmed glasses. "Here we thought this mayoral election was over before it started, and now it looks like we'll have us a three-way race."

"Three? But I thought only Mr. Tattersall —"

"That McKinley fellow came in a few hours back to do the same thing you're doing."

McKinley? Morgan McKinley was running for mayor of Bethlehem Springs? But he was a stranger in this town. He owned a home here but spent no time in it. He'd made no effort to meet his neighbors or learn what mattered to those who lived in Bethlehem Springs. Why would he think he should be mayor?

"Who'd've thought it'd come down to a saloon keeper, a newcomer, or a woman?"

Mr. Jones shook his head. "Looks like it'll be a surprise who we call Mr. Mayor no matter who wins."

Mr. Mayor? Not if she could help it. Madam Mayor was more like it.

With a defiant lift of her chin, Gwen said, "It should make for an interesting race, shouldn't it?"

"That it should. Wait till I tell the missus. She won't believe it."

With a word of thanks, Gwen took the necessary paperwork and left the clerk's office, her confidence already waning. Did she stand a chance of winning now? People knew Hiram Tattersall couldn't be trusted. At least all the people who didn't frequent his saloon did. But what about Morgan McKinley? He might be little known, but he was a wealthy man from a prominent family, presumably a sober one. Would the voters choose him over her?

She recalled the man she'd met on the road earlier in the day. Black hair and piercing dark eyes. An angular face and lean build. He would cut a dashing figure standing at a podium.

But Gwen had something he did not — a desire to better her town because she belonged to it. He could be intelligent, charismatic, wealthy, or a dozen other things that might win him votes, but she had love for Bethlehem Springs and its citizens. That was something he didn't have, couldn't have.

"We'll just see what you're made of, Mr. McKinley," she whispered as she walked toward home. "We'll just see."

Gwen had reached the corner of Idaho and Wallula when she was hailed by Charles Benson, a man who fancied himself her suitor no matter how often she spurned his attentions. Perhaps she was too gentle with her refusals.

"Good afternoon, Miss Arlington." Charles crossed the street. "You're looking particularly lovely today. Is that a new bonnet you're wearing?"

"You're very kind, Mr. Benson. But no. The hat isn't new."

"Well, it looks new on you." He motioned in the direction of her house. "May I walk you home?"

She stifled a groan. "If you wish."

He fell into step beside her. "Did you hear that Gloria Birdwell is coming to Bethlehem Springs in July? I heard her sing in Boise last summer. She is nowhere as beautiful as you, Miss Arlington, but she does have an extraordinary voice, to be sure. It's no wonder she's called the Songbird of the West."

Gwen quickened her pace, as if she could out-walk the question that was sure to come next.

"It would be my great honor to escort you to the concert, Miss Arlington. Would you grant me the pleasure of your company?"

"How kind of you to ask, Mr. Benson." Thank goodness she was almost home. "But I'm afraid I must decline. I don't know if I will be able to attend, as wonderful as it sounds."

"Well, perhaps you would allow me to ask again as the time grows closer."

Everything in her wanted to say she would rather he didn't ask again, but politeness overruled. "If you wish." Reaching the bottom step of her front porch, she stopped and faced Charles. "Thank you for escorting me home, Mr. Benson. Have a pleasant afternoon."

With a nod of her head, she hurried up the steps and into the house before he could say anything more. Once safely inside, she leaned against the door and breathed a sigh of relief.

She supposed there was nothing *wrong* with Charles. He was polite, good natured, and undeniably handsome. And yet she felt no desire to spend time in his company. But her lack of interest hadn't discouraged him.

Not in the least. Charles was nothing if not persistent.

Gwen pushed away from the door and crossed to a small table set against the wall. A mirror hung above it. She stared at her reflection as she untied the netting that covered her face and held her straw hat — the large crown swathed in yellow silk chiffon — in place. It was, as Charles had said, a pretty hat, but it wasn't new or even worth mentioning.

Why was it men thought a woman's appearance required flattery? Why not ask what she was reading or what she thought about America's position regarding the war in Europe? Why not inquire about her thoughts on temperance and the chance that Idaho might become a dry state? Why didn't they care what was beneath the pretty bonnet on a woman's head? On *her* head?

She removed her hat and set it on the table, then walked through the parlor and dining room and into the second bedroom, which served as her library. A large desk filled one side of the room. She sat in the chair behind it, pulled several sheets of paper from a drawer, and picked up a pen.

"I will not be judged by appearances," she whispered. "I will make the people of this town hear me."

At the top of the paper, she wrote: *What I want to accomplish as mayor of Bethlehem Springs.*

In his youth, Morgan had lived in stately mansions, hobnobbed with the best of society, and spent his summers in Italy, France, and a few more exotic locations. He'd been accustomed to servants seeing not only to his needs but to his most frivolous wishes as well.

He thanked God he hadn't turned into a worthless fool, the way some men of his acquaintance had. He could have, if not for his mother.

Danielle Hubert McKinley had come from the finest of New York families — the Huberts, able to trace their ancestry back to English and European royalty. But Danielle's heart, filled with the love of God, had yearned to leave the world a better place for having been there.

Before her husband died and her own health began to fail, she'd taken her son — and later, his younger sister — with her on visits to poorhouses, jails, and hospitals. Many a time, Morgan had sat on a chair on the top floor of a noisy tenement house, the scent of rotting garbage rising from the street below. He'd watched his mother ladle soup into a sick woman's mouth and seen the tender way she spoke to those with dirty faces, ragged clothes, and rotten teeth. Never had he seen her act as if she were someone's better. Not even once.

Later, when chronic pain became her companion and she'd relied on others to tend to her needs, his mother seldom complained. Instead she encouraged her caregivers and thanked them for all they did on her behalf.

And to everyone — those for whom she cared and those who cared for her — she shared the hope she had in Christ. Pauper or prince, it made little difference to Danielle McKinley.

It was in the latter years of his mother's life, as Morgan took her to spas in England and Europe looking for some way to ease her pain, that the idea for the New Hope Health Spa was born. He'd seen the relief she'd found in the warm mineral waters, but had also seen that those places had room only for the wealthy.

"The poor need this too, Morgan," his mother had said. "Oh, that there would be such a place — one that welcomed everyone, rich and poor. And one where God was invited to move and to heal. Make it happen, son."

All of this went through Morgan's mind as he stood in the front parlor of the house he owned in Bethlehem Springs.

While the room was small in comparison to the ballrooms and halls of his boyhood homes, it was large enough for entertaining members of this town's elite society. And if he, the outsider, wanted to win the election for mayor, then he *must* entertain. He had only six weeks to become a fixture in the minds of the town's citizens. From now until the election, he must spend more time in Bethlehem Springs than he spent at the resort. It was as simple as that.

Fagan had informed him that his opponent, one Hiram Tattersall, was not particularly well liked. That was good news. Still, Morgan surmised Harrison Carter would not be glad to know he was running for office. If the chairman of the county commissioners gave his support to Tattersall, the election might not be easily won, despite Morgan's best efforts.

He left the parlor and went into what he planned to use as his study. A large table filled the center of the room, its surface covered with plans and drawings and account sheets he'd brought with him from the building site. After glancing at the papers, he moved them to one end, clearing the space he needed to begin strategizing his campaign.

An hour later, he had filled four sheets of paper with the chicken scratches he called writing when a knock sounded on his front door. He wished he could pretend he wasn't home, but he couldn't. His automobile was parked in plain sight. However, his visitor — in addition to interrupting his train of thought — had served to remind him of one more thing to add to his list.

Hire household staff, he scrawled before rising from his chair and walking toward the front of the house. He opened the door to find Kenneth Barker, the minister of the Methodist church, standing on the porch.

Several times over the past year, Kenneth Barker had visited the resort site. On his third visit, he'd invited Morgan to join him at the Methodist church some Sunday.

"I would, Reverend Barker, but we hold our own service here," Morgan had said. "A lot of our workers wouldn't go into town for church, but they'll sit in the tent with others while some of us share words from the Bible."

"Ah, then you care for the spiritual condition of the men in your employ."

"Yes. I do."

"I'm glad to hear it," the reverend answered. "I predict that you and I shall become friends, Mr. McKinley. I do, indeed."

Morgan had thought then that he liked the idea of becoming friends with Kenneth Barker. The problem was time. His was all used up by the demands of the resort's construction.

"Oh, good. You are here." Kenneth removed his hat. "I saw your automobile in the drive. Hope I'm not interrupting."

"You're always welcome, Reverend. You know that." Morgan stepped back, pulling the door open wide. "Come in."

"Thank you."

Morgan led the way into the parlor. "It's a bit dusty. Mrs. Cheevers cleans on Thursdays." He motioned toward a chair. "I'd offer you something to eat or drink, but I didn't bring much with me from camp and I haven't made it to the market yet."

"Sounds to me as if you need a wife to look after you, my friend." With a wink, he quoted Proverbs, " 'Who can find a virtuous woman? For her price is far above rubies. The heart of her husband doth safely trust in her, so that he shall have no need of spoil. She will do him good and not evil all the days of her life.' "

As the two men sat down, Morgan said,

"I'd love to meet such a woman." *If one exists in these modern times.* "But it isn't easy when one's moved around as much as I have." *And it isn't easy when many young women are only interested in my money.*

"Ah, but it seems you're putting down roots in Bethlehem Springs."

"Making a stab at it anyway."

"Why don't you join us at church on Sunday and you can make the acquaintance of a number of our eligible young ladies."

Morgan's mind filled instantly with a vision of the attractive blonde he'd met on the road that morning. He wondered if Kenneth knew her and, if so, if Morgan would meet her on Sunday as well.

"Speaking of our town" — the reverend leaned forward — "have I been rightly informed that you are running for mayor?"

Kenneth's question drove out all thoughts of pretty blondes in buggies. "News travels fast."

"It does, indeed. Then it's true?"

"It's true."

"Well, thank the good Lord. You may be a newcomer to our town, but I believe you'll win easily. No one thinks Mr. Tattersall would be a competent public servant. It pains me to say it, but the man is rarely sober. I'm surprised he could be bothered to complete the paperwork required to enter the race. And as for the other candidate, I'm not sure Bethlehem Springs is prepared to elect a woman as mayor."

"A woman? What woman are you talking about?"

It was Kenneth's turn to chuckle. "I guess not *all* the news travels fast. Miss Gwen Arlington has declared her candidacy for office. It's now a three-way race."

"But the clerk said nothing to me when I was in the municipal building this morning. In fact, he told me —"

"She declared for office this afternoon."

Miss Gwen Arlington. Probably one of those dour-faced suffragettes, the type he'd seen back East and in England. Not that Morgan didn't applaud their cause. He believed in equality for women under the law, as had both of his parents. Still, there was something about those radical women in bloomers who marched about with signs and chained themselves to pillars and posts that set his teeth on edge.

"Have you met Miss Arlington?" Kenneth asked.

"No, I don't think so."

The reverend chuckled. "If you'd met her, you would remember."

So he was right. Miss Arlington was one

of those unforgettable radicals. No wonder
Kenneth was glad Morgan was in the race.

FOUR

When Harrison Carter heard the news that both Morgan McKinley and Gwen Arlington were running for the office of mayor, he wanted to hit something — or someone. However, he hid his foul temper until his secretary left the office. Then he rose from his chair and stepped to the window looking down on Main Street, his hands clasped behind his back, his brow furrowed in thought.

Morgan McKinley could not be allowed to win the election. He had to be stopped. Harrison wanted him gone from Bethlehem Springs, not becoming its mayor. McKinley had to be forced to abandon that confounded resort and return to his home in the East — or wherever else he wished, just so long as he didn't stay here.

Thus far, Harrison had helped frustrate McKinley's plans, though he hadn't managed to stop them altogether. He did not doubt he would ultimately succeed in damaging the profitability of the venture. McKinley might be wealthier than most, but from all reports, he was also a shrewd businessman. There would come a time when he realized he was throwing good money after bad. That's when Harrison would step in and offer to buy the land.

Not that he cared a fig about the hot springs or the resort. No, there was something much more valuable up there: gold. Lots and lots of gold.

And Harrison meant for it to be his.

But first he must decide what to do about this election. If Hiram Tattersall became mayor, there would be no problem. The man was a fool and would do whatever Harrison told him to. But now the citizens of Bethlehem Springs had a better choice of candidates, and it was doubtful Tattersall would win. Harrison couldn't come out in support of the man. Folks would think he'd lost his mind.

That left him with Gwen Arlington.

Hmm. A tiny slip of a thing. Pretty. Unmarried. If he recalled correctly, she made her living giving piano lessons, and she also wrote articles for the local newspaper. Uninteresting pieces of fluff, in his opinion, but she would have a following of sorts. Her father owned a cattle outfit northeast of town and had some influence in the community, having lived in the area since before Bethlehem Springs was anything more than a wide spot in the road. That might give her some advantage.

Still, Harrison had no intention of underestimating Morgan McKinley's potential as a candidate.

He released a sigh. He'd best pay a call on Miss Arlington and offer his services and support. Once she was elected mayor, he wanted her to look to him for advice, as past mayors had done. He wasn't about to lose the behind-the-scenes influence he'd enjoyed for many years.

Come to think of it, Gwen Arlington might make the perfect mayor. A woman would be much easier for him to control.

Tick . . . Tock . . . Tick . . . Tock . . .

Set atop the piano, the metronome marked perfect time. Unfortunately, the same could not be said for Felicity Evans. Her fingers stumbled over the keys in fits and starts.

"Felicity," Gwen said when the pitiful performance ended. "Have you practiced your lessons every day?"

"Yes, Miss Arlington."

"*Every* day?"

55

The girl's dark pigtails flopped against her back as she nodded. Then, after a moment's thought, she shook her head. "No, Miss Arlington. Not every day. But most of 'em."

"You know you shall never be proficient if you don't practice daily."

"I know." Felicity sighed. "But after school, my friend Billy and I've been building a tree fort down by the river and I forget about getting home to practice, and then it's time to help Ma with supper and —"

"Does your mother know you're neglecting your practice?"

Felicity lowered her gaze to her fingers, still resting on the piano keys. "No, Miss Arlington."

"Your mother works hard in the bakery in order to earn the money to pay for your lessons. You shouldn't waste it."

"No, Miss Arlington."

Gwen suppressed a smile. "Promise me you'll practice thirty minutes every day in the coming week, and I won't tell your mother that you've been forgetful about it this past week." She closed the sheet music that leaned against the top panel of the upright piano. "That will still leave plenty of time for fort building with Billy."

Felicity looked up, her face beaming. "Yes, Miss Arlington. I promise."

"Good." Gwen rose from the bench. "Then you're excused."

Her student jumped up and started toward the door.

"Felicity, aren't you forgetting something?"

The girl stopped, turned back, a confused expression on her face. Then, with a grin, she grabbed the sheet music from Gwen's outstretched hand and raced out of the house, the screen door slamming closed behind her.

Gwen chuckled. Felicity was one of her less talented pupils, but she remained a favorite all the same. Gwen supposed Cleo must have been a lot like Felicity when she was a child. Tomboys, the both of them.

I wish I'd known Cleo when we were little.

Gwen closed the piano's fallboard to keep the dust off the keys and slid the bench closer to the instrument. A cup of tea was now in order. But the sound of footsteps on her porch drew her gaze to the front door before she could start toward the kitchen.

Harrison Carter removed his hat when he saw her through the screen. "Good day, Miss Arlington."

"Mr. Carter." She moved toward the entry.

Her guest — they were acquainted, although she didn't know him well — was a tall man of about forty with a distinguished sprinkling of silver in his thick, dark hair and a thin mustache riding his upper lip. His striped necktie, silk waistcoat, and leather shoes said he liked fine clothing, and his generous waistline proved he enjoyed fine foods.

"I hope I'm not intruding," he apologized when she reached the door.

"Not at all. I just finished with my last student for the day."

He glanced over his shoulder. "I believe that was Myrna Evans's youngest who ran past me on the walk."

"Yes."

His gaze met hers again. "I've come to see you about the mayoral election."

"Oh?"

Despite receiving encouragement from her father and sister as well as Nathan Patterson, Gwen couldn't expect everyone to be pleased when they learned she was running for public office. This was the twentieth century, but some folks remained stuck in the Victorian Age. Not everyone believed women were capable of filling roles traditionally held by men. She supposed —

"If I'm not being too presumptuous, Miss Arlington, I'd like to offer you my support."

Gwen managed to keep her mouth from

falling open in surprise. While she didn't know the councilman more than to say hello on the street, he seemed the sort of take-charge man who would not take kindly to a woman mayor.

"Could we sit down and talk awhile?" he asked.

She felt heat rising up her neck and into her cheeks. "Forgive me, Mr. Carter." She opened the screen door. "Please come in."

"If you don't mind, could we sit on your porch? The weather is exceptionally fine to-day."

"Of course." She stepped outside and led the way toward the painted chairs near the north corner of the house.

Once they were both seated, Harrison rested his hat on his right knee and gave her a smile. "I confess I was taken by surprise when I learned you planned to run for office, Miss Arlington. I was also greatly relieved. Hiram Tattersall is not qualified to be our mayor."

If that's how he felt, why hadn't he declared himself a candidate?

"I know what you're thinking," he said, "and the answer is simple. I promised my wife I wouldn't run for mayor."

She felt herself blushing a second time, wishing her thoughts hadn't been so easily guessed.

"Between my commissioner duties and my law practice, my wife and children see too little of me as it is. And to be frank, the mayor's salary would not provide adequately for the Carter household. However, I care a great deal that the right person be elected mayor, which is why I intend to back you."

"But you don't know me, sir. Not well. Why do you think I'm the right candidate?"

He appeared to give her question deep thought before answering, "To be frank, Miss Arlington, I'm sure there are several men in this town more qualified than you. You are young and have no experience in matters of city government. However, you are not a drunkard as is Mr. Tattersall, and you are not an outsider as is Mr. McKinley. You are involved in the community already, as evidenced by your articles in the *Daily Herald,* and this area has been your father's home, if not yours, for more than thirty years." He cleared his throat before adding, "With the proper guidance from men who do have experience, I'm sure you will serve our town well."

Gwen should appreciate his words more than she did. He hadn't spoken anything but the truth. And yet there was something off-putting about his manner. He was polite, yes, and yet overbearing too. Presumptuous, even.

"Whatever assistance you need, Miss Arlington — whether before the election or afterward — rest assured I will gladly render it. In fact, my wife and I would like to have a supper party in your honor. Our way of endorsing your candidacy."

"That's very good of you."

"Not at all. It's important that I do this. I am not without influence in Bethlehem Springs, so my support will start your campaign on solid footing. And while I believe you're the better candidate, we mustn't take anything for granted."

"I won't." She sat a little straighter in her chair.

"Good." Harrison stood and set his hat on his head. "Then shall we make that supper for next Friday evening? I'll have Susannah come see you about the details."

"Yes. Of course. Whenever it is best for you and Mrs. Carter."

"Good. Good. Then I'll be going. And remember, Miss Arlington. Whatever assistance I might render is yours. You need only ask. I am here to advise you." He gave a brief bow at the waist, then turned and walked away.

I should be grateful for his offer of support.

She frowned. *So why don't I feel grateful?*

Inez Cheevers rested her folded hands on her ample belly. "My word, Mr. McKinley. If this don't beat all. Of course I'll be glad to do more than the occasional cleaning. And if you don't mind me saying so, it'll be good to see this house lived in like it was meant to be." She gave an emphatic nod of her head. "You leave it to me to find you the rest of the servants you'll require. I've got some folks in mind who I think will suit."

"Your assistance is greatly appreciated, Mrs. Cheevers."

"Saints alive! I do believe this election could get exciting."

Morgan smiled at her. "I hope I'll have your vote."

Inez — a short, plump woman with gray hair that resembled a bird's nest, wisps flying in all directions — held herself erect, her expression serious. "How a person votes is a private matter. You should know that."

"You're so right, Mrs. Cheevers. I should know that." He chuckled. "I promise never to ask you again."

Her smile returned. "Well, I had best be about my business then. You can expect me here first thing in the morning. Oh, will you want any of the staff to live in?"

The McKinley home of Morgan's youth had employed a large household staff — butler, cook, housekeeper, housemaids, footmen. Servants abounded when he and his mother stayed in hotels and spas in England and on the Continent. But since coming West, Morgan had become used to seeing to his own needs. He slept on a cot in a tent like the rest of the men. He washed and mended his own clothes too. Fortunately, there was a cook at the work site. They all ate better because of it. It would take some getting used to, living in town and having a full staff there to cater to his needs.

"I think you should, sir," Inez stated, drawing him from his musings.

He nodded. "Do as you think best, Mrs. Cheevers."

"Thank you, sir, for your faith in me."

After the housekeeper left, Morgan went into the kitchen. He stared at the stove, hungry but unwilling to cook. This seemed like a good time to visit one of the three restaurants in town. He could eat a good meal and possibly even shake a few hands. No time like the present to start his campaign.

It was a pleasant time of day for a walk.

Everything seemed softer at this midpoint between afternoon and evening. As Morgan made his way along Skyview Street and down the hillside toward the center of town, he considered the odd twists of fate that had brought him to Bethlehem Springs.

If his father, the man Morgan had admired most in all the world, hadn't died at the age of forty-five.

If his mother hadn't suffered for years with chronic pain.

If Morgan hadn't seen the spas of Europe that catered to the privileged.

If he hadn't talked to so many doctors and nurses in so many places and come away with so few answers.

If he hadn't met Fagan Doyle, a man familiar with the American West.

If God hadn't planted the desire in his heart to bring help and hope to the hurting.

Lost in thought, Morgan almost walked past the South Fork Restaurant, a modest-sized eatery located between the office of the *Daily Herald* and a ladies' hat shop. He might not have stopped if it weren't for the delicious odors wafting through the open doorway.

When he stepped inside, he took quick note of about half a dozen other diners, but then his gaze settled on the woman at a table at the far end of the restaurant. It was her — the woman he'd come upon on the road yesterday morning. She glanced up, saw him looking at her, and frowned. Then she quickly lowered her gaze.

Not exactly the response he would have hoped for.

"Good evening, sir," a waitress in a black dress and white apron said to him as she approached. "One for supper?"

"Yes."

She led the way to a table and placed a menu on the red and white checked tablecloth. "The special tonight is meat loaf with green peppers and onions."

"Sounds good." He sat down, removed his hat, and set it on the chair next to him. "I'll have that."

After the waitress walked away, Morgan looked again toward the attractive blonde, eating her supper. Eating alone. There must be something wrong with the men of this town to allow that to happen.

Behind him, the waitress greeted another customer. A moment later, he heard his name.

"Good evening, Mr. McKinley."

He looked up at the man now standing to his left. "Mr. Patterson." He offered his hand to the owner and editor of the *Daily*

Herald. "Good to see you." With a tip of his head, he motioned toward the chair opposite him. "Would you care to join me?"

"Don't mind if I do." The newspaperman sat down.

"This meeting is fortuitous. I planned to visit you tomorrow to discuss some advertising."

Nathan Patterson lowered his voice. "If it has to do with your campaign, then maybe we'd best wait to discuss it at my office. No point sharing your ideas with your opponent."

"My opponent?" Morgan looked around the restaurant a second time. He didn't know Tattersall was in here. Failing to find the saloonkeeper, he looked back at Nathan.

The newspaperman's eyes widened and then he started to laugh.

"What's funny?" Morgan asked.

"You don't know, do you? You really don't know?"

"What?"

Nathan rose to his feet, took three steps toward the young woman who had captured Morgan's interest not once but twice. "Excuse me for interrupting, Miss Arlington, but I'd like to introduce you to Mr. Morgan McKinley."

Morgan caught his breath. *She* was his

opponent? She didn't look *anything* like what he'd expected. Where was the radical, wild-eyed suffragette he'd had in mind? This couldn't be Gwen Arlington. Couldn't be the woman running against him for mayor.

"How do you do, Mr. McKinley. I believe we crossed paths yesterday morning on the road."

"I remember." He stood. "It's a pleasure to make your acquaintance, Miss Arlington."

She smiled, the sort of acknowledgment that made a man's brain turn to mush. "The real pleasure will be when I trounce you in the election, sir." Her words dripped with honeyed sweetness, but her blue eyes told him she was deadly serious.

Morgan was not the sort of man to shy away from a challenge, not even one uttered by such a beautiful opponent. "We shall see, Miss Arlington. We shall surely see."

FIVE

" 'We shall see, Miss Arlington,' " Gwen muttered as she turned slices of bacon in the skillet with a fork. " 'We shall surely see.' " She sniffed. "Yes, we shall, Mr. Mc-Kinley."

She'd slept little during the night, her thoughts turning again and again to her brief meeting with Morgan McKinley at the restaurant. The best part about it had been his surprise when he learned who she was. Whatever he'd expected in his opponent, it wasn't her. That pleased her, for it meant he'd been thrown off guard when Nathan introduced her. She wanted to keep him that way.

She took a plate from the cupboard and eating utensils from the sideboard and set them on the counter. Returning to the stove, she scooped the bacon from the skillet, drained off the extra grease, then scrambled an egg in the center of the pan.

Morgan McKinley's most striking feature, Gwen thought now, were his eyes. Such a dark brown they were. Almost black. He also had strong features — high forehead, long nose, angled jaw — and there was something about his mouth that made her think he must smile often. It was a handsome smile, to be sure.

Of course, this analysis of his appearance was merely so she might best him in the election. She had to weigh his pros and cons. Knowing his good looks might increase his appeal, especially among women voters, was something she had to expect and overcome.

She carried her breakfast plate to the table and sat down in her accustomed chair. Bowing her head and closing her eyes, she silently asked the Lord's blessing on her meal, then added a request for wisdom for the day.

"And confidence, Lord," she whispered. "Keep me confident."

When Nathan had sat at Morgan's table yesterday, a chill had shot through Gwen. Nathan had promised to back her in the election, but that had been before Morgan declared his candidacy. Now she wondered if the newspaperman had changed his mind. If so, running for office could be an exercise in futility.

"Lord, don't let me waver or begin to fear. Please guide my words and my steps."

She inhaled deeply and reminded herself that the election wouldn't be over until it was over. Until then, she would do all she could to ensure that she won.

The first item on the day's agenda was to go to the paper and speak to Nathan. Even if he chose to back another candidate, he was still a fair journalist. He would want to interview her, get her opinions on matters of interest to the voters of Bethlehem Springs. And he would want her to place advertisements in his paper as well.

Gwen finished eating her breakfast, washed the dishes, and then went into her bedroom to dress for the day. From her wardrobe, she chose a rather austere brown and white dress and a pair of brown shoes. After sweeping her hair atop her head and fastening it with pins, she covered it with a short-brimmed straw hat. She wanted her appearance to speak for her: intelligent, businesslike, serious, able to lead. She thought she'd succeeded.

With another quick prayer for God to go before her, she set off for the center of town.

Morgan was headed for the newspaper office when he saw Gwen Arlington approach from the opposite direction. He stopped to observe her just as she paused to speak to a mother and child on the sidewalk. After a brief exchange with the woman, Gwen leaned down to address the child. A moment later, her laughter carried to him on the breeze.

An angelic sound.

The thought alarmed him. He didn't want to be derailed by her laughter or her beauty. He had work to accomplish. Besides, Morgan had learned the hard way that external beauty often didn't translate into beauty of the soul. His personal "hard way" was named Yvette Dutetre. Exquisite, passionate, emotional Yvette. His former fiancée. She'd loved his money more than him, and when she betrayed him the hurt had gone deep.

He pushed the memories away as he resumed walking. That was all long ago and mattered not at all to him now.

The scent of ink and dust greeted him when he entered the newspaper office a few moments later. Nathan Patterson sat at a desk littered with paper and books, a pair of glasses perched on his nose, reading copy and scribbling notes to himself in the margins.

Nathan held up the index finger of his left hand without looking up. "Just give me a second."

"No hurry."

"Oh, Mr. McKinley." He set down his nub of a pencil. "Sorry. I was expecting my wife. What can I do for you?"

"I wanted to discuss my candidacy for mayor, how I might best reach the citizens of Bethlehem Springs."

The newspaperman rose from his chair. "I'll be glad to discuss different options, but you should know —" He broke off as the door opened again.

Morgan looked over his shoulder, thinking he was about to meet Nathan's wife. Instead he saw Gwen Arlington standing in the doorway. He removed his hat. "Good morning, Miss Arlington."

"Mr. McKinley." Her tone made it clear she wasn't thrilled to see him there.

"I take it we have both come to the *Daily Herald* for the same purpose. Our campaigns?"

Gwen shifted her gaze from Morgan to Nathan. "I'll come back at another time."

"Wait," Nathan said, stopping her departure. "Come in and sit down. Both of you. Please."

Her obvious determination to avoid looking at Morgan again caused him to smile. Beauty she might have, but she didn't try to use it to disarm him. He liked that about her.

Gwen walked past him, head held high, shoulders back. She sat in one of the two chairs opposite the editor's desk. Morgan sat in the other.

"All right," Nathan said. "Here's how it's going to be. Mr. McKinley, I told Miss Arlington that the paper would back her candidacy if she ran against Tattersall. When I told her that, I never dreamed, after all the weeks leading up to the deadline to declare, that we would end up with three candidates."

Morgan cast a sideways glance at Gwen. The slightest hint of a smile was curving the corners of her mouth. Well, he supposed she had a right to smile, but she hadn't won yet.

"A promise is a promise." Nathan sat again. "Miss Arlington, I don't mean to go back on my word. However, even you must admit that things are different now. I want to give you and Mr. McKinley a fair shake, so here's what I intend. I'll give both of you — and Tattersall, too, if he wants it — space in the paper to discuss your platforms and what you think the mayor should be doing for Bethlehem Springs over the next four years. And then we'll do a comparison interview with me calling the shots."

That hint of a smile slipped from Gwen's lips. Morgan knew she had to be disappointed by this turn. He, on the other hand, couldn't be more pleased. It meant he wouldn't begin his campaign with the newspaper already aligned against him. He believed he could trust Nathan Patterson to be fair.

"If in the week just prior to the election it appears you two are in a dead heat and splitting the vote might allow Tattersall to win, then I will endorse whoever I believe is the strongest candidate."

"Sounds fair enough," Morgan said.

Leaning forward, his forearms resting on the cluttered surface of his desk, Nathan looked at Gwen. "I know that isn't what you were hoping for, Miss Arlington. Not even what you expected. But this I promise you: I will be fair and will remain open minded throughout the campaign. What I want most is for the person who'll be the better mayor to win. I believe that is what you must want as well."

Gwen's posture was ramrod straight. "*Do* you think Mr. McKinley would make the better mayor?"

"Not at this time." Nathan smiled slightly as he shook his head. "I believe it's up to you to win or lose the election."

"I agree. And I intend to win." She stood. "Thank you, Mr. Patterson." She turned, her gaze meeting with Morgan's. "Good day."

Morgan didn't move from his chair until he heard the door open. Then he felt compelled to rise and go after her. "Miss Arlington," he called as he stepped onto the sidewalk. "May I have a moment more of your time?"

She took three additional steps before she stopped, hesitated, then turned to face him. "If you wish."

"I hope you feel Mr. Patterson's decision is a fair one."

"Yes." She took a deep breath and released it. "I suppose it is, given the circumstances."

"You must understand I didn't know you would be my opponent when I decided to run for mayor."

"How could you have known?" Gwen tipped her head to one side. Her blue eyes studied him. "Why *are* you running, Mr. McKinley? You've only lived in the area for a year or so, and even then you've spent almost no time in town. What makes you think you know what will be good for the citizens of Bethlehem Springs when you've kept yourself a stranger?"

"That's a good question. One I plan to address when I write my piece for the newspaper."

"But you don't want to tell me your answer now."

"Well" — he shrugged his shoulders — "you *are* my opponent in this election, Miss Arlington. There's no point giving you more advantages than you already enjoy."

"It's wise of you not to underestimate me, sir, for I intend to use every advantage at my disposal."

"I never underestimate my opposition."

"Not even when the opposition is a woman?"

Morgan couldn't help himself. He laughed. "*Especially* not when the opposition is a woman."

Gwen fought the urge to smile. She wouldn't fall victim to this man's attempts to appear friendly. He didn't fool her. "If you'll excuse me, Mr. McKinley, I really should be going."

"Of course." Still grinning, he tipped his hat to her. "Good day to you, Miss Arlington. I believe the next few weeks shall prove quite interesting for us both."

It struck her then that as much as she

disliked him, he had a certain charisma, an obvious charm. It was possible he could use it to best her in the election. She would have to remain wary and alert. She would have to remind others that he'd made no attempt to become part of the community until he wanted to win an election. How did they even know he would stay in Bethlehem Springs once his resort was completed? He had no ties here, and from all she'd heard about his wealth, he could go anywhere in the world. Why should they believe he would settle in Bethlehem Springs?

No, he was not someone to be trusted, and she would *not* lose this election to him. So help her, she wouldn't.

Six

Crinkled sheets of paper cluttered the table and the floor around Gwen's feet. For more than an hour, she'd tried to write her article for the newspaper — the one that would explain what she hoped to accomplish as mayor. Everything she penned sounded . . . well, silly.

With a groan of frustration, she rose and began to pace from dining room to parlor and back again, hands clasped behind her back.

"Maybe I won't make a good mayor," she said aloud.

"Of course you will."

Gwen looked up to find Cleo standing in the back doorway.

"I'm here to help." Her sister swept off her dusty hat and hung it on the coat rack near the door. "Just tell me what you need."

Gwen lifted her hands in a gesture of confusion — or was it despair? "I don't know what I need, Cleo, but I'm certainly glad you've come."

The sisters embraced.

Looking over Gwen's shoulder at the dining room table, Cleo asked, "What's all that?"

"I'm trying to write something for the *Daily Herald.*" Gwen stepped back from her sister. "Mr. Patterson is going to run an article written by each of the candidates. It's my best chance to state the reasons why I would make the better mayor, but everything I write sounds so . . . so trite."

"I reckon you're trying too hard."

Gwen sighed. "Maybe I don't have any good reasons. Maybe I'm kidding myself, thinking I'd be a good mayor. Maybe the town doesn't need me after all."

"You've got plenty of reasons, and you're not kidding yourself. You're needed, all right."

"Once the citizens of this town get to know Mr. McKinley, I may not stand a chance."

"I swan." Cleo made an unladylike sound in her throat. "What twaddle are you spouting, Gwennie?"

Gwen sank onto one of the high-backed chairs at the table. "He has a kind of charisma. He's well spoken, well dressed, and he has . . . I don't know . . . He's so sure of himself."

"You don't say." Cleo sat down across from Gwen. "Sounds like you've had a chance to talk with him some since you met him on the road."

"Mr. Patterson introduced us at the South Fork Restaurant on Thursday night, but we didn't say much more than hello." *Not counting when I warned him I meant to trounce him in the election.* She picked up a pencil and began to sketch flowers on a sheet of paper. "Yesterday we met again at the newspaper." She remembered the sound of his laughter when he told her he didn't intend to underestimate her. Even now she felt the sound deep in her soul.

Cleo tipped her chair onto its hind legs. "Hmm."

"What do you mean by that?"

"Nothing." She brought the chair down again. "Just letting you know I'm listening."

"Thanks," Gwen said, disheartened. It was nice to have a sympathetic ear, but what she needed were ideas. Lots and lots of ideas.

Cleo stood. "Let's take a walk."

"I don't have time for a walk. I need to work on this article."

"No." Her sister rounded the table and took hold of her arm, drawing her to her feet. "You need to take a walk."

"Cleo —"

"No argument, baby sister."

Gwen rolled her eyes. Cleo was the older twin by only ten minutes but loved to pretend it was more than that. "Don't bully me, big sister," she returned, feeling her spirits lighten a little.

"Put on one of those pretty hats you like to wear, and let's take us a stroll. The weather's fine. Doesn't come any finer."

Gwen knew that look on Cleo's face. Nothing would change her sister's mind. Cleo was like a dog with a bone when she got like this.

"Come on, Gwennie."

"You win. I'm coming."

Once the sisters were outside — Gwen wearing a pale straw hat decorated with a blue grosgrain ribbon, Cleo wearing her dusty brown Stetson — Cleo linked arms with Gwen and turned her left onto Wallula Street and then right onto Shenandoah.

"You know, sis," Cleo said, breaking the easy silence. "When you first came to Idaho, I never thought you'd stay. You were so educated, so refined and cultured and all. But I was wrong. You love this place."

"Yes, I do."

"It isn't perfect, but it's ours."

Gwen could have argued that point. She thought Bethlehem Springs was as close to perfect as any place could be. So much so that she'd chosen to live in town rather than on the ranch with her father and fraternal twin. Bethlehem Springs suited her as no other place had. She loved that the streets weren't all straight lines, that they didn't run north-south and east-west in perfect, square blocks. She loved that the new mixed with the old. She loved that the stately sandstone municipal building was across the street from the livery stable with its faded red paint.

Cleo tilted her head toward the schoolhouse. "Did you know that Miss Thurber has been teaching the children of Bethlehem Springs for the past twenty-eight years? In fact, she grew up here and went to school in that same building."

"Yes, I've heard that before. We're lucky to have her. She's very dedicated. She told me she sometimes buys supplies with money out of her own salary because the school budget doesn't stretch far enough." Gwen shook her head. "That doesn't seem right, does it?"

"It sure doesn't."

Gwen paused a moment on the sidewalk, her gaze still on the schoolhouse. "Don't you think it looks a bit dejected?"

"A fresh coat of paint would go a long way in helping that."

Gwen nodded. Yes, paint would help. But the school needed far more than that.

They continued walking. As they approached the firehouse on Bear Run Road, they were greeted by a man hosing down the driveway in front of the station.

"How's everything, Mr. Spooner?" Cleo called to him.

"Just peachy, Miss Arlington. Same for you and your sister?"

"Same for us."

"That's good. Nice day for a walk."

"We couldn't agree more."

He nodded his head and returned to his work.

After they were out of earshot, Gwen said, "After church last Sunday, Mr. Spooner told me that they could have saved the Goodman home if they'd had the new hoses. He said some of the hoses on the fire wagon didn't carry more than a thimbleful of water before the seams burst. The volunteer brigade's been complaining for more than a year, but the mayor never did anything. If he had, the Goodmans would still have a home."

"That's shameful."

"Thank God there hasn't been another fire since then. The whole town could go up in flames."

Cleo *tsk-tsked* in response. A few minutes later, when they turned onto Main Street, she pointed at the High Horse Saloon. "I heard Tattersall's got a room set up for gambling in the back of that place. It's supposed to be hush-hush, but if even I've heard about it, how come the law hasn't done something to stop it?"

"Because Mayor Hopkins looked the other way."

"Uh-huh. And who's going to enforce Prohibition if it becomes the law? Won't be Tattersall if he gets elected."

Gwen stopped and turned toward her sister. "Bethlehem Springs does need me."

Her sister grinned. "Isn't that what I told you? Now you remember that the next time doubt comes knocking at your door."

"I will. I promise."

"Good girl."

Like his father, grandfather, and great-grandfather before him, Morgan McKinley was a man of single-minded purpose, one able to focus on a goal and pursue it without wavering from the chosen path. For as long as he could remember, he had been that way, both in his personal life and his business life. It had served him well during his school years, later as he'd sought healing and relief from pain for his ailing mother, and more recently, in the planning and construction of the New Hope Health Spa.

That's why his persistent thoughts about Gwen Arlington troubled him so.

As he sat at his desk, supposedly writing something for the *Daily Herald,* he recalled the sweet curve of her mouth when she smiled. He remembered the soft scent of her lilac cologne that had teased his nostrils as they sat next to each other in the *Daily Herald* offices. How could a woman appear so gentle and refined and yet be such a headstrong, opinionated, obstinate —

"Stop." He stood and stepped to the window of his study.

The last thing he needed was to be distracted by a female. Any female. But especially this particular one. He needed to think of her as he thought of Hiram Tattersall: just his opponent in this election. Think of her as he would any man who stood in his way, any man who wanted to keep him from achieving his objective.

He groaned. Even in his wildest dreams, he wasn't sure he could picture Gwen Arlington as a man.

"Excuse me, Mr. McKinley."

He turned from the window, glad to be interrupted by Inez Cheevers, no matter what she wanted. "Yes?"

"If you've got a moment, sir, I'd like to introduce the staff I've hired."

"Of course." He strode across the room, following the housekeeper out to the entry hall.

Standing near the front door was a girl of no more than eighteen, her chin tucked to her chest and her eyes downcast; a middle-aged woman with a hooked nose and the shadow of facial hair across her upper lip; and a man of sixty or more whose shoulders were stooped and legs bowed.

"Mr. McKinley, I'd like you to meet Miss Louise Evans who I've employed as the housemaid."

Morgan extended his hand to the girl. "How do you do, miss?"

"I'm well, thank you, sir." Her voice no more than a whisper, she shook his hand but didn't look up.

Morgan glanced toward Inez with a raised eyebrow.

The housekeeper shrugged, then motioned toward the older woman. "This is Opal Nelson, your new cook. She worked in one of the finer restaurants in Boise for many years, but she and her husband moved to Bethlehem Springs this year. Mr. Nelson works at the bank."

"It's a pleasure to meet you, Mrs. Nelson."

"Likewise, Mr. McKinley."

"And this," Inez finished, "is Roscoe Finch. He'll be tending to the upkeep of your house and yard and anything else we need him to do around the place. He's a fine carpenter, by all accounts, and with the right clothes, he could serve as your butler when you entertain."

Morgan tried to imagine the man in butler's attire, but failed. "Welcome, Mr. Finch."

"Thank you, sir. Glad to be of service."

"Mrs. Finch isn't here as she's in Boise visiting her sister, but she'll be taking care of the laundry for the household." Inez rested her hands on her belly. "I've given Louise the attic bedroom. Mr. and Mrs. Finch will take the room off the laundry in the basement. Mrs. Nelson won't be living in, but we've agreed she'll arrive for work each morning at six and return to her home after supper every day except Wednesdays, which she'll have off."

Morgan nodded his acceptance to the arrangements.

"Very well, then." The housekeeper looked at the staff. "Let's be about our business, shall we? Mr. McKinley has his work to do, and we have ours."

The new employees scattered, leaving Morgan alone in the entry hall. Rather than returning to his study, he opened the front door and stepped outside onto the veranda that wrapped around the house. From this hillside location, he was afforded an unobstructed view of Bethlehem Springs. And if he wasn't mistaken, he could see the rooftop of Gwen Arlington's home on Wallula Street.

Hers was a modest home made of red brick, single story, perhaps five or six rooms in all. A white picket fence surrounded a well-tended front yard, flowers and shrubs in abundance. A stone walkway led to the covered porch where wooden chairs and a swing invited people to sit and relax in the cool of the evening. He knew all this because he'd made a point of driving past it yesterday.

It hadn't taken much effort for Morgan to learn some details of Gwen's life: raised by her mother in New Jersey; moved to Idaho at the age of twenty-one after graduating from a women's college; taught piano lessons and wrote occasional articles for the newspaper; devoted to her sister and father; attended the Presbyterian church on Sundays; pursued by one Charles Benson whose father owned a sawmill to the south of town. But Morgan would like to know a lot more.

For practical purposes, of course. The more he knew about Gwen Arlington the more likely he was to win this election.

And he meant to win. The success of New Hope could depend upon him becoming the next mayor of this small mountain town. He wasn't about to let a pretty face best him. The sooner Gwen Arlington realized it, the better for all concerned.

SEVEN

Gwen's favorite day of the week was Sunday.

She loved cooking for her father and sister, but even more, she enjoyed the discussions that transpired after they'd eaten their Sunday dinner and moved to either the parlor or, in nice weather, the front porch. Once settled comfortably, they shared the main points of the sermons they'd heard from the pulpits, Gwen quoting Reverend Rawlings, the minister at All Saints, and her father and sister sharing the words of Reverend Barker from the Methodist church.

Then, invariably, Gwen and her father would debate opposing points of Christian doctrine held to by their respective denominations. Cleo tried to stay neutral and sometimes acted as referee.

This Sunday had followed the familiar pattern.

Leaning against the porch rail — looking

more comfortable now that she'd changed out of the dress she wore to church and into her trousers, shirt, and vest — Cleo set her glass of iced tea on the floor. "Gwen, your roses are prettier than ever, and it's only May." She straightened and moved to the steps. "I'm particularly fond of those." She pointed to a bush near the front gate. "What color would you call that?"

"Peach." Gwen exchanged an amused glance with her father. Mentioning the roses was Cleo's way of indicating it was time for the debate to cease. "I'll cut you some and put them in water for you to take home."

She rose from the swing and went into the house, retrieving a pair of scissors from a drawer in the kitchen. When she came outside again, she saw Cleo had descended the steps and was bent over the rose bush in question, sniffing the petals.

Gwen drew near. "You should plant some roses at the ranch. They would be beautiful along the south side of the house. I could give you some starts."

"Gwennie, I just look at a plant like I'm going to tend it and it keels over dead. I'm far better with horses than green things."

"I'd be happy to show you how —" The words died in her throat at the sight of Morgan McKinley on the other side of her fence.

"Good day, Miss Arlington." He touched his hat brim. Then his gaze shifted to Cleo. "And I believe you are Cleo Arlington. I saw you and your father in church this morning but didn't have an opportunity to be introduced."

Gwen felt her eyes widen. This was the first she'd heard of that. Why hadn't Cleo told her he'd been there?

"I'm Morgan McKinley."

"Pleasure to meet you," Cleo answered. "We were admiring my sister's roses. Aren't they pretty?"

He was looking at Gwen when he answered, "Very pretty, indeed."

She felt an odd quiver in her stomach.

"Out for an afternoon stroll?" Cleo asked.

"Yes. I felt the need to walk after dinner. I have a new cook, and I'm afraid I ate more than I should have."

"I know what you mean. Gwennie's a mighty fine cook herself." Cleo stepped to the gate and pulled it open. "Why don't you come on up and meet our father? He'd probably like some male company."

Forget what their father would like. Gwen would like to kick her sister in the shin.

"That's kind of you, Miss Arlington. Thank you."

"It's too confusing, all this 'Miss

Arlington' nonsense, what with the two of us. Call me Cleo. That's proper enough for me. I'm not a candidate for anything." She led the way toward the porch. "Care for some iced tea, Mr. McKinley?"

"Yes, thank you. I would. And feel free to call me Morgan."

When that man left, Gwen was going to throttle her sister. Throttle her within an inch of her life.

She pasted on what she hoped was a pleasant expression and returned to the porch swing.

That Gwen wasn't happy to have Morgan sitting on her front porch in the chair next to her father was as obvious to him as the nose on her face. Oh, she tried to hide her feelings, but he wasn't fooled nor surprised. The surprise was that he wanted to change her feelings. He wished her to be comfortable around him. Despite being her opponent, he wanted her to like him, which wasn't logical in the least.

"Thanks for the iced tea," he said to Cleo. Then, lifting the glass toward Gwen as if toasting her, he added, "It's very good."

She nodded but said nothing, the swing moving gently forward and back.

It was her father, Griffin Arlington, who

broke the silence. "You've shocked a lot of people, Mr. McKinley, by declaring for office. Some are wondering why it took you more than a year to live in that house you bought. Not to mention your appearance in church this morning for the first time."

Morgan nodded, certain there was more to come.

"Living out where we do, I don't have a vote in town affairs, and you don't owe me an explanation if you don't want to give one. But I'd sure like to know why you came to Bethlehem Springs. Seems to me there must be plenty of other places to build that resort of yours. This isn't the only one with hot springs."

"That's a fair question, Mr. Arlington, and I don't mind answering it. I had a number of sites to consider, several of which would have been suitable places to build the resort. All of them had benefits and drawbacks, including the one north of here."

He decided against saying he believed God directed him to build in Idaho. People usually wanted more concrete explanations than that, and so that's what he gave them. "But after weighing every factor, I came to believe this would prove to be the most successful site."

Gwen shifted on the swing. "You think it

will be the most profitable location." Her words seemed to be half-question, half-statement.

"Success isn't always measured by profits, Miss Arlington. But yes, I do believe the resort will turn a profit." Morgan leaned back in his chair. "And, I might add, it will do a world of good for the town too."

"I don't imagine very many of our citizens could afford to stay at your resort."

Should he tell her what his mother, before her death, had envisioned for this spa? No, he didn't think he would share that information. For the moment they were adversaries, and he'd best remember it.

Breaking the silence, Cleo said, "So tell us what your resort's going to do for Bethlehem Springs."

"That's easy enough, Miss Arlington."

She shook her head. "Call me Cleo. Remember?"

"Cleo." He smiled at her. "The resort is already employing a number of men during the construction phase. Carpenters. Bricklayers. Stonemasons. General laborers. And when it's time for our opening, we'll need maids, bellmen, waiters and waitresses for the restaurant, a chef and chef's assistants, attendants who will work in the bathhouses, masseurs, stable boys, a physician, a couple of therapists, and several nurses." He lifted his hands, palms up. "As you can see, we'll need many, many people to work at New Hope, and I naturally hope to be able to hire as many as possible from the area."

He could have mentioned the possibility that a railroad spur would be brought up to Bethlehem Springs. But that was too tentative at present. Without the cooperation of the town and county, without his ability to buy more land from them, the railroad would never agree to come here. And lack of train service would definitely be a hindrance for New Hope.

"And it goes without saying," he continued, "that the resort will bring with it a strong tourist trade, which will benefit other businesses in Bethlehem Springs. They'll come into town to attend a performance at the opera house or to eat in one of the restaurants, or they'll want to buy a new dress or a new hat or any number of things that the resort doesn't provide." He glanced from Cleo to her father to Gwen and back to Cleo again.

"That all sounds good," she said, "but it begs another question in my way of thinking."

Something told him that Cleo Arlington always spoke her mind, and he decided he liked that about her. No pretense. No gilding of the lily. No pretending to be anything she wasn't just to impress someone. She was who she was.

And if Inez Cheevers hadn't told him Cleo and Gwen Arlington were twins, he wouldn't have believed it.

"If you're all so determined about making that resort of yours a success, why are you running for mayor? Won't that take you away from the work that brought you here?"

Morgan nodded. "Yes, it will, but I have good people working for me who can manage things on my behalf."

Softly, Gwen said, "You didn't answer Cleo's other question. Why do you want to run for mayor?"

He turned his attention upon her. "Because I can do the job and do it well. And as a businessman, I've discovered that the governing bodies hereabouts are not always as helpful as they should be. They make it harder for new businesses to come to the community. I want to change that. I want to bring progress to Bethlehem Springs, and I want to see the town and its people flourish." He challenged her with his eyes. "Don't you, Miss Arlington?"

Gwen almost sputtered with indignation.

What a question! Of course she wanted her town to flourish. But she didn't believe an outsider was the right person to make that happen. The mayor of Bethlehem Springs should be intimately acquainted with the people who lived here.

"I believe in progress, Mr. McKinley, and I want prosperity for those who live here. But I don't believe you know our town well enough to make those things happen in the right way."

"Sometimes an outsider can see things more clearly than those on the inside."

Gwen felt heat rising in her cheeks. What gall! Had he no humility whatsoever? As if they needed him to rescue their town, the same way he'd wanted to rescue her when his motorcar startled Shakespeare.

He smiled.

Was he laughing at her?

"Miss Arlington, I believe I have intruded on you and your family long enough." He held out his empty glass to her. "I thank you all for your hospitality."

He *was* laughing at her. He must be, for only a blind man wouldn't have seen how he'd angered her. She took the glass from his hand, making certain their fingers did not touch.

Morgan rose from the chair and placed

his hat on his head. "It was a pleasure to meet you, Mr. Arlington. Cleo." He nodded one last time at Gwen. "I look forward to further discussions about how we might improve Bethlehem Springs." Then he turned and walked away, disappearing through the gate a few moments later.

"A pleasant fellow," her father said.

"Pleasant?" Gwen felt as if the veins in her temples might explode. "He was condescending and . . . and supercilious. Why, even his churchgoing must be to help him win the election. Wasn't this the first time he's been to your services? Isn't that what you said? What a hypocrite. Doesn't he know God won't be mocked?"

"Gwennie," Cleo said, "I think you're being a bit hard on the man. You don't know that's why he came to church. You don't want to be judging him unfairly."

Gwen looked from her sister to their father and back again. Had Morgan McKinley won them over so easily? Her own family! Well, she wasn't so easily swayed. And if he'd thought this would make her rethink her own candidacy, he was in for a rude awakening.

EIGHT

Harrison Carter folded the morning's newspaper and placed it on the table next to his breakfast plate. What he wouldn't like to say to Nathan Patterson about this edition!

"Susannah?" He looked toward the opposite end of the table. "Is everything in readiness for tonight's supper party?"

"Yes, Harrison. Of course it is."

He had not expected otherwise. His wife was the epitome of efficiency. Thirteen years his junior, Susannah had been groomed for marriage to a man of his station. Trained by her mother to properly manage her husband's household, to serve as the perfect hostess, and to bear and raise his children while doing everything in her power to please him, she was genteel, compliant, and attractive. Everything a wife should be.

Harrison pushed his chair back from the table and stood. "I'll be home in time to change before our guests arrive." He picked up the newspaper, then strode to her end of the table and leaned down to kiss the cheek she turned to him.

The Harrison Carters owned the largest home in Bethlehem Springs. It was built by a man made rich in the Idaho gold rush fifty years earlier; Harrison had purchased the three-story mansion for a song after the owner lost his fortune in the financial panic of 1893. Some men were fools — and he was glad of it. He often profited from the mistakes of others.

When he stepped out his front doorway a short while later, Harrison found his automobile and driver waiting for him. The drive to his office took only a matter of minutes, but it afforded him another chance to peruse the newspaper.

"Why They Are Running for Mayor," the headline blared. Beneath it were three articles, written by the candidates, about what they hoped to accomplish if elected.

Hiram Tattersall, as could be expected, came off sounding like the buffoon he was. Gwen Arlington's piece was articulate and insightful. Unfortunately, so was Morgan McKinley's.

His eyes narrowed as he folded the paper once again. Two things were needed. First, he must convince Tattersall to withdraw. He didn't want him taking even one vote away from Harrison's chosen candidate. Second, he needed to discover — or manufacture, if necessary — something that would discredit McKinley. The second would be more difficult than the first, especially since the election wasn't that far off.

The motorcar rolled to a stop on Main in front of the law office. The driver was quick to get out and open the door for his employer.

"Be ready to take me home at five-thirty," Harrison said as he disembarked.

"Yes, sir."

He glanced up at the sign on the building. *Harrison Carter, Attorney-at-Law.* What the sign did not say was that Harrison was an ambitious man who knew what he wanted. And that once he knew, he went after it.

What he wanted now was that land McKinley had purchased just weeks before Harrison received confirmation — confidential confirmation — that there was a wealth of gold hidden in the mountains to the north of town. If he'd known anyone else had been interested in purchasing the land, he would have made an offer sooner. But he hadn't known.

It wasn't right that someone like McKinley could sweep in here and take what Harrison had meant to be his. And somehow he must persuade McKinley this wasn't the right place for him after all.

Standing outside the main lodge at the resort, Fagan Doyle slapped the newspaper against his thigh and laughed. "Boy-oh, I'm thinkin' you'll have no easy win over Miss Arlington."

Morgan nodded his agreement. He too had been impressed with Gwen's article in that morning's *Daily Herald.* It revealed intelligence and integrity, as well as her heart. It should give her an edge at the ballot box.

Not liking the direction of his thoughts, he cleared his throat. "Bring me up to date on the construction. Anything particular I should know?"

Fagan's grin disappeared. "Sure, and there is one thing you should know." He jerked his head to the right, then turned in that direction.

Morgan fell into step beside him.

"I don't know when it happened. When everyone's workin', it makes for a racket. All the hammerin' and such. Still, 'tis hard to believe we never heard a thing."

"Heard what?"

Just as Morgan asked that question, they

reached one of the larger storage sheds — the one holding the window glass that had arrived by freight wagon two weeks earlier. Fagan yanked open the door. Morgan stepped inside and waited for his eyes to adjust to the dim light. When they did, he felt his stomach sink. Shattered glass lay everywhere.

"Not a whole pane left amongst 'em," Fagan said.

Morgan stepped deeper into the shed. Glass crunched under his shoes.

Who did this? Is it related to what happened up at the dam?

As if reading his mind, Fagan said, "Young boys up to a bit of mischief, I'm thinkin'. The shed door wasn't locked, though I promise it will be from here on in."

Morgan drew a deep breath as he turned to face his friend. "I'll order more windows as soon as I'm back to town." He stepped outside into the sunlight. "In the meantime, we'd better hire some guards with dogs to help patrol the site."

"Aye."

It wasn't the cost of replacing the glass that bothered Morgan nearly as much as the time it would cost them. Each delay piled on top of another. Sometimes it felt to him as if the resort would never be completed.

The two men headed back toward the lodge.

"Did I make a mistake, Fagan?"

"What mistake would that be?"

Morgan rubbed his forehead. "Believing I should build this resort in Idaho where I don't know anyone. Right now it seems like the whole world is working against us."

" 'Fagan,' me blessed mother used to say, 'don't be bangin' your shin against a stool that isn't there.' " He raised an eyebrow. "God almighty has spoken to your heart, Morgan McKinley. So you've told me and so I believe. Quit doubtin' yourself. 'Tis not like you."

His friend was right. It wasn't like him. Morgan usually had an abundance of confidence. Maybe the frustrations of the past few weeks had cracked his self-assurance. Or maybe he just needed a few good nights of sleep. He hadn't slept well since moving to town.

The two men completed a survey of the lodge, the bathhouse, and the pools. Morgan made some notes to himself, including one about another visit to the municipal building to inquire again about land-use permits, variances, and options to buy.

An hour later, his business finished, he mounted his horse and rode toward Bethlehem Springs. He let the gelding have its head while his thoughts continued to churn and tumble, while he worried and fretted about construction delays and vandalism and manpower and mounting costs.

But eventually the calm of the forest that surrounded him seeped into his consciousness. He reined in, bringing the horse to a standstill, and stared at the towering pines that swayed and whispered in a gentle breeze.

Then shall the trees of the wood sing out at the presence of the Lord, because he cometh to judge the earth. O give thanks unto the LORD; for he is good; for his mercy endureth for ever.

He drew a deep breath and released it slowly, the tension going with it. "Your mercy endures forever."

A Steller's jay swooped across the road only a few feet in front of him, causing the horse to sidestep and toss his head. The bird landed on a branch of a nearby ponderosa pine. A moment later, it was joined by another, their dark-blue feathers in striking contrast to the yellow-green of the pine tree's needles.

Then shall the trees of the wood sing out at

the presence of the Lord!

Morgan nudged the gelding's sides with his heels and started down the road once again.

The delays in construction were irritating but not critical. Replacing the window glass would take both time and money, but not an insurmountable sum of either. He needed to relax and trust God. Keep the faith, as Fagan always told him.

"Hey, Morgan!"

At the sound of his name, he looked around. There came Cleo Arlington, cantering her black and white pinto across the bridge. He stopped and waited for her, greeting her with a touch of his fingers to hat brim.

"Did your automobile break down?" she asked as she drew near, slowing her horse to a walk, then to a stop.

"No. The car is fine. My horse needed exercise so I decided to ride him up to the resort."

"You headed back to town now?"

"Yes."

"Mind some company?"

"Of course not."

"Dad and I enjoyed visiting with you last Sunday."

He'd bet money her sister wouldn't say

the same.

"One of our ranch hands brought the newspaper back from town earlier today. Seems to me you and Gwennie think more alike than you do different."

The horses moved forward in unison.

Morgan chuckled. "Maybe that's why she seemed so smart to me when I read her piece."

"Could be. Sure could be." She gave him a hard stare, but her smile remained broad. "Know what, Morgan? If it weren't for Gwennie, you'd have my vote. That is, if I could vote in the town's elections, which I can't."

"Thanks anyway, Cleo. It's kind of you to say so."

"Pity you'll have to lose to my sister."

"What makes you so sure I'll lose?"

"Some things a gal just knows. Especially when her twin's involved. It's a kind of special connection we've got."

He raised an eyebrow. "I heard you're twins, but it's a bit hard to believe."

"Don't I know it. My gorgeous sister, as pretty and ladylike and genteel as you please." She dropped the reins onto her horse's neck and held out her hands, palms up, then shrugged. "And me."

He immediately regretted what he'd said.

The last thing he wanted to do was hurt Cleo's feelings. "I'm sorry. I didn't mean —"

"Easy, Morgan. My hide isn't that thin. The boys at the ranch would have me for breakfast if it was." She shrugged again. "I am what I am, just what the good Lord made me. That suits me fine."

She pulled a watch from her pocket, then released a whistle. "I'd better get me a move on. I promised Gwennie I'd help her get ready for the shindig Carter's putting on for her. Guess you knew he's supporting her candidacy."

Morgan went still at the name. What was Harrison Carter's interest in Gwen? Was he courting her? Or was he just trying to keep Morgan from winning?

"If Gwen's elected mayor, those two will be working together plenty, so it's good he believes in her. And I guess there isn't anybody in town who's got more pull than Carter. Lots of folks turn to him for advice, him being a lawyer and all."

Morgan made a sound to let Cleo know he was listening, but in his mind he imagined Harrison with Gwen. A disturbing image.

" 'Course, I can't say I know Carter or his wife well myself. We don't exactly move in the same social circles." She laughed.

Morgan felt the tension leave his shoulders. "I didn't know he was married."

"Yeah. His wife's about my age, I think. Pretty. Real quiet thing. She and their two children go to mass at the Catholic church. I wouldn't swear to it, but I don't think Carter ever darkens a church door, Catholic or otherwise, except for weddings and funerals. Maybe that's why I don't cotton to him much."

Morgan didn't cotton to Harrison either, particularly now that he was showing so much interest in the election.

NINE

The supper party was only a few hours away, and Gwen still couldn't decide whether to wear the rose-pink dress or the lemon-yellow one. She liked them both.

"Oh, Cleo. Hurry up." She checked the clock on her dresser. "You were supposed to be here by now."

A voice called to her from the front of the house. "Halloo."

Oh, mercy. It was her nosy next-door neighbor, Edna Updike. The worst gossip in town. Such a difficult woman, and one who could talk for hours without seeming to draw a breath. Gwen didn't have time to deal with her now. She shouldn't have left her door open, despite wanting to let in the fresh air.

"Miss Arlington. Are you there? Halloo."

Patience. Give me patience. She took a quick breath, put a smile on her face, and left the bedroom.

Edna had her forehead pressed against the screen as she peered into the house. When she saw Gwen, she said, "Oh, good. You are at home. I was hoping to speak to you."

"How are you, Mrs. Updike?"

"My rheumatism's been acting up lately, but I'm well enough for a woman my age."

Gwen waited for her neighbor to take two steps back, then pushed on the frame of the screen door to open it. "Won't you come in?"

"Thank you." She breezed past Gwen. "It really is fine weather we're enjoying, isn't it? I was telling Mr. Updike this morning that I don't remember a prettier May in all the years we've lived in Bethlehem Springs. Of course, you haven't lived here near as long as we have, but don't you think this is the finest May ever?"

"Indeed."

Edna plopped her plump form onto the sofa. "Did you know our Lady had her pups this week? Five of them. That's a large litter for a small dog. I thought at first the littlest wouldn't survive, but she seems to have enough milk now and they're all thriving, including the runt." She looked around the parlor. "This really is the most pleasant room, Miss Arlington. You have quite the flair for decorating. So appealing."

"Thank you." Gwen sank onto a chair. "What is it you wished to speak to me about?"

"Why, the newspaper, of course. What else?"

"Oh." She resisted the urge to sigh.

"You surely are not serious about this election nonsense, Miss Arlington. Goodness, dear child. Being mayor is not a proper vocation for a woman, especially not a young, unmarried one such as yourself. Surely your father did not know you intended to do this or he would have forbidden you to consider it."

"Yes, Mrs. Updike. My father did know. As a matter of fact, he encouraged me."

Edna clucked her tongue. "I declare. And what of your minister? He has undoubtedly advised you to withdraw."

"No." Gwen shook her head. "He has not."

"Then Reverend Rawlings has forgotten his duty as a man of the cloth. He should remind you that women are never to have authority over men. The Bible says so. Women are not equipped to assume leadership roles. We are the weaker vessels, after all."

Gwen quelled her irritation. Her neighbor was in her late sixties, set in her ways, and unlikely to change her mind about anything. "Mrs. Updike, I know you mean well. Truly, I do. I appreciate your concern. But the Bible has several examples of women who held authority. What about Miriam, the sister of Moses, and also Deborah, who was a judge? Isn't a judge a little like a mayor?" She smiled to soften her words.

"That's the Old Testament," Edna responded, accenting the words with a *harrumph* at the end. "Christians live under the new covenant."

"Then what about Priscilla and Phoebe? They were leaders in the early church. I believe when women are called the 'weaker vessel,' it means our physical strength, not that we are inferior." She leaned forward. "It isn't my wish to be argumentative, Mrs. Updike, but I was taught we must never use one verse of Scripture out of context from the whole."

Edna gave her a cool stare. "Miss Arlington, you are more like your sister than I suspected." She stood. "You shall regret this. Mark my words. It will be your ruination. No man of good standing will look upon you with favor." She wagged her finger at Gwen. "Your Mr. Benson will soon look elsewhere for a bride if you persist in your current way."

"Since he is not *my* Mr. Benson, he is free to look wherever he wishes. I do not intend to marry. Not him or any other man. I don't intend to surrender the freedoms I enjoy as a single woman. Too many men in this world want a servant, not an equal partner. They don't want someone who can walk beside them rather than behind." Gwen's temper grew hotter with each word. "And I'm delighted to know that you think I'm like Cleo. There's no one I admire more than my sister."

From the parlor doorway came Cleo's hoot of laughter. "Now there's something I don't hear every day."

Edna sputtered something about tending to the puppies and hurried out without a word of good-bye to Gwen or a word of greeting to Cleo. Rather than rise and follow her neighbor, Gwen covered her face with her hands and released a groan.

Wry amusement laced Cleo's voice. "I take it Mrs. Updike isn't thrilled about you running for mayor."

"I'm doomed to spinsterhood because of it." Gwen lowered her hands. "And possibly risking my salvation."

Cleo snorted. "Gwennie, given you're a Presbyterian and of the Calvinist persuasion, you can't possibly believe that."

Despite herself, Gwen smiled. Cleo had an uncanny way of knowing just what to say to make her feel better.

"Now, what're you doing just sitting there? Don't you have a party to get ready for and an election to win?"

"Yes, I do."

"Then let's get to it, sis. Times a wastin'."

Cleo urged Gwen toward her bedroom much as she would herd cows into a corral. Once Gwen was seated at her dressing table, Cleo plucked the pins from her hair until it cascaded down her back. "Guess who I rode into town with." She began stroking Gwen's hair with the brush. "Morgan McKinley."

"Oh?"

"Yeah. He's had a hard time believing we're twins, just like most folks do."

Gwen met her sister's gaze in the mirror, wondering what else he'd said to her.

"Before we parted company, he asked if I was going to the Carter shindig with you." Cleo grunted. "As if you could drag me to something like that."

"All you would need is a new evening frock and —"

"Gwennie, haven't you learned by this time that you can't make a silk purse out of a sow's ear?"

Gwen grabbed her sister by the hand and

twisted on the dressing stool to look at her. "Don't say such things about yourself. You are *not* a sow's ear."

"Maybe not." Cleo smiled gently. "But I don't belong with the Carters and their like either. It's not just that I don't belong. I don't *want* to belong. I like who I am."

Gwen sighed. "I envy you, Cleo. You're so sure of who you are and what you want to do. I wish I was more like you."

"Poppycock. You're already who you want to be. I just heard you saying so to Mrs. Updike. You're just nervous about tonight. That's all."

Cleo took Gwen by the shoulders and turned her to face the mirror again. "Now let's get your hair fixed or you'll never get to that party on time."

Gwen knew everyone seated around the long table in Harrison and Susannah Carter's dining room — the *Daily Herald's* Nathan Patterson and his wife, Christina; Samuel Benson, owner of the Pine Company sawmill, his wife, Flora, and their son, Charles, who was seated to Gwen's right; Jedidiah Winston, the Crow County sheriff, and his unmarried daughter, Rose; Mike O'Rourke of the Golden Gorge Mining Company; Reverend Walter Rawlings;

Mayor Thaddeus Hopkins; and the four other county commissioners along with their wives. All sixteen present were dressed to the nines.

As the party dined on rainbow trout, roasted potatoes, creamed vegetables, and a chocolate confection for dessert, a three-piece orchestra — violin, cello, and harp — played softly in a nearby room. Overhead, a chandelier glittered, its glory reflected in the gold-rimmed china and fine crystal goblets. Black-and-white uniformed servants saw to the guests' every need.

Charles leaned near to Gwen. "You are a surprising woman, Miss Arlington. I had no idea you had political aspirations."

"I surprised myself in that regard, Mr. Benson."

"Please allow me to assist you in any way I can." He spoke in a husky voice, implying some sort of intimacy between them.

Why must he do that? It was actions such as this one that had made her neighbor refer to Charles as "your Mr. Benson."

She lifted her water goblet and took a sip before answering him. "That's very kind of you. Of course, there isn't much to do, other than convince voters I'm the right candidate, and that is something I must do myself." She gave him a smile, hoping it looked genuine. "Isn't it?" Without waiting for Charles's response, Gwen turned to her left and said to her host, "Thank you again for doing this, Mr. Carter."

"I'm pleased to do so. Tattersall isn't qualified, and since I'm quite unhappy with that resort McKinley is building, I couldn't very well support him."

She hadn't known Harrison opposed the resort. "Why is that, Mr. Carter?"

"I don't believe it will be good for Bethlehem Springs."

She recalled Morgan's response to a similar question. His answer had made sense to her — employment for many in the area and an influx of tourist trade for the businesses in town. Didn't everyone see the benefits of those things, even if they thought a resort would ultimately fail?

Before she could voice her thoughts, Harrison stood and tapped a knife against his water goblet. *Ting . . . ting . . . ting . . . ting . . .* The room fell silent and all eyes turned toward the host.

"I would like to thank you all once again for coming tonight." He looked at each person as he spoke. "As you know, we have three candidates for the office of mayor of Bethlehem Springs. As you must also know by now, I have given my support to Miss

Gwen Arlington." He applauded as he looked at Gwen. Everyone else followed suit. "I certainly hope you will join me, for the sake of our fair town, in seeing that she is elected."

With darkness blanketing Bethlehem Springs, Morgan leaned his shoulder against an awning post on the side porch and stared at Harrison Carter's mansion, located on an opposing hillside. Lights glowed from every window of the house, and music could be heard, even from a half mile away.

Morgan wondered if the guest of honor was enjoying herself. One thing was certain: she wouldn't be among strangers. Bethlehem Springs was not a large town. Most who lived here could call their neighbors' children by name and would have a fair idea of the personal business and romantic involvements of those they saw on the street. Townsfolk who didn't have small businesses of their own — dress shop, haberdashery, mercantile, shoe store, bank, feed store, law office, restaurants — worked at the sawmill to the south of town or in the sole remaining mine to the west. Even those who lived in the county on cattle ranches and small farms were well known because this was where they purchased supplies and went to church.

All of which meant Gwen was among friends. They would support her because she was one of them already.

Morgan pushed off the post, turned, and walked inside. Unlike the Carter mansion, few lights burned within these walls. Silence engulfed him.

Too silent. Too empty. Maybe he should invite his little sister to come stay with him again. Not that he thought Daphne would accept. She was having far too much fun traveling with their distant cousin.

It bothered him that Gwen had Harrison Carter's endorsement. He couldn't shake the feeling that the commissioner wasn't all he tried to appear. Maybe Morgan was wrong, but his instincts were usually good ones.

As for Miss Arlington? He'd believed at first she was a beautiful woman who thought rather highly of herself. He'd had to readjust his opinion after reading her campaign piece in the paper. In fact, earlier in the week he'd perused the newspaper archives to better acquaint himself with matters of interest in the town. In doing so, he'd read quite a number of Gwen's columns. On paper, at least, she came across as intelligent, thoughtful, and caring.

But still beautiful. Still very beautiful.

He pictured Yvette Dutetre as he'd seen her during the days of their courtship and engagement. Tall and willowy, with amber eyes, light-brown hair, milk-white skin, and a flawless beauty that caused men to stop and stare, mouths gone dry. Morgan knew their response because he'd been just like them. Strolling with Yvette along the streets of Paris or entering a glittering ballroom with his fiancée on his arm had made him proud because he'd won her affections.

But what he hadn't seen — what he'd missed completely during their courtship and the months of their engagement — was that her beauty was only skin deep. While he'd been falling in love, she'd been plotting how to spend his family fortune while taking another man into her bed. Discovering the truth — just one week before their lavish wedding was set to take place — had been a rude awakening.

The memory of his narrow escape still gave him chills.

He'd stayed free of romantic entanglements since leaving Paris five years ago. His mother's worsening illness and their frequent travels had aided him in his determination not to fall victim to another pretty face. But his mother was gone, and he was putting down roots in Bethlehem Springs. He had best be on his guard. Now was not the time to let a woman — any woman — invade his thoughts.

Especially not the woman who might stand in the way of the successful completion of his resort.

Sheriff Winston leaned a shoulder against the fireplace mantel. "If you ask me, Governor Alexander is asking for trouble, pushing to make Idaho a dry state. We'll need more officers all around the state if we're expected to enforce it."

"So you don't support the prohibition of alcohol?" Gwen asked.

"Sumptuary laws can be slippery things, Miss Arlington."

"But isn't public drunkenness a problem in many cities? And even here in our own small town?" Although neither of them mentioned Hiram Tattersall, Gwen felt certain the sheriff knew who was in her thoughts when she asked her question.

"Yes, we've had a few problems with it, but I'm still not convinced that the passage of Prohibition is the answer. I guess we'll find out soon enough. The governor is a determined man, and I think we'll see the law pass before year's end." He took a sip of sherry from the glass he held in his hand. "And what about you, Miss Arlington? Where do you stand on the issue?"

Before Gwen could answer, Harrison Carter stepped to her side. "I'm sure that when she is mayor, Miss Arlington will seek counsel from those more experienced in such matters." He looked at her. "It isn't necessary for you to have an opinion of your own on everything."

Gwen swallowed the retort that sprang to her lips, determined not to be rude to her host. But it was aggravating that he hadn't given her a chance to respond to Sheriff Winston. She *did* have an opinion about Prohibition. No doubt, she would have an opinion about anything and everything concerning town government once she was mayor. And she wouldn't be shy about sharing those opinions either.

Susannah Carter joined the threesome by the fireplace. Slipping her hand into the crook of her husband's arm, she leaned close to him. "Harrison," she said softly, "some of our guests are leaving."

Relief swept through Gwen. At last she could depart without insulting anyone. She looked at the mantel clock. "My goodness. I didn't know it was so late. It's almost midnight. I must go as well."

She followed her host and hostess to the front door and said good-bye to the other guests as they stepped into the night. Finally, only she and Charles Benson — who had insisted on accompanying her home in her buggy — remained.

After putting on her wrap, she turned toward Harrison and Susannah. "Thank you again for the lovely evening."

"It was our pleasure," Susannah replied.

"Indeed," Harrison said. "We want to do whatever it takes to make certain you are victorious."

"I'm grateful for your support." Then, although she hadn't realized it was even in the back of her mind, she said, "I hope we can talk soon about why you feel Mr. McKinley's resort won't be beneficial to Bethlehem Springs."

"Miss Arlington" — Harrison gave her a patient smile; it felt as if he was about to pat her on the head, like a good little girl — "I believe that's something else we can discuss after you're elected. Once you and I are working together to manage our town and county governments, I will be only too glad to help steer you through such matters. Certainly you needn't be concerned with it now." He turned toward Charles.

125

"Thank you for offering to see our guest of honor home. It's good of you to do so."

Charles stepped to Gwen's side and placed the palm of his right hand under her left elbow. "It's my pleasure, sir."

Gwen felt as if she'd been brushed aside like a bothersome fly. Besides, she didn't want Harrison to steer her anywhere. She'd only wanted to know why he opposed the resort. It was a simple enough question, one that deserved an answer.

Charles said, "Are you ready, Miss Arlington?"

Somewhat reluctantly, she looked at her self-appointed escort. "Yes. I'm ready."

"Good night, Miss Arlington," Harrison said. "We'll talk again soon."

Charles escorted Gwen to her buggy and helped her onto the seat. As he walked around the rear of the buggy, Gwen turned her gaze toward the gentle, rolling hills on the north side of town. Up there, in the shadows of the night, was Morgan McKinley's home.

She wondered what his opinion on Prohibition was — and if others would listen when he chose to share it.

TEN

Gwen awakened the next day feeling frustrated and irritated, and no matter what she tried — Bible reading, prayer, a firm mental talking-to, scrubbing the kitchen with more vigor than was normal — she couldn't seem to shake the feeling.

As her final student, Owen Goldsmith, flew through his scales and chords on Saturday afternoon, Gwen's thoughts returned to the previous evening at the Carter home. She still felt out of sorts over Harrison's unwillingness to answer her question about the McKinley resort. Had he meant to brush her aside or had she simply asked at an inopportune moment? Perhaps she was being overly sensitive. One of her worst faults was to bristle when she felt ignored by reason of her gender. However, she had earned that fault through experience. Too many men of her acquaintance thought she — and all females — should think of nothing but how to manage a home and raise children. Ridiculous! Did they believe God gave her a mind but didn't want her to use it?

"How was that, Miss Arlington?" Owen asked, drawing her attention back to the present.

"Very well done. You've been practicing, haven't you?"

"Yes'm. Ma says I've gotta play a lot if I wanna be good."

Gwen nodded. "Your mother is right." She flipped through a stack of sheet music. "I believe you're ready for something a bit more challenging. Here's a short piece by Frederick Chopin. Let's give it a try."

The first time through was slow and choppy. The second time through sounded much better. By next Saturday, the boy would have it memorized. He was such a gifted student. One day in the not too distant future, he would surpass her ability to instruct him on the piano. It was no stretch to believe that if he received a proper education, if he stayed in school through all twelve grades, his talent would take him far beyond the borders of Bethlehem Springs.

With the minute hand on the mantel clock marking the hour, Owen slipped from the piano bench, then shoved his right hand

128

into his pocket. "Almost forgot. Ma sent the money for my lessons, last week and this." He dropped the coins into Gwen's hand. "She said thanks for waitin'."

Many would not consider it a great deal of money, but Gwen knew it was a financial sacrifice for the Goldsmith family. "Tell your mother she's welcome, and remember to thank Mrs. Evans for letting you practice on her piano."

"Yes'm." He grabbed the sheet music. "See you next week." He started for the door, then stopped and spun toward her again. "Miss Arlington? You still gonna give me lessons if you're the mayor?"

"Yes, Owen. I'm still going to give you lessons."

"That's good, 'cause Ma said she wouldn't vote for you if it meant you not teachin' me no more." With that, he dashed out the door.

Gwen slid the bench under the keybed before putting the remaining sheet music into a wicker basket on the floor next to the piano. One day, Owen might play on a piano in a place like Carnegie Hall, but his grammar would need to improve before then. And that probably wouldn't happen without changes in the Bethlehem Springs educational system. The town needed more teach-

ers, more books, perhaps even a new building.

As mayor, education for the children of
Bethlehem Springs would be her top priority.

A rap on the doorjamb drew her gaze to
the front door. On the opposite side of the
screen stood Morgan McKinley.

"Good afternoon, Miss Arlington. Am I
intruding? I saw that young fellow leave,
and I was hoping I might have a moment of
your time."

She moved toward the door. "Owen was
my last student for the day."

"I heard him playing. Or was that you?"

She opened the screen, but rather than
inviting him in, she stepped onto the porch.
"How is it I can help you?" She didn't mean
to sound unfriendly, but she was afraid she
did.

If it bothered him, he didn't let it show. "I
am in need of a secretary, and I was hoping
you might be able to recommend someone."

And you couldn't ask someone else? It
seemed a flimsy excuse for this visit.

As if reading her thoughts, he said, "I
asked Mrs. Cheevers, but she had no sug-
gestions. So I went over to the church, but
Reverend Barker is on a pastoral visit to
someone who lives near the sawmill and he

isn't expected back until this evening. And then I thought of you. Since I was close by, I decided to stop and ask you."

"I might be able to come up with a few names. Give me a few days to think about it." She narrowed her eyes. "Tell me, Mr. McKinley. Do you plan to remain in Bethlehem Springs after you lose the election?"

"After?" Amusement lit his eyes. "Not *if?*"

She smiled despite herself. "After, not if."

"I assure you, Miss Arlington" — he returned her smile — "I plan to spend plenty of time in Bethlehem Springs, no matter what happens in the election."

Gwen felt as if her stomach had done a somersault. Perhaps two or three. *Gracious. What an odd sensation.*

Morgan enjoyed watching the emotions that played across her face. He almost thought she might like him a little. Or at least didn't dislike him as much as she'd seemed to in the past.

Reluctant to leave just yet, he glanced toward the chairs at the far end of the porch and asked, "Do you mind if we sit down?"

She surprised him by acquiescing with a nod, and he followed her as she walked to the porch swing. He settled onto one of the chairs. Briefly their gazes met before she turned to look at the flowers in her garden. A touch of pink colored her cheeks, and he realized that she was made uncomfortable by his staring.

To break the lengthening silence, he cleared his throat and asked, "How was the party at Commissioner Carter's last night?" Her eyes widened, and he knew he'd startled her with the directness of his question. "Mind telling me who was there? Or would that be aiding and abetting the opposition?"

Gwen shook her head. Whether in answer to Morgan's first question or the latter, he didn't know.

"Miss Arlington." He leaned forward in the chair. "I am *not* the enemy. I don't wish you ill. Surely you could see from our articles in the newspaper that our ideas and desires for Bethlehem Springs are more alike than they are different."

A new emotion appeared on her face — regret. "That *is* what I've done, isn't it? I've made you the enemy." She released a soft, self-deprecating laugh. "I apologize, Mr. McKinley. An enemy is quite a different thing from a political opponent."

"At least it is in our case. I'd like to believe we could be friends, no matter what happens in the election."

Friendship. Was that what he wanted from

her? He wasn't so sure.

"There is no reason you shouldn't know who came to the gathering last night." Gwen raised a hand to her nape and twirled a wisp of blonde hair around her index finger. "The entire board of commissioners and their wives were present. Mr. Patterson from the paper and his wife. Mr. Benson from the mill and his wife and son. Our county sheriff, Mr. Winston, and his daughter. Mr. O'Rourke from the mine. Reverend Rawlings from All Saints Presbyterian." After a pause, she added, "I believe that's everyone. No, wait. Mayor Hopkins was there too."

The guest list didn't surprise Morgan. Money and power. That's what mattered to a man like Harrison.

A frown crinkled Gwen's brow. "Are you aware that Mr. Carter believes your spa is not in the best interests of the people of Bethlehem Springs?"

"Yes, I'm aware of it. What about you? Do you believe it isn't in the town's best interests?"

"I may not understand all the ramifications." Her answer showed both wisdom and caution. Her eyes narrowed a little as she looked at him. "I know the reasons you say the town will profit by the resort, but I think I'd like to understand a little more why you want to build a resort. Here or anywhere. You haven't built a resort or a hotel anywhere else. Nor has the McKinley family been involved in those enterprises. So what makes you want to do it now and here of all places?"

Ah, she had done her own bit of investigating. Good for her.

He leaned back in his chair again. "It began with my mother's illness. I was in college when the symptoms first appeared. Periods of pain throughout her body, usually intense. A general weakness at times. At others, total exhaustion." It was his turn to look toward the flowers in Gwen's garden. "There were times when she didn't get out of bed for a week or two at a time. Different doctors diagnosed different conditions, and they tried numerous remedies. Her greatest physical relief came from the warm water therapy and massage she received at spas in Europe."

Morgan's reply didn't paint a complete picture of his mother's struggles with debilitating pain, but he couldn't bring himself to be more descriptive.

He looked at Gwen again. "But it was her faith in God that gave her the strength and courage to endure. New Hope was her dream, and while she didn't live long enough to see it built, I mean to make it a reality in her memory. The McKinleys have enjoyed financial blessings for many generations. That's what allowed her to receive the help she did. But she dreamed of a place where anyone could come. The poor who suffer from polio. The young and old who live with incurable pain. Those without faith who need prayer."

"Do you mean to say that your spa will not cater to the wealthy?"

"Not to them alone."

There was something different about the way she looked at him now. Could it be a glimmer of admiration?

Encouraged, he said, "If you'd like, Miss Arlington, I could take you up to the site next week. Let you see for yourself."

"I would like that, Mr. McKinley. If it wouldn't be too much trouble for you."

"No trouble at all. I have some obligations to see to on Monday and Tuesday. How about Wednesday?"

She shook her head. "I give piano lessons on Wednesdays."

"Thursday then?"

"I visit my father and sister on the ranch on Thursday. We like to have lunch together."

Had she changed her mind? Were these just excuses?

"But I suppose I could meet you at the resort site and then to go the ranch from there. Would that be convenient for you?"

Morgan liked the idea of a drive with Gwen seated beside him. He wanted them to spend that time together. After all, it could be beneficial. He might be able to detail more of his plans, something he couldn't do if they arrived and departed separately.

"I have a better idea," he said. "Let me drive you up in my motorcar. When we're finished at the resort, I'll take you to the ranch. It will be much faster."

"How would I get home?"

"I'll come back for you. All you would need to do is tell me when to return."

"That would be too much to ask, Mr. McKinley."

He smiled. "You aren't asking. I'm offering."

"But —"

"I'll pick you up at nine o'clock Thursday morning. That should give us ample time at the site and still get you to the ranch for lunch."

Her expression revealed her struggle as she weighed his offer. He thought for a moment that she would refuse and was surprised by the disappointment he felt in return.

A small sigh escaped her. "All right, Mr. McKinley. I'll be ready at nine o'clock Thursday morning."

"Wear a scarf over your hat." He rose from the chair. "It gets windy in the automobile."

Gwen watched as Morgan walked down her front pathway with an easy, yard-eating gait. Once on the sidewalk, he looked back and waved before heading east on Wallula Street toward the center of town.

Had it been wise to agree to drive with him to his resort? She didn't know. But something had shifted in her heart as he talked about his mother and his plans for the spa she'd wanted to build. He had seemed anything but controlling or high and mighty. What sort of man built a spa that would cater to both the wealthy and the unfortunate?

One with a kind heart.

All the same, she wasn't sure it was wise to spend time alone with Morgan McKinley. She wanted voters to elect her as the next mayor, and he wanted the same. He might not be her enemy, but still . . .

Was it dangerous to allow him to become a friend?

Eleven

Dedrik Finster looked up from his mail sorting. *"Guten Tag, Fräulein.* Good you come in. You have letter from your *Mutter."* He turned toward the individual slots on the far wall.

Gwen crossed the post office to the counter.

"Long time between letters. Your *Mutter* is well, I hope."

"I hope so too." She took the proffered envelope from the postmaster's hand. "Thank you."

"Is true, you will be mayor?"

"I want to be, Mr. Finster. I will do a good job. I hope you'll vote for me."

"I will decide. Vote very important."

"Yes, I know it is." While Mr. Finster's English wasn't perfect, she knew he was proud of his American citizenship and felt privileged to be able to vote in an election. "You should cast your ballot for whoever you think will serve our town the best." She gave a little wave. "Please say hello to Mrs. Finster for me."

"I will, *Fräulein*. I tell her."

Gwen hurried down the sidewalk toward home, eager to read her letter. As happy as she was in Idaho, she still missed seeing her mother and looked forward to hearing from her. She hoped the transcontinental telephone wires would soon reach Bethlehem Springs, making it possible for her and her mother to speak to each other. It had been such a long time since she'd heard her mother's voice.

On the porch, she made a beeline for the swing. Settling onto it, she opened the envelope and unfolded the pretty stationery.

Dearest Guinevere,

It's been nearly two months since I've written to you or your sister. I have meant to write often but have not had the opportunity until now.

Your grandfather fell and broke his right leg in three places, and even though we hired a nurse, Mother and I see to many of his needs ourselves.

"Oh, no. Poor Grandfather."

140

You can imagine how out of sorts Father is, being confined to his bed, unable to go into his office whenever he pleases. His secretary (poor man) spends much of the day at the house, despite the doctor's urging that Father rest more. Mother says she cannot see why we should pay the physician good money when Father refuses to follow any of his advice.

Gwen couldn't help but smile. She could hear exactly how her grandmother would have said those words — loving but exasperated.

Before Father's accident, I was visiting with Stuart Martin and his sister at their home on Long Island. I believe you met the Martins at your coming out. Stuart has proven quite the persistent suitor, and I believe he may be on the verge of proposing marriage to me.

Gwen noticed her mother didn't mention she wasn't free to *accept* Stuart Martin's proposal. Had that even occurred to her?

When Gwen was about seventeen, she'd asked her mother why she never got a divorce. Elizabeth Arlington had replied that she would not remove the protection of her wedding ring until it was about to be replaced by another.

"Oh, God," Gwen whispered, an ache in her heart, "please lead my mother home to You."

With all that is going on here, I'm sure you will understand why I must decline your invitation to come stay with you in Bethlehem Springs for the summer. I do miss you terribly. Perhaps it's time for you to return to your grandparents' home. You could bring Cleopatra with you, and we could spend a lovely holiday at the shore.

After Gwen settled in Bethlehem Springs seven years before, she'd tried to explain to her mother why she, Elizabeth, should come for a visit, why she needed to see Cleo and let Cleo get to know her. Gwen understood the deep hurt her twin felt because of her mother's desertion. She wanted to see healing between those two.

But in their mother's mind, she'd left Idaho — a place — not her husband and daughter. That they had remained behind wasn't her fault, just an unavoidable circumstance. There was no need, Gwen's mother had written back, for her to return to Idaho when Cleo was free to visit Hoboken at any time.

Despite her mother's selfish actions and thoughtless behaviors, Gwen loved her and tried not to judge her too harshly. Still, her refusal to visit Cleo was something she found hard to forgive.

Oh, I nearly forgot. Do you remember the Wellington boy, the young man I once encouraged you to consider as a suitor? He became involved with a woman of poor family and there was something about a child, although I never learned the particulars. Certainly he disgraced his family's good name. He took his own life last month. A shocking turn of events. It was in all the newspapers and has been the talk of every social event I've attended.

Thank goodness you had the good sense to see through him years ago. He wasn't at all what he appeared to be.

Her mother's letter went on for another two pages of gossip about neighbors and friends from her social circle. Nothing of interest to Gwen who cared little about the things her mother found so important.

Well, I must close. This is my day to join your grandfather for lunch at his bedside. His preferred topic of conversation is matters of business, which I find boring. I do hope he will be able to get about on his own soon so I can get on with my life.

Say hello to Cleopatra and your father for me, and tell your sister I will write to her soon. Sending my love.

Mother

Gwen sighed as she refolded the letter. Sometimes she felt more the parent than the child. She wanted to chastise her mother, to scold her, to tell her to grow up, to encourage her to think of someone other than herself every now and again.

"I'm sorry for feeling that way, Lord," she whispered as she slipped the stationery into its envelope. "But Mother can be so exasperating at times."

Morgan ran his gaze down the list of supplies one last time before handing it to Bert Humphrey. "May I tell Fagan the supplies will be ready for pickup on Friday?"

"Sure can. I've got everything here in my storeroom." The proprietor of the mercantile set the list on the counter. "I'd like you to know, Mr. McKinley, I'm grateful for your business. It's been a boon for me and the missus this past year, I can tell you."

Morgan acknowledged the man's thanks

with a nod, then asked, "How is Mrs. Humphrey feeling?"

"She's somewhat better. Though it's hard to make her keep to her bed, the way the doctor wants. She's used to working here in the store with me and is feeling mighty restless." He shrugged. "I was telling Miss Arlington awhile ago that it's too bad that spa of yours isn't open already. Maybe it would help her. But then, I probably couldn't afford to take advantage of it no how."

"That's where you're wrong, Mr. Humphrey. New Hope will be affordable for all. I give you my word."

"Do tell."

Morgan nodded again, even as he felt a stab of frustration. If the county commissioners, led by Harrison Carter, kept interfering, kept preventing him from acquiring the necessary use permits and land purchases, it would be difficult for anyone, rich or poor, to benefit from New Hope. Overcoming the roadblocks was the reason he'd decided to run for mayor. Running for mayor meant opposition to Gwen Arlington. And Gwen — with the lovely hair that curled into tiny fish hooks at her nape and the soft-scented cologne that wafted about his nostrils whenever he drew close to her — was the reason he hadn't slept much for the last two nights.

Two more customers entered the store, bringing a convenient end to his discussion with Bert Humphrey. He bid the man a good day and left the mercantile.

Outside on the sidewalk, he checked his watch. He had appointments with several businessmen this afternoon. Glad handing. Speech making. Kissing babies. He couldn't say any of it was a favorite pasttime.

Maybe that was because his candidacy had begun with admittedly selfish motives. He had something to gain if he became mayor — overturning unfair and restrictive laws that made life difficult for honest men of business. Yes, he would make a good and open-minded mayor, should he be elected. Still . . .

He frowned.

It was different for Gwen Arlington. She had nothing to gain. She wanted to serve her neighbors and the tradesmen and even the children of Bethlehem Springs. She cared about them. Morgan believed she too would make a good and open-minded mayor. Perhaps a better mayor than he would make, even though she lacked practical business experience.

Was it right for him to continue, knowing all that?

On the other hand, would the people of Bethlehem Springs elect a woman? And if they wouldn't elect a woman and Morgan withdrew, that would leave Hiram Tattersall to serve as mayor. His gut told him Tattersall would be a puppet for Harrison Carter, just as the other county commissioners and the current mayor were, and that Morgan could not allow.

No, he couldn't withdraw from the race. He had to stay the course — and pray that the people of this town would choose the right person come Election Day.

TWELVE

Standing in the hall near the front door, Gwen checked her appearance in the mirror. A gauzy pink scarf covered the crown of her hat and was tied snugly beneath her chin. She hoped it would keep her face and hair clean while she and Morgan motored to the construction site.

After slipping her arms into a duster coat, she took her purse from the entry table and opened it to double-check that her mother's letter was there. Cleo would want to read it, especially if she hadn't received one of her own.

The *put-putter-put* of an approaching motorcar reached her ears, causing a tiny shiver of anticipation to race up her spine. Morgan was here. It was time for them to leave.

But why this sudden excitement? This was nothing more than a fact-finding excursion. It was her duty as a candidate for mayor to be well informed.

She stepped onto the porch and closed the door behind her. No reason to wait for him to get out of the car. She had no need to be escorted to the vehicle.

"Good morning, Miss Arlington," Morgan called as he brought the automobile to a halt. "Lovely day for a drive, isn't it?" Reaching over to open the passenger door, he smiled.

What was it about his smile that made her feel so unsteady? It didn't used to have that effect on her. What had changed between last week and this? Was his offer of friendship enough to make the difference?

"Watch your step."

She drew a quick breath. "Thank you, Mr. McKinley." After sitting down, she closed the passenger door and folded her hands in her lap, eyes forward.

"We should be up to the site in a little more than half an hour."

Gwen saw Edna Updike staring out her parlor window. Although she couldn't tell for certain, given the distance between them, she imagined the woman wore a frown of disapproval. After all, Gwen was about to drive off in an automobile with a man without the benefit and protection of a chaperone. Scandalous!

Morgan steered away from the curb, driving down Wallula to Main, then taking Main out of town. Once they were on the road heading north, he spoke above the noise of the engine. "Do you drive, Miss Arlington?"

"Drive? Do you mean an automobile?" Without waiting for his answer, she shook her head. "No."

"That surprises me. I somehow thought you would."

How was she to take that comment? Was it a compliment or an insult? She couldn't be sure.

There hadn't been a drop of rain in several weeks, and it wasn't long before their coats were covered with a fine layer of dust. Morgan expertly steered the Model T around ruts carved earlier in the spring when the ground had been softer.

They rode in silence for a while. Then Morgan said, "I've been wondering something, Miss Arlington."

She looked at him.

"How much do you charge for piano lessons?"

What an odd question for him to ask.

He glanced her way, obviously expecting a reply.

"Twenty cents for a half-hour lesson in my home. Another nickel if I go to the student's home."

"Very reasonable," he said, his eyes back on the road. "And do you give lessons to adults as well as children?"

There was that strange sensation in her stomach again. "Sometimes."

"Would you consider taking me on as a pupil?"

"Why do you want to learn to play, Mr. McKinley?"

He glanced at her a second time. "Does there have to be a reason?"

"There should be, yes."

"Well . . . I've always had an appreciation for the musical arts, even as a boy. But my father preferred I pursue other interests while I was in school. Sports in general. Football in particular. After I graduated from university, I was involved with my father's various business interests. Later I traveled with my mother after she became too ill to travel alone, and we never stayed in one place for any extended period of time." He removed one hand from the steering wheel and raked his fingers through his wind-tousled hair. "Now that I'm settled in Bethlehem Springs, I'd like to pursue an old interest." He smiled again without looking at her. "Is that reason enough?"

Although she was certain it would be better to remain silent, she asked, "Do you have a piano in your home so you could practice?"

"Yes. A rather fine one, I believe. It came with the house."

It wouldn't be wise to give him lessons. She felt that in her bones. But since he seemed so determined, perhaps she had best try another line of reasoning. "I don't recommend that you begin lessons, Mr. McKinley, if you'll be spending all your time at the building site in a matter of weeks. It takes dedication and determination to learn to play a musical instrument."

"There you go again, assuming I'm going to lose the election."

His comment amused her. She had begun to enjoy this competition of theirs. "Since I plan to win, I believe that means you must lose."

"Then I'll make you a promise. Even if I lose the election, I will still be dedicated in my playing of the piano. I'll practice every day."

She couldn't help smiling now. "All right, Mr. McKinley. If you are truly determined to learn to play the piano, I will instruct you. I could do it Tuesdays or Fridays."

"Let's make it Tuesday." He slowed the motorcar to a stop, then reached into his pocket and extracted a quarter. "At my home." He reached over and took hold of her left hand, opened it, and dropped the coin onto her gloved palm, then folded her fingers over it. He didn't release her hand immediately.

Gwen's smile faded. She found it difficult to move, to think, to breathe. She scarcely knew where she was as she stared into his eyes.

"Shall we say three o'clock?" he asked, a smile tugging at the corners of his mouth.

She nodded. That seemed the only response possible.

It was more difficult than it should have been for Morgan to let go of Gwen's hand. That he felt a growing attraction to his lovely opponent was becoming clear to him. Whether or not that attraction would prove a disaster — for him, for the resort, for the election — remained to be seen.

Silence surrounded them as they resumed the drive, Gwen pretending great interest in the passing countryside. After they passed the bridge that led to her father's ranch, the road curved into a narrow canyon, hugging the river on the right side that tumbled and foamed over boulders and ancient logs.

"If things go as planned," Morgan said,

hoping to make both of them feel a little less uncomfortable, "that's where the railroad will lay tracks." He pointed to the flat terrain on the opposite side of the river.

"Do you really think the Union Pacific will bring a spur up this way?"

"They will if the county and town do their part. We've had several meetings with the men who make those decisions, and it looks encouraging. Of course New Hope will cover some of the costs, which is a good incentive."

Gwen seemed to consider his words before asking, "When do you plan to open the resort, Mr. McKinley?"

"We'd hoped to have our first guests staying with us this fall, but it looks now like it will take us until early next spring, depending upon what sort of winter we have."

She said nothing more, and Morgan decided to leave her to her own thoughts until they reached the resort.

A short while later, they arrived at the building site. The air was filled with sounds of hammering and sawing and the shouts of one man to another. Noticeable progress had been made since Morgan's last visit. The exterior of the lodge was nearing completion. Soon the craftsmen would begin work on the interior.

Just as the motorcar's engine fell silent, Morgan heard Gwen whisper, "Oh, my."

A perfect response. He grinned. That's how he wanted everyone to react when they arrived at New Hope.

As Morgan walked around to the passenger side of the motorcar, Fagan Doyle hurried toward them from the direction of the bathhouse. "Morgan, you weren't expected today. But it's glad I am you've come."

"Problems?"

"No, but we've got some questions about the pools that need answered."

He nodded. "I'll meet with you before we leave." He turned and opened the car door, holding out a hand to Gwen to assist her to the ground. "Fagan, I'd like to introduce Miss Arlington. Miss Arlington, this is Fagan Doyle."

Fagan doffed his hat. "It's pleased I am to make your acquaintance." Then to Morgan, "You should've warned me, boy-o. Sure and I wouldn't have any man jack atop a ladder or roof right now. They're likely to fall off when they see her pretty face."

"Then perhaps I should keep my face covered, Mr. Doyle. I would hate to be the cause of an accident."

Did Morgan detect a less-than-pleased

edge in her response to the compliment? It did seem that she could turn prickly at the most unexpected moments. What woman didn't like a bit of flattery?

Morgan removed his duster and tossed it into the rear seat before turning to Gwen to ask, "Would you like me to take your coat? It seems to be warming up."

With a nod, she unbuttoned the light-weight overgarment. "Thank you, Mr. Mc-Kinley."

The scent of her cologne teased him as he slipped the coat from her shoulders. It was all he could do not to bring it close to his face and breathe deeply.

What had come over him lately? He was acting like . . . like a lovesick pup. Heaven help him! He needed to nip this behavior in the bud.

He took several long, slow breaths before turning around. Gwen had removed the scarf from her hat and now stood looking at the lodge.

Pretty didn't begin to describe her.

He cleared his throat. "Let's look inside the lodge first, shall we?"

Gwen hadn't envisioned anything close to this place. Not in her wildest dreams. Not here in Idaho, outside a small town like

156

Bethlehem Springs.

Morgan escorted her through the lodge, detailing what things would look like when finished. The elegant fireplaces. The large sitting room. The library. The modern kitchen and large dining hall. The guest rooms. In her mind, she saw it all as he described it.

Next came a tour of the bathhouse and the pools. He explained the different kinds of therapy that would be available to guests of the resort and told her there would be doctors and nurses on staff.

"And up there" — he pointed toward a draw about a hundred or more yards up an incline — "is where the prayer chapel will be."

"A prayer chapel?"

"I learned from my mother that physical healing is not enough. My wish — and my mother's wish — is that New Hope will be a place where people can come for spiritual healing first. And then, if God wills it, be healed of their physical ailments. Or, at the very least, their pain lessened."

"It doesn't sound like a profitable enterprise."

Softly, he answered, " 'For what shall it profit a man, if he shall gain the whole world, and lose his own soul?' "

She couldn't argue with the familiar Scripture. Still, if enough guests — *wealthy* guests — didn't come to stay at New Hope, how could the resort be of benefit to Bethlehem Springs? Without turning a profit, New Hope would eventually close its doors, the railroad would cancel the route — if it ever started in the first place — and businessmen in town would experience great disappointment. It seemed a great risk to her.

"Miss Arlington, I am not a fool."

"I never said you were, sir."

He cocked an eyebrow, as if to say he'd read her thoughts and knew she was being disingenuous.

Heat rose in her cheeks.

"Walk with me." He motioned toward the draw where the chapel was to be built. Gwen fell into step beside him, knowing he shortened his strides to accommodate hers.

"Miss Arlington, my great-grandfather, my grandfather, and my father were all successful men of business, each increasing the family fortunes, each generation building upon the success of the last. My mother's family was likewise blessed. As Providence would have it, I am the heir on both the maternal and paternal sides. And I, in turn, have had my own successes in the business world, although modest by comparison." He clasped his hands behind his back. "I don't tell you this to impress you. There have been times when my family's prosperity has seemed more of a curse than a blessing. After all, Jesus himself said it's easier for a camel to go through the eye of a needle than for a rich man to enter the kingdom of God. I'm ever mindful of that warning."

Listening to him, Gwen's heart stirred. Other than her father, she rarely encountered men who spoke about their faith outside of church.

Morgan stopped when they reached the draw. His gaze swept over a stand of aspens, leaves applauding in the breeze, a shallow brook bubbling out from beneath the underbrush. "On paper this resort undoubtedly looks impractical, but sometimes God requires us to step out in faith. You know" — he glanced at her — "like the Israelites had to wade into the water before it parted before them."

Perhaps he wasn't the man she'd thought him when they first met. Perhaps it wouldn't be unwise to let herself like him. Perhaps they could become friends after all.

For a long while they stood there, looking at each other. The sounds of construction faded into the distance, as did the rustle of leaves and the gurgle of the mountain stream. Nothing seemed to exist but the two of them, alone in the late morning sunlight.

Gwen felt her body sway toward him, as if drawn by an invisible cord. Perhaps fearing she was about to fall, Morgan lifted his hands and lightly grasped her by the upper arms. Her heart hammered, blood pulsing in her ears, breath shallow and quick.

"Gwen," he whispered.

It seemed right to hear her given name on his lips.

"You're so beautiful."

Those three words were like a splash of cold water on her face, waking her from some hypnotic state. She took a step back, out of his grasp.

"I . . . I think we should go now, Mr. McKinley."

He looked as if he might protest, but he didn't. "Yes, perhaps you're right. We should be on our way. Your father and sister will be looking for your arrival."

Wordlessly they made their way down the hillside to the motorcar.

THIRTEEN

Gwen felt a rush of relief when she saw her sister leave the main corral and walk toward the motorcar. The drive down from the construction site had seemed to take forever. That moment of temptation — when she'd nearly leaned into Morgan's embrace — had replayed in her mind again and again. She'd felt out of breath ever since. Even now . . .

"Gwennie! We weren't expecting to see you arrive this way." Cleo grinned. "Howdy, Morgan."

"Good day, Cleo." Morgan hopped out and came around the front of the automobile to open the door for Gwen. "I took your sister up to the resort so she could judge for herself whether it will or won't be good for the community."

Cleo said, "I wouldn't mind a look-see myself. Maybe I could ride up there someday and let you show me around too."

"Anytime you want, Cleo. You're always welcome. Just let me know when."

Oh, please let's not talk about the resort. Let's not talk about anything that will delay his departure. Let him leave . . . so I can breathe again.

Gwen stepped down from the car. "Cleo, would you mind taking me back to town later? I don't want to keep Mr. —"

Her sister turned toward Morgan. "I reckon you'll be staying for lunch, won't you?"

"Well, I —"

" 'Course you will. Won't let you go until you eat something." Cleo linked arms with Gwen and drew her toward the house. "So tell me how the campaign's going. Has Mr. McKinley thought of backing out yet?" Cleo glanced over her shoulder at Morgan. "Now would be a good time."

"I'm not ready to concede as of yet," he answered.

"Pity." Cleo laughed. "It's going to be mighty embarrassing for you, come Election Day."

As the sisters climbed the steps onto the porch, their father appeared through the front doorway, wiping his hands on a towel. "There you are, Gwen. I was wondering if you'd make lunch. You're later than usual."

He leaned forward and kissed her cheek. As he straightened, he looked beyond her shoulder. "Mr. McKinley, this is a pleasant surprise."

"Thank you, sir."

"Joining us for lunch?"

What did her father and sister have against her? Shouldn't they *know* she would rather he leave? Leave *now!*

Morgan answered, "Cleo was kind enough to invite me. If it isn't too much bother, I'll accept."

"No bother at all. We like to have company, but don't get much of it. Do we, Cleo?"

"No. Not nearly enough."

Griff motioned toward the chairs on the porch. "Make yourselves comfortable. Cookie's got chicken frying in the skillet, and it ought to be about ready. I'll go check on it."

"I'll go, Dad," Gwen said. "You stay and talk to Mr. McKinley." She hurried into the house before her father could reply.

Once inside, she drew a slow, deep breath and released it. There, that was better. Her equilibrium returned. Her feet stood solidly on the ground. It would take more than a man whispering her name to cause her to forget herself.

"You're so beautiful." If he'd said anything but those words. If he'd seen her, if he'd seen the *real* Gwen, maybe . . .

No. She shook her head. No, that wouldn't have made any difference. She didn't want to become involved with him. Not with him or any man. Only as a woman alone could she accomplish her goals, live her own life, be free to pursue the paths God led her down. Hadn't the apostle Paul written that it was better to be single so one was free of entanglements?

She stepped through the door into the large kitchen of the ranch house. Cookie, the irascible man who'd cooked for Griff Arlington's family and ranch hands for the past thirty years, stood at the stove, turning chicken in the skillet. If anyone had ever known his real name, they'd forgotten it by now.

"Hello, Cookie. Dad wants to know how long until lunch."

He looked over his shoulder. His cheeks were flushed, and there was a sheen of perspiration on his forehead. "You're late, girl. Chicken's almost burnt to a crisp."

"Sorry." She smiled, knowing he exaggerated. Cookie would never allow food to burn in his kitchen.

"Tell Griff you can set yourselves down at

the table. I'll have the grub out in a jiffy."

"Thank you, Cookie. I'll tell him."

Morgan couldn't remember when he'd enjoyed a meal more. The fried chicken, biscuits and gravy, and creamed vegetables were delicious. But it was the people seated at the table that made it perfect. Observing the Arlington family's affection and appreciation for one another made him miss his own family more than he had in a long while. Not that he'd ever been as close to his younger sister as Cleo and Gwen were to each other.

Daphne was ten years his junior and they'd spent only brief periods of time together since she was six or so. For most of her growing up years, he'd been away at school or traveling. Later, when he was home, she'd been off to school. Their paths had seldom crossed for long. These days, they wrote to each other, but those letters were brief — his all about the spa, hers all about her travels.

Cleo's voice pulled him from his reverie. "So what did you think of the resort, Gwennie?"

Everyone at the table looked at Gwen. In return, she looked from her sister to her father and back again. But not once did she glance in Morgan's direction. He wondered if that had anything to do with the moment when he'd almost kissed her. He rather hoped it did.

"I was impressed. It is grander than I'd envisioned. And Mr. McKinley seems to have thought everything through in great detail."

Morgan leaned forward. "So you don't agree with Mr. Carter? You don't think New Hope is a bad thing for Bethlehem Springs?"

This question, at last, drew her gaze. Both her expression and her tone were serious as she answered. "No, Mr. McKinley. I don't agree with him. You have convinced me that New Hope will be a boon for the community. As you pointed out earlier, you have already hired many local men. I recognized some of them today." An unexpected smile tugged at her lips. "When I'm mayor, I shall lend you and your spa my full support."

He was glad she no longer seemed upset with him. "I believe you are a bit premature, Miss Arlington. The election hasn't happened yet."

"Perhaps my comment is prophetic rather than premature."

"Touché!" Cleo slapped the palm of her right hand against the table. "You might as well concede, Morgan. You're never going to beat my sister."

He chuckled. "All the same, I think I'll leave my hat in the ring."

"It's a free country." Cleo pushed her chair back from the table. "If you'll excuse me, I've got some horses to tend to."

Morgan knew that once Cleo left the dining room, he would have to leave the ranch — without Gwen. And he wasn't ready for that. If he dawdled, perhaps he could convince her to drive back to town with him. So he said, "Mind if I tag along, Cleo?"

"With me?" She raised an eyebrow.

"Sure. I'd like to see more of the place. I've never spent much time on a cattle ranch, and I'm curious about your operation."

"Guess I've got no objections."

Morgan rose. "It was a delicious meal, Griff, and the company was delightful. Thanks for inviting me to join you." He looked at Gwen and gave her a slight bow. "Miss Arlington, it was a real pleasure showing you New Hope."

"For me too, Mr. McKinley," she answered softly, any hint of a smile gone.

Morgan followed Cleo out of the house, noting that her stride was almost as long as his own. Again he wondered at the differences between the sisters. Not just their physical differences but also the obvious differences in their speech and carriage and manner of dress.

"I've got an injured mare in the barn that needs doctoring," Cleo said. "Doubt you'll find much interest in watching that."

"You might be surprised. My interests are wide and varied."

She stopped short and looked at him, her gaze shrewd. "But I'm guessing Gwen's what interests you now. Am I right?"

He considered his answer carefully. Should he hedge a bit or be flat-out honest? As the listener was Cleo Arlington, he chose the latter. "You guessed right. I am interested in knowing more about your sister."

"Because she's your opponent?"

"Not entirely."

One corner of her mouth curved upward. "She's got your spurs tangled, doesn't she?"

"Beg your pardon?"

"You like her."

"Let's just say I'm intrigued."

"That's what I thought. Well, that's fine. That's real fine." She motioned with her head, then continued walking, Morgan falling into step beside her once again.

Daylight from the open doorways chased the darkness of the barn into corners. The air smelled of dust and hay and animals. Cleo paused long enough to grab a cloth, some bandages, and a bottle of liniment before heading for the nearest stall. Inside it was a sorrel horse with a blazed face, sorrowful eyes, and a bandaged left foreleg.

"What happened?" Morgan asked as Cleo entered the stall.

"She tangled with some barbed wire. For a while, I thought we might have to put her down, but she's coming along. I don't think she'll be any good for herding cattle, but she'll make a good kid's pony."

Morgan leaned his arms on the top rail of the stall and watched as Cleo squatted next to the mare's leg and removed the soiled bandages.

"Bet the first thing you'd like to know is how Gwen and I turned out so different from each other." She looked over her shoulder at him. "Right?"

A more direct woman he'd never met. "Yes, that would be a good place to begin."

"When Gwen and I were two, our mother decided she didn't want to live in Idaho, so she up and went back to New Jersey to live with her parents. She took Gwen with her and left me with our dad. Of course Dad didn't think she would stay back there for long, but that's how it worked out. Gwen didn't get to return to Idaho until she was twenty-one, right after she finished college."

"And your mother?"

"She still lives with our grandparents in Hoboken." Cleo reached for the liniment. "And she's still trying to convince Gwen to come back to civilization, but so far Gwennie hasn't listened. I don't reckon she'll have much time for traveling once she's mayor either."

Morgan didn't rise to the bait.

Cleo stood and looked at him. "My sister's a whole lot more than beautiful and refined. She's smart too. Don't go thinking she's not."

"I won't."

She pointed her finger at his chest. "And don't you hurt her. Because if you do, it'll be me you'll have to answer to."

"You have my word. I won't hurt your sister."

Evening had cast a soft shadow over Bethlehem Springs by the time Morgan left Gwen at her door. She stood on her porch and listened to the sound of his motorcar until it faded into silence. When she could hear it no longer, she went inside the house, dropping her hat and duster carelessly over the nearest chair.

Cookie had sent her home with a few pieces of cold fried chicken and a biscuit, but exhaustion had stolen her appetite. She put the leftovers in the icebox, then went outside to feed and water Shakespeare.

"Hello, boy." She laid her cheek against the bridge of the horse's nose while scratching his throat with her left hand. "Did you miss me today?"

Shakespeare snorted.

"Well, I missed you." She sighed as she drew back, looking into the horse's big dark eyes. "It was a miserable afternoon. I've never been so miserable, and Dad and Cleo were no help at all. They *like* Mr. McKinley. I can tell they do." *Even I like him. A little. Just a little.* "Oh, I never should have agreed to ride to the resort with him in his automobile. I should have let you take me up there. Then I wouldn't have been forced to spend a minute more with him than I wanted."

The horse pawed at the floor of his stall.

"I know. I know. You're hungry."

She brought hay to the stall and dropped it into the manger, then grabbed the bucket and took it to the pump, where she filled it with fresh, cold water.

"He asked me to give him piano lessons. Can you believe that? He's building a resort, running for mayor, and he wants to add piano lessons to the mix. And I agreed! Why did I do that? What was I thinking?" She hung the bucket once again on the hook inside the stall. "I don't need his twenty-five cents."

Shakespeare chomped on his hay, unmindful of her dilemma.

Gwen rested her hands atop the stall rail, then placed her chin on her wrists. "Of course, I don't have to give him lessons. I could cancel, couldn't I?"

Yes, she could cancel. She *would* cancel. First thing tomorrow, she would let him know she couldn't give him those lessons after all.

FOURTEEN

Gwen arrived at Morgan's home at three minutes to the hour the following Tuesday afternoon. She had meant to cancel the lesson. More than once she'd begun a note to tell him she couldn't do it. The notes had ended up unfinished in the trash.

A woman wearing a black dress and matching apron answered her knock. "You must be Miss Arlington." The woman opened the door wide. "Mr. McKinley told me to expect you. I'm Mrs. Cheevers, the housekeeper. Please come in."

"Thank you." Gwen stepped into the entry hall. "I believe we've met before, Mrs. Cheevers. At the Humphrey girl's wedding last year."

"Oh. Of course." The housekeeper motioned with her right hand. "If you'll make yourself comfortable in the front parlor, Mr. McKinley will join you soon. He's in a meeting with Mr. Doyle."

Mrs. Cheevers led her into a beautifully appointed room with a high ceiling and tall windows that afforded a view of the town and the mountain range to the south. The piano, which stood near one of those windows, had been polished to a high sheen.

"May I bring you some refreshment, Miss Arlington?"

"No, thank you." Gwen made her way to the piano and slipped onto the bench.

Her grandparents owned a grand piano similar to this one. Her own lessons had begun on that instrument when she was six years old, before her hands could properly span the keys. She recalled many an hour in the music room of her grandparents' home in Hoboken, practicing her scales over and over again.

Mr. Kirby, her teacher, had been a strange-looking little man with thick glasses that rode the tip of a birdlike nose. "Do it again, child. Concentrate this time," he'd told her.

Sometimes Gwen had cried in frustration, but her tears hadn't moved her mother. Elizabeth Arlington had wanted Gwen to learn to play and learn to play she would. A musical ability, she'd told Gwen repeatedly, was one of the social graces. Every young lady of quality played an instrument.

Her mother couldn't have guessed that Gwen would one day be paid to teach others.

"Poor Mother," Gwen whispered as she placed her fingers on the ivory keys. "What a disappointment I am to her."

She heard men's voices and twisted on the bench an instant before Morgan and Fagan Doyle came into view.

When Morgan saw her through the parlor doorway, he smiled. "Ah, you're here already." He stepped into the room.

"It's now past three o'clock."

"Is it?" He checked his watch. "I hadn't realized. I am sorry to have kept you waiting." He glanced over his shoulder. "Fagan, you remember Miss Arlington. She's here to give me a lesson on the piano."

Gwen slid to the end of the bench as the two men approached.

" 'Tis a pleasure to see you again, Miss Arlington." He gave her a broad wink. "Be patient with Morgan. I wouldn't call him daft, but still . . ." He shrugged as his voice faded to silence.

"Be on your way, Fagan." Morgan feigned a scowl.

Fagan laughed. "He has no sense of humor, that one. None at all. Have a care, miss."

"I will, Mr. Doyle." She grinned at him, enjoying the easy banter of the men. "Thank you for the warning."

As Fagan left the room, Morgan looked at Gwen and in a stage whisper said, "I most certainly *do* have a sense of humor. If I didn't, I wouldn't survive having Fagan for a friend."

His eyes, she thought, contained so much life, and his laugh was deep and rich. Had she noticed that before?

Swallowing hard, Gwen reached into her bag and withdrew the sheet music she'd brought with her. "We should begin your lesson, Mr. McKinley."

"Of course." He moved to the left side of the bench and sat beside her, his shoulder almost touching hers.

It was quite warm in the room. Perhaps she should ask that a window be opened.

Morgan put his fingers on the piano keys, his left little finger resting on lower C, his right thumb resting on middle C.

Gwen gave him a sharp look. "You've had lessons before."

"Yes, but that was years ago."

"But I thought —"

He pressed middle C with his thumb, three times in quick succession. "My parents and I heard Percy Grainger play in the

London recital that established his reputation as a virtuoso. I'll never forget it." Slowly, Morgan played the notes of the C-major scale with his right hand. "I was twenty years old at the time. Percy Grainger was nineteen. I remember wanting to learn to play just like him."

How easily he spoke of his travels in England and Europe, of the grand hotels and spas he'd visited, of seeing one of the great pianists of their day perform in London. Morgan had led the sort of life her mother could only dream of, the kind of life she'd wanted for her daughter if only Gwen would have married well.

Poor Mother.

Gwen's maternal grandparents were well-to-do merchants in New Jersey. Part of the *nouveau riche,* their money had opened many doors for Elizabeth and Gwen. But some doors at the highest echelons of good, long-established society had remained firmly closed. Gwen hadn't cared, but her mother had.

What would Mother think if she could see me now?

Morgan's left hand began the scale, moving from left to right, but he struck a sour note as he crossed his middle finger over thumb. He stopped, chuckled, then looked at her. "As you can tell, I'm no virtuoso."

Gwen swallowed again. "You'll get better." Her heart beat an uncertain rhythm in her chest. "It only takes practice."

How easy it would be to lean to his right and kiss her lips. Morgan longed to know if she tasted as sweet as she looked.

As if she'd read his mind, her eyes widened and color infused her cheeks. She slipped from the bench and stood beside it, clenching her hands at her waist. "Please play that scale again, Mr. McKinley."

He shouldn't be thinking about how easy it would be to kiss her or how sweet she looked. That wasn't why he was here. He concentrated again on the piano keys. His playing felt awkward, his fingers stiff. How many years had it been since he'd sat on a piano bench, his fingers touching ivory? Too many.

"Do you know your C-major chords?"

"Yes." He positioned his hands, hearing the notes in his head even before he played them.

"Now the G-major scale."

He thought about it a moment. Ah, yes. F-sharp. He played the scale, first with one hand, then the other, and finally together.

Gwen moved to the bend in the piano

beside the open lid. Her expression was grave. "You deceived me, sir."

His fingers stilled.

"You let me believe you were a beginner."

He wished he could deny the accusation, but he couldn't. Though he hadn't lied to her, he also hadn't revealed the whole truth. Sometimes omission was the same as a lie.

"How well can you play?"

"Not as well as I'd like. That's why I asked for the lessons."

She studied him with a narrowed gaze.

"I didn't intend to deceive you, Miss Arlington, but I did and I'm sorry." He stood, shoving the bench away with the back of his knees. "I apologize. Please forgive me."

Seconds passed like minutes as she appeared to weigh his words. He felt like a prisoner awaiting the verdict. Would it be freedom or the gallows? Would she remain or walk out the door?

At last, she spoke. "Tell me about the instruction you've received."

"I had a few lessons when I was a boy of about ten or so, but like I said, my father had other aspirations for me." He shook his head, envisioning his father. "Don't misunderstand me — he was a wonderful man. But he held strong opinions about the proper roles for men and women. Musical interests were not for his son." He chose not to tell Gwen what his father would have thought of a woman running for mayor. "I was twenty-six when he passed away. I hadn't lost the desire to learn to play the piano, so I hired an instructor who taught me the basics. But then my mother's health worsened, and I started traveling with her. I played whenever I could. I even mastered a few songs, but my technique wasn't good."

His mother hadn't cared about his technique. Over and over again, she'd asked him to play "Amazing Grace," "Jesus, Lover of My Soul," and other favorite hymns. She'd loved it even when he could only play the melody with his right hand. "It comforts me," she had said to him countless times.

Morgan cleared his throat as he tamped down the poignant memories.

"How long has it been since you played?" Gwen's voice was filled with compassion, as if she'd heard the words he hadn't spoken.

"About four years."

"Nothing is lost. You'll remember what you learned, I promise you. It's just a bit rusty." Gwen motioned toward the piano keys. "Let's begin our lesson again, shall we?"

She smiled at him.

And in that moment he realized something. A man couldn't plan if or when he would find a woman who would win his regard. It simply happened. Such was the case with the enchanting Miss Arlington. Despite his intentions to remain free of attachments, despite all his promises to himself, he'd fallen for her like a lemming tumbling over a cliff into the ocean, headlong and mindless of the danger. And unless he missed his guess, it was much too late to save himself. Although she might not know it yet, Gwen already held his heart captive in her hands.

Good thing he knew God's timing was perfect. He couldn't say much for his own.

Gwen was not so naive that she didn't recognize the light of interest in Morgan's eyes. She'd seen it in men's eyes before. She saw it in Charles Benson's eyes every time they were together. And yet Morgan's gaze seemed different. As if he saw beneath the surface and knew the real Guinevere Arlington.

Which was a ridiculous, romantic notion, and she was not a ridiculous, romantic woman. Besides, in her experience, few men saw beneath the surface when it came to women.

She drew herself up, trying hard to look

every inch the teacher. "Please play the C-major scale again. A little faster this time." Then, to make certain her thoughts didn't continue to wander where they shouldn't, she moved to stand behind Morgan.

The remainder of the lesson progressed in a normal fashion with her student running through the scales and chords, roughly at first but improving with each try. Gwen suspected she would soon hear him play more difficult melodies.

And though she was loath to admit it, she looked forward to listening to him play again, next week and the one after that and the one after that.

FIFTEEN

Harrison Carter closed the office door and turned toward his visitor. "What can you tell me? Why was she in his home?"

Elias Spade, a short, bespectacled man, shook his head. "Miss Arlington's giving McKinley piano lessons."

"I don't believe it."

"It's true, sir. She was there just over half an hour, and I could observe the two of them clearly. My view was unobstructed."

Harrison crossed to the window that overlooked Main Street. Kitty-corner from his law offices stood the sandstone municipal building that housed both county and city governments. For more than a decade, all the major decisions regarding what was and wasn't done in this area had been made in Harrison's office first. He wasn't about to let anything upset the order of things.

Piano lessons. What was she thinking? Foolish girl.

This was why women shouldn't be involved in politics or business. They had no head for it. They were naive and unable to make the types of decisions men made on a daily basis. Women belonged in the home and not in the halls of government. To think he would be saddled with this foolish female for the next four years set his teeth on edge.

Maybe he shouldn't have given her his support. But what else could he have done? If he'd backed Tattersall, he'd have been labeled crazy. And while he could have run for mayor himself, he knew his own interests were better served in his position as head of the county commissioners.

He cursed softly. He would have to assert a little more control over Miss Arlington.

"What more have you learned?"

Spade answered, "McKinley owns the land free and clear. No mortgage. No encumbrances. Almost a hundred acres." He cleared his throat. "And from what I hear, he's got some connection to the governor or some senator. I'd be careful if I were you."

"Moses Alexander isn't interested in what's happening in Bethlehem Springs. He's too busy trying to make Idaho a dry state to notice us." Harrison sat in an oversized leather chair. "What about Mc-

Kinley's business practices? What about his family?"

"Sorry, sir. Nothing you don't already know."

Harrison felt his temper rising. "What am I paying you for, then?"

"Mr. Carter, Morgan McKinley is one of the fifty wealthiest men in the country. What he doesn't want anyone to know, they aren't going to know. I've done my best, but there just isn't anything more to be learned."

"Get out." Harrison waved his hand. "Get out of my sight."

Elias Spade didn't waste any time following the order.

Harrison got up from his chair and began to pace the length of the office, hands clasped behind his back. He had to stop McKinley from completing that resort, had to force him to give up and sell the land — at a price far less than it was worth. Let him build his resort someplace else. Any place but where it was right now.

Gwen sat back on her heels and wiped the back of her left gardening glove across her forehead. It was unusually warm for early June, and her flowers loved it. Unfortunately, so did the weeds. But she would persevere until every last one of them was gone. Her flowerbeds were one of her joys.

And as much as she disliked the weeding chore, the task did provide time for praying about and thinking through matters that bothered her. Take, for instance, Mr. McKinley. He bothered her a great deal.

She hadn't seen him since Tuesday, not since she'd gone to his home for his first piano lesson. Yet he continued to weigh on her mind. And whenever she thought of him, she felt a strange — what? A strange longing. As if something were missing in her life.

She yanked another weed from the earth.

What a ridiculous notion. Nothing was missing from her life. She was content in every way. Content in her own small home. Content with teaching her music students and writing her pieces for the *Daily Herald*. Content tending to her colorful garden. Her life was full of friends and worthwhile activities, and her faith gave her purpose. She didn't need anything more. Not a single, solitary thing.

If she'd wanted more, she could have had it. She could have married Bryant Hudson when she was nineteen. Bryant was from a family of good society, old money, dignified and responsible. Her mother and his parents had arranged the marriage, and she'd liked

Bryant well enough at first, before she truly got to know him. They'd become engaged with the usual fanfare and had planned to wed as soon as she finished her schooling — schooling he believed was a waste of time and money.

From the start, her fiancé had made it clear he cared nothing for Gwen's thoughts or opinions. When she brought up items she'd read in the newspaper to him, especially matters of politics or economics, he would look at her as if she'd grown a second head. In his mind, such things couldn't be of any interest to a young woman.

Gwen straightened and brushed loose hairs away from her face.

Oh, how close she had come to making a tragic error. She might have ignored all the warning signs and married him despite her growing uneasiness. But then had come the day when she'd mentioned to Bryant her plans to attend a meeting led by supporters of woman's suffrage. He had forbidden her to go.

In a flash, she'd seen her future. She would be expected to pretend she hadn't a serious thought in her head. She would be expected to decorate her husband's arm and her husband's home, nothing more — another possession he could brag about to his friends. Bryant didn't love her, held no special affection for her, would never think of her as an equal partner in marriage.

She'd ended her engagement that very day and had promised herself to never again give anyone else control over her life.

Sadness washed over Gwen, remembering how her poor mother had taken to her bed, distraught over the news of the broken engagement. Maybe, if her mother had tried to understand Gwen's decision, things wouldn't have become so strained between them. But then, if things hadn't been so strained, maybe Gwen wouldn't have come West to meet her father and sister and maybe she wouldn't have made Bethlehem Springs her home. So she supposed it was all for the best.

Rising from the ground, she removed her gloves and dropped them into a basket with her gardening tools. As she turned toward the porch, she heard an automobile putter to a halt on the street. Her heart gave a little hiccup, then quickened. A moment later, Morgan appeared at her front gate.

He smiled when he saw her. "Good day, Miss Arlington." He tipped his hat, looking dapper in his light-colored summer suit.

"Mr. McKinley." She brushed at the dirt and grass stains on her apron. She must look a fright.

"You've been gardening."

"Yes."

He opened the gate and stepped into the yard. "You have the loveliest gardens in town."

Her face warmed at his compliment.

"I am here on a matter of business."

"Business?"

"Regarding the campaign."

"Oh." She picked up the basket and moved toward the porch, hoping to put her thoughts in order. "Do sit down, Mr. McKinley, while I get us something cool to drink." She motioned toward the chairs.

"Don't go to any trouble for me. I know I'm intruding."

"Not at all." What was wrong with her? Let him state his business and leave. "I won't be but a moment."

She set the basket on the porch, opened the screen door, and stepped inside. The mirror over the table in the entry told her that not only was her hair disheveled but there was a smudge of dirt on her forehead as well. She whipped off her soiled apron and used one corner of it to wipe the dirt from her face as she headed for her bedroom. Once there, she quickly brushed her hair back into its proper place, all the while telling herself that the only reason she cared about her appearance was because of the election. She did not want to feel at a disadvantage with her opponent.

Yes, of course. That was the reason.

In the kitchen, she poured iced tea into two tall glasses, sweetened the drinks with sugar, and carried them back to the front porch. She found Morgan sitting on the swing, one arm draped casually over the back of the seat, his right ankle resting on his left thigh just above the knee. He looked at home, as if he'd sat thus a hundred times.

Oh, this would not do.

She handed him his glass of tea. "Do tell me what business brought you to see me." Although the swing was her favorite place to sit, she chose instead to settle on the wooden chair farthest from it — and from him.

"Reverend Barker has invited the mayoral candidates to participate in a debate next Saturday in the basement of the Methodist church. The room is big enough to hold a large group. I'm sure there would be a great turnout for the event. However, Mr. Tattersall is undecided at this time about whether or not he wants to participate. So I have come to see if you will accept the invitation."

The Methodist church had become Morgan's church since he moved to town. Would he have an advantage because of the location? Would her fellow Presbyterians stay away? Surely not. Besides, her sister and father attended the Methodist church as well, and they were supporting her in the election.

Morgan took a sip of his iced tea, then said, "Of course, if you and Tattersall both decline, I suppose I shall simply give a speech."

Over my dead body! "That won't be necessary. I accept."

"Splendid. I believe it shall prove an interesting evening." He drained the last of his tea. "Although, as I've mentioned to you before, you and I are not so far apart in what we hope to accomplish in office."

Rather than agree with him, she reached for his empty glass. Perhaps they did share many of the same views, but she would still make the better mayor. He couldn't possibly care about the town or its citizens as much as she did. He hadn't lived here long enough. He'd spent almost the whole of the past year up at that resort of his. That's what would be his undoing.

Morgan rose from the swing and set his hat back on his head. "Thank you for the tea, Miss Arlington, and for allowing me to intrude upon your gardening."

Gwen rose to walk with him toward the steps.

"By the way, I'd like you to know that I've been practicing the piano every day."

"Would that all of my students were as dedicated."

He smiled down at her, a look that caused her breath to catch. "I have every intention of impressing my teacher when she comes to my home next Tuesday." He tipped his hat one final time, went down the steps, and strode toward his waiting automobile.

Heaven preserve me. This man would be her undoing if she wasn't careful.

Dear Daphne,

It has been far too long since I have written to you, dear sister, and I apologize. I would use the excuse of how busy I've been with work on the resort, but that's all it would be. An excuse. Please forgive me. I hope this letter finds you well. How is our cousin Gertrude? Please give her my regards.

You may be surprised to learn this, but I am running for the office of mayor of Bethlehem Springs. I confess that I entered the race because we've had problems with the local decision makers at both the town and county levels, and those problems have caused a number of delays for New Hope. I had hoped I would already have an agreement with the railroad to bring a spur up to Bethlehem Springs, but until some land-use matters have been resolved, I don't believe the railroad will look at my proposal seriously.

One of my opponents for office is a woman. Miss Guinevere Arlington is her name, although she is called Gwen by her family and friends. It is my hope that I will one day be considered her friend too. It is Miss Arlington who has caused me to enjoy this run for office more than I anticipated.

Will you be traveling abroad again this summer? If not, I wish you would consider a visit to Bethlehem Springs. I have hired a proper staff to care for my home and the needs of any guests who might come to stay. Do think about it, dear sister. I have been reminded recently of the importance of family. Since you and I are the only McKinleys left, I would like us to know one another better than we do.

I remain your affectionate brother,

Morgan

Sixteen

"Ah, Miss Arlington." Charles Benson doffed his hat to Gwen as she rounded the southwest corner on Wallula and Main. Almost as if he'd been waiting for her. "A glorious Sunday morning, isn't it?"

"Yes, it is, Mr. Benson." She quickened her pace as she crossed the street, the front doors of All Saints Presbyterian in view.

Charles stayed beside her. "Eager to get to church?"

"I'm always eager to worship the Lord."

"Of course. Aren't we all?"

She thought not but didn't say so.

"Townsfolk are buzzing about the election because of you."

"Are they? Why is that?" Her tone was somewhat sharper than she'd intended it to be.

"Well . . . I mean . . . no one expected a woman to run for office. Especially a young unmarried woman such as yourself."

She stopped and faced him, clutching her Bible close to her chest. "My age and gender should have no bearing on my qualifications. Nor should my marital status. I am fully qualified and able to serve as mayor. I care deeply about the issues that concern the people of Bethlehem Springs. I should think that would be all they cared about."

Poor Charles. He seemed at a loss for words now.

"The service will start soon, Mr. Benson. We don't want to be late." She hated using the word *we*, certain he would read meaning into it that wasn't there. However, she saw no way around it. After all, Charles and his family were members of All Saints too.

Morgan McKinley, however, was not a member — yet he was the very man she saw first upon stepping into the vestibule. How alarming that her heart tripped at the sight of him.

"Good morning, Miss Arlington."

"Good morning."

"Surprised to see me here?"

His smile was one of his best features. In fact, she liked it so much she forgot his question.

"How do you do," Morgan said to Charles, offering his hand. "I'm Morgan

McKinley."

"Charles Benson."

His question found its way back into her head. "Yes, I admit I am surprised. You're a Methodist, aren't you?"

He lowered his voice as he leaned toward her. "I wanted to see you at worship. One can learn a lot about a person that way." He glanced at Charles, then back at her. "May I sit with you? This being my first visit to All Saints."

No! "If you wish, Mr. McKinley." Why did she say that?

She moved toward the sanctuary. Although she didn't look, she knew he was right behind her. She heard him greeting other congregants, working his charm, as he followed her to her usual pew.

He didn't need to sit with her just because it was his first visit. He obviously knew many of the people here. Oh, he was a cad to do this to her in her own church. Was there no limit to the lengths to which he would go to win the election?

When she was seated, she glanced to her right to see if Charles meant to sit with them. Apparently not. He had joined his family across the aisle and up one row.

She should have looked for another single female and sat beside her. She wasn't required to sit in this pew. As it was, it looked as if she was *with* Morgan McKinley. Nothing could be further from the truth, but that was surely how it appeared all the same.

Thoughts churning, Gwen didn't realize the service had begun until Morgan rose to his feet, hymnal in hand. She stood too. A few bars into the hymn, she learned he had a wonderful singing voice, the kind that made others turn their heads to see to whom it belonged. Then they smiled, taking pleasure in listening to him. And there she was, sharing his hymnal, the two of them side by side for all to see.

How had her Sunday morning gone so wrong?

It hadn't been Morgan's aim to make Gwen uncomfortable. Nor had his decision to join her there had anything to do with the campaign. Not really. He'd simply wanted to see her again, and church had been the logical place on a Sunday morning. Reverend Rawlings was a good preacher, although Morgan thought the man could use some of Reverend Barker's fiery enthusiasm.

Which caused him to wonder why Gwen chose to worship at All Saints Presbyterian instead of Bethlehem Springs Methodist with her sister and father. He would have to ask her — once she was no longer mad at him.

When the last hymn was sung and the last amen spoken, Morgan turned toward Gwen. "I enjoyed the service and appreciate your hospitality, Miss Arlington. Thank you."

She didn't quite meet his eyes as she replied, "You're welcome, Mr. McKinley."

He stepped into the center aisle, then motioned for her to precede him. As he followed her out of the sanctuary, he took pleasure in watching the way she carried herself. She was a tiny thing. Couldn't weigh more than a hundred pounds soaking wet. But her back was ramrod straight and her head held high, as if she hoped to make herself a few inches taller by sheer force of will. If anyone could do such a thing, it was probably Gwen Arlington.

At the church doorway, she paused long enough to shake the reverend's hand and tell him she enjoyed the sermon. Morgan did the same.

"It was our pleasure to have you with us today, Mr. McKinley," Walter Rawlings said. "Could it be you might become part of our congregation?"

"Sorry, Reverend." From the corner of his eyes, he saw Gwen go down the steps. "I was only visiting."

The man chuckled. "And I believe I know why." His gaze shifted toward Gwen, who was now in conversation with several other women.

Morgan let the comment go unacknowledged, instead saying, "There's going to be a mayoral debate next Saturday at the Methodist church. I hope to see you there."

"I'll certainly do my best."

"The details should be in tomorrow's *Herald*."

"I'll look for them, Mr. McKinley."

Morgan set his hat on his head and stepped into the bright sunlight of midday. He didn't know if Gwen saw him, but that was the moment she moved away from her women friends and walked across the street, soon disappearing around the corner on her way toward home.

It was tempting to go after her. He could apologize for making her uncomfortable. He could invite her to dine with him. He could —

No, he'd best let it go for now. He'd already bungled things enough for one day.

He turned north and walked through town on his way toward home. There was little activity along Main Street on a Sunday. A few horses were tied at the hitching post outside the High Horse Saloon and one automobile was parked on the street. Tattersall obviously had no scruples about having his business open on a Sunday. That wouldn't last long. Prohibition could come to Idaho as early as the first of next year.

What would Tattersall do if that happened? He'd have to close down the High Horse. Could that be why he was running for office? To make sure he had a job? No. Tattersall didn't strike him as a man who considered the future much beyond the next week.

He'll probably become a bootlegger. Just what Bethlehem Springs needs.

Once past the municipal building, the street made a steep climb up the hillside. Halfway up, with the sun feeling hot upon his back, Morgan stopped to remove his suit coat, then tossed it over one shoulder, the collar hooked on an index finger. He'd almost reached the top of the hill and the turn onto Skyview when a boy on a bicycle came racing around the corner, headed straight for him. Morgan gave a shout of warning and jumped to one side, barely avoiding being hit. The boy veered hard to the left, wheels skidding in the dirt and gravel, and then the kid parted company with the bike, rolling and bouncing down the incline before coming to a dusty halt on his back.

Morgan dropped his suit coat and hurried to the boy. "Hey, there." He knelt beside the lad. "You okay?"

The boy — perhaps eleven or twelve years old, he'd guess — gave Morgan a dazed stare.

"Are you okay?"

"I . . . I think so."

"What's your name?"

"Owen. Owen Goldsmith." The boy sat up, giving his head a slow shake as he did so. When he saw the long, ragged tear in the knee of his left pant leg, he groaned. "Ma's not going to like seein' that. These are my Sunday best."

Morgan leaned forward. "Your knee's bleeding too." He parted the torn fabric to look at the scraped knee. The wound had dirt and gravel imbedded in the bleeding flesh. "Think you can walk on it?"

" 'Course I can." Owen gave him a disgusted look, one that said the question was dumb.

Subduing a grin, Morgan stood and waited while the boy got to his feet. Owen took one step — and grimaced, his face gone pale. Even if the bike could be ridden — not likely from the look of the front wheel — he couldn't have managed it with that knee.

"Where do you live?" Morgan asked.

"On Shenandoah, the other side of Wallula."

"That's a long way, limping and pushing a bike with a twisted wheel. Come with me to my place and I'll drive you home in my automobile."

Owen's eyes got as big as saucers. "Really? I can ride in your car?"

"Sure can." Morgan pointed. "My house is just around the corner there. Let's go." He stepped over to the bicycle, lifted it by the cross bar, and started up the hillside, checking his stride so as not to outdistance the boy.

When they reached Morgan's suit coat where he'd dropped it in the road, Owen picked it up. "I'll carry this for you."

"Thanks."

They walked in silence until they reached the top of the hill and turned onto Skyview. That's when it struck Morgan where he'd seen the kid before — leaving Gwen's home. "You take piano lessons from Miss Arlington, don't you?"

"Yeah." There was an implied *What of it?* in his tone.

Morgan wondered if some of Owen's

friends gave him a hard time about playing the piano. "She's my teacher too."

The kid shot him a look of disbelief. "Aren't you kinda *old* to be takin' lessons?"

"Never too old to learn something new."

Owen grunted.

"And Miss Arlington's a good teacher. Don't you think? I know I've enjoyed her thus far."

"Yeah, I suppose she's good." The kid squinted his eyes. "You sweet on her or somethin'?"

Fortunately for Morgan, they'd reached his home. He ignored Owen's question and pointed toward the garage. "My motorcar's in there. Want to try to clean up that knee before I take you home?"

"No. It can wait." It was clear he wanted to get into the Ford touring car as soon as possible.

Within minutes, the damaged bicycle and its owner were in the automobile and Morgan was driving down the hillside on Shenandoah, headed toward the Goldsmith home. As he passed through the intersection with Wallula, he couldn't help glancing toward Gwen's home and wishing he hadn't upset her the way he had.

Because Owen was right. Morgan *was* sweet on Miss Arlington.

Seventeen

Gwen was standing in the kitchen, the door to the back porch open to catch the breeze, when she heard the *put-putter-put* of an automobile. Her heart leapt at the sound. Was it Morgan's car? Was he coming here? But no. The sound didn't stop. It continued on, fading as the automobile continued down the street.

She opened the oven door and removed the pan holding the pot roast and vegetables.

She didn't care, of course, that it might have been Morgan's automobile. It could as easily have been Harrison Carter's or one of the two or three other local men who owned motorcars.

But it had sounded like Morgan's to her.

A groan of frustration slipped from her lips. This was silly, the way she thought of him so often. Silly and totally unlike her.

I was rude to him this morning.

It was true. She'd walked away while he

talked to Reverend Rawlings. She hadn't spoken a word of good-bye. He had seemed appreciative that she'd allowed him to sit beside her, and she had responded with irritation and rudeness.

"I wanted to see you at worship. One can learn a lot about a person that way."

What had he meant by that? Had he been sincere? And why did it matter to her anyway? If it weren't for the election, they might never have met, and even if they had, they would have had nothing more than a passing acquaintance.

She recalled that moment, up at the resort site, when she'd felt herself sway toward him, when she'd thought he might kiss her, when she'd thought she might welcome his kiss, when —

"Gwennie," Cleo said, "the table is set. Can I help with anything in here?"

"What?" Gwen turned to face her sister, who stood in the kitchen doorway. "I'm sorry. I was woolgathering." Not for anything in the world would she tell Cleo where her thoughts had been — or upon whom.

"Just wondered if I can help you with anything."

"No. Dinner's ready. Tell Dad to come inside. I'll have everything on the table in a moment."

■ ■ ■ ■

Morgan followed Owen up to the boy's house, carrying the damaged bicycle. Before they reached the front porch, the door opened and a woman — presumably Owen's mother — stepped outside. Her brown hair was streaked with gray, and her face was lined with worry.

"Owen? What happened?"

"Nothin', Ma. I fell off my bike, that's all."

The woman's eyes shifted to Morgan.

"I saw him take the spill, Mrs. Goldsmith." He set the bike on the ground, leaning it against the porch. "When I saw the bike was damaged, I offered to bring Owen home. His knee's banged up."

The woman knelt on the porch to examine Owen's injury, saying not a word about the torn trouser leg.

From the look of things, Morgan guessed the Goldsmith family was none too prosperous. The house could use a coat of paint, and the porch sagged at one end. He wondered if they would have the funds to fix that bicycle wheel. Probably not. The kid's spill would mean no bike riding for a while.

Mrs. Goldsmith stood and looked at him. "I'm afraid I don't know your name so I can thank you properly."

"I'm sorry." He removed his hat. "I'm Morgan McKinley."

"Oh, you're the other candidate for mayor."

"Yes, I am."

"I'll be voting for Miss Arlington. I've known her for a number of years, and she is a fine young woman."

He smiled to let her know he took no offense at her honesty. "That's all right. I understand. I'm sure my worthy opponent has many friends who feel as you do. But I hope I can change at least a few minds."

"Well, there's a good chance you'll get my husband's vote. He doesn't much cotton to the idea of a woman mayor." From the stiff way she held herself and the tone of her voice, it was obvious her husband's attitude grated on Mrs. Goldsmith. But her expression softened as she added, "I do thank you for your kindness to my son, Mr. McKinley."

"Glad I could be of service, ma'am." He pointed at the tear in Owen's trousers. "You take care of that knee."

"It don't even hurt anymore," the boy replied.

Morgan put his hat on his head. "Good day to you both."

"Good day, Mr. McKinley."

Morgan turned on his heel and strode back to his car. He couldn't help but wonder if the votes for mayor might be split along gender lines. Would the women of Bethlehem Springs vote for Gwen and the men for him? Hmm. Might be that quite a few men would vote for her simply because of how pretty she was.

If I wasn't running, I'd vote for her myself.

The family was seated around the table, her father saying grace, when Gwen heard the *put-putter-put* of the automobile again. Almost against her will, her eyes opened and she glanced toward the front door in time to see Morgan drive past. Only a brief glimpse, but to her chagrin, her heart hiccuped at the sight of him. To make matters worse, when she turned to bow her head again, she caught Cleo watching her with a knowing gaze.

This Sunday was going from bad to worse.

She whispered, "Amen" at the close of the blessing, then passed the platter of meat to their father.

"Everything looks delicious as usual." He began to carve the roast into thick, juicy slices.

"Thank you, Dad."

"I heard that Mr. McKinley attended church at All Saints this morning." There was a hint of mirth in Cleo's voice. "Did you see him there?"

Gwen pretended not to notice that her sister was fishing for information. "Yes, I saw him."

"Did you speak to him?"

Gwen felt heat rise in her cheeks as she scooped some potatoes and onions onto her plate. "Yes, we spoke briefly."

"He's gained the support of many of the men in our congregation," their father said. "I suppose that's to be expected. But Cleo and I will do our best to change their minds before the election. Too bad we live too far out to have an actual vote."

Would any of them be able to do enough? Gwen hated knowing that many men of her acquaintance would still choose Morgan because he was a man. It hurt worse that many women would vote for him for the same reason. A lot was riding on next Saturday's debate. More than she'd thought when she accepted the offer to participate.

Will it be so terrible if he wins? Perhaps not, but she wasn't giving up.

At least he seemed to want the same things for Bethlehem Springs that Gwen wanted — better schools, new jobs and prosperity for the people of the town, fairness and integrity in the local government. That was some comfort.

Cleo intruded on Gwen's thoughts, saying, "If it's all right with you, Gwennie, I'd like to come back tomorrow and stay with you for the rest of the week. Then I can visit every home and business in Bethlehem Springs and encourage everyone to turn out for the debate on Saturday. Don't you worry. You'll show them that you're made of the right stuff. Morgan's a likeable sort, but he hasn't got the heart for this town the way you do. They'll see that for themselves come Saturday."

"Oh, Cleo. I hope you're right."

After a quick look around — no one else in sight — Harrison Carter climbed the steps that led to the living quarters above the High Horse Saloon. He rapped sharply on the door and waited. When his knock wasn't answered, he let himself in. The apartment was dark, the curtains drawn over the windows.

"Tattersall?"

He was about to leave when he heard sounds from what he assumed to be the bedroom.

"Tattersall, I'd like to speak to you a moment. It's Harrison Carter."

More sounds from the other room, louder this time, followed by a string of curse words. Moments later, Hiram Tattersall appeared in the doorway, sliding his suspenders up to his shoulders, his upper body clad only in his underwear.

Hung-over, no doubt.

Tattersall blinked a few times, yawned, then said, "Never expected to see you here."

"Neither did I."

"And on a Sunday to boot."

"Tattersall, I'm here about the election. I want you to withdraw your name from the ballot."

"You what?" The man scratched his left armpit.

"I want you to withdraw as a candidate for mayor."

"Why should I?"

Harrison's eyes narrowed. The man was such a fool. Didn't he know who he was talking to? "There are many reasons, but suffice it to say that if you do not, you will find your saloon tied up in so many legal entanglements that Prohibition will be the least of your concerns. Because it just may be that I can find you've broken enough laws that they'll send you to the state penitentiary." He took a step closer to Tattersall and lowered his voice. "Because not to do as I request could be the worst thing you ever do. Do I make myself clear?"

Perhaps Hiram Tattersall wasn't a complete fool. He stopped asking questions. Gave up any pretense of arguing. "Guess I wasn't going to win anyway. Not with you backing that little gal."

"You'll see to the details tomorrow, I trust."

"Yes, sir, Mr. Carter. I'll see to them tomorrow."

"Good." Harrison turned toward the door. "I'm sure you are doing so for the good of the town. Good day, Tattersall."

EIGHTEEN

A refreshing breeze blew off the mountains as Gwen walked toward the mercantile, carrying a basket in the crook of her arm. The sky was a pristine blue, dotted with cotton-ball clouds. It was the same sort of day that had made her fall in love with Bethlehem Springs that first summer in Idaho.

A tiny bell sounded overhead as she stepped into the store. From a room in the back, she heard Bert Humphrey call, "Be right with you."

"No hurry, Mr. Humphrey."

She started down one of the aisles. If Cleo planned to stay with her all week, she would need to stock up on supplies. Her sister might be female, tall, and thin, but she had an appetite as big as any of the cowpokes who worked the Arlington ranch. Not to mention her sweet tooth. Gwen planned to bake a cake later this morning, hopefully before her sister arrived.

The bell chimed again, and Gwen looked back to see who had entered the store. It was Owen's mother, Kitty Goldsmith, carrying a basket of eggs in her arms.

When their gazes met, Gwen said, "Good morning, Kitty."

Kitty gave her a slight smile that must have taken all her energy. The woman always looked exhausted. Her life was not an easy one, caring for her three children and for her husband, Patton, who had been injured in an accident at the sawmill three years earlier. To support their family, Kitty sold fresh eggs, worked as a seamstress, and took in laundry. Patton did odd jobs, as he was able — which wasn't often enough.

"It's a beautiful morning, isn't it?" Gwen said, wishing she could help ease her neighbor's burdens. Kitty was only six years Gwen's senior, but she looked twenty years older. "It won't be long before true summer is upon us."

Kitty nodded. "I hope it won't get too hot too soon."

"I hope so too." She shifted the basket to her other arm. "I wanted to tell you how well Owen is doing with his piano lessons. You must be so proud of him."

Another little smile, this one staying a fraction longer. "I am."

"Do you go with him when he practices at the Evans's house?"

Kitty shook her head.

"Then come with him to his next lesson. I know you'd be blessed by his progress."

"I'll try." She sighed. "I'm just grateful his hands weren't injured when he fell yesterday. They could have been."

"His hands? What fall?"

"Owen had an accident on his bicycle yesterday. The wheel was bent up. It's ruined, far as I can tell. Heaven knows when there will be any money to repair it or replace it."

"You say his hands are okay. Was he otherwise injured?"

"He scraped his knee but nothing serious. Mr. McKinley saw the accident and drove him home in his automobile. Owen loved that part. He's never had the opportunity to ride in a car before."

Gwen recalled the sound of the motorcar passing her house the previous day. Not once but twice. That must have been where he'd gone. To take Owen home.

"He's a very genial man, isn't he?" Kitty continued. "He was so kind to Owen. But I told him you would have my vote."

Gwen patted Kitty's hand where it rested on the handle of her basket. "I appreciate your loyalty."

"After all the kindnesses you've shown my family, how could I do otherwise?"

Her neighbor's reply took her aback a little. "I hope you think I will make a good mayor. I wouldn't want to be elected for any other reason."

Whatever Kitty might have said next was interrupted by the appearance of Bert Humphrey from the back of the store. "How can I help you ladies?"

"I've brought you some eggs, Mr. Humphrey," Kitty answered as she walked toward him.

"He's a very genial man, isn't he?"

Indeed. Mr. McKinley was genial — and too much on her mind.

To distract his thoughts from the lovely Gwen Arlington — and to remove the temptation of going to see her uninvited once again — Morgan drove to the building site late on Monday morning. The workers had made noticeable progress since his last visit.

Fagan greeted him with a cheery "Halloo!" as he strode across the yard. "Sure and I didn't expect to be seeing you again this soon."

"I'm surprised myself. It's a hard habit to

break, being up here every day. But it looks like I'm not needed. No more vandalism, I take it."

"One of the guards thought he heard someone moving around the bathhouse a couple of nights back, but if anyone was there he was scared off. No sign of him come morning. No mischief done."

Morgan nodded, not happy to hear there might have been another trespasser prowling around the site. Still, as there'd been no damage —

"Stonemasons ought to begin their work inside the lodge next week."

"What about the prayer chapel?"

"The men have made a good start on it. Sure and I'm thinking it won't take long to finish."

"Good. I want the chapel given high priority, Fagan."

"I'll pass that word along to Christopher. He'll see to it."

The two men walked side by side toward the lodge. Once inside the enormous lobby, Morgan stopped and breathed in the scent of lumber that filled the air. In his mind's eye, he saw the room completed and fully furnished. He imagined guests of all ages and of all classes sitting throughout, visiting, laughing, their faces shining with improved health. In the dining room, he pictured guests drinking tea in the afternoon or eating a delicious, healthy meal in the evening.

With everything that he was, everything he believed, he was convinced the New Hope Health Spa was supposed to be here, on this land, in this place. He couldn't allow Harrison Carter and his political cronies to impede the completion of this resort.

Ask Rudyard.

Morgan turned toward Fagan, but his friend was inspecting the doorframe and obviously had not spoken to him.

Ask Rudyard.

The words tugged at him, insistent on being understood.

Rudyard . . . Rudyard . . .

His eyes widened. Of course. Senator William Rudyard. A long-time friend of his mother's. Was it possible he could be of some help? The senator was a man of influence, both within Idaho and beyond. Yes, he just might be able to help Morgan — with his problems with the commissioners *and* with winning the election. He would contact him immediately.

Maybe it was time for him to arrange for a dinner party. The reason for hiring a household staff was so he could entertain, to build rapport with other citizens of Bethlehem Springs, and as a result perhaps win their votes in the election. He couldn't depend upon the debate to bring him all the votes he would need to win.

Trouble was, whenever he pictured himself sitting down at the long dinner table with a room full of guests, he always imagined Gwen seated at the other end.

Cleo was full of excitement when she arrived in the early afternoon. "Have you heard?" she asked Gwen as she led her horse toward the small stable at the back of Gwen's lot. "Tattersall withdrew from the race for mayor this morning. Now it's between just you and Morgan."

"Yes, I heard."

Gwen didn't know whether to feel worried or glad. If everyone who'd planned to vote for Tattersall — surely there couldn't be very many of them — chose to vote for Morgan, it could mean he had the edge. On the other hand, it was a relief to know there was no chance that a known drunkard would be their next mayor.

"How did you hear about it so quickly?" she asked as Cleo removed the saddle from her gelding and led the animal into the second of two stalls.

"I saw Charles Benson as I rode into town, and he told me." Cleo pushed her hair away from her face. "He asked after you."

"I hope you told him I was well."

"Poor Charlie. Do you suppose he'll ever give up on winning your heart?"

"I hope so. I haven't encouraged him in the least."

"Gwennie, if you so much as smile at a man, he's going to take it as encouragement. You oughta know that by now."

"Sometimes you say the silliest things."

Cleo laughed. "And you haven't a clue about the power you have over men. You're the prettiest woman within five hundred miles, and they want to swarm around you like bees to a hive."

Irritated now, Gwen turned and hurried toward the house. It was bad enough when men thought her nothing more than a pretty face with an empty head. It was worse when her beloved twin teased her about it.

Maybe I'd be taken seriously if I started wearing trousers and smoking a pipe. She shuddered at the thought.

"Gwennie?" Cleo stepped into the kitchen, contrition in her eyes. "I'm sorry. You know I don't mean to upset you like that. I was only funning you."

Gwen turned, her vexation already spent.

"I know." She could never stay angry with her sister for long. "You're forgiven."

"Thanks, sis." Cleo clasped her in a tight embrace. "Truth is, I've got a bit of man trouble of my own."

Gwen took a step back so she could look her sister in the eye.

"His name's Tyler King, a new hand working at the ranch. Been there about a month now. Gwennie, whenever he comes around, my heart starts racing like a hummingbird's wings. I get all discombobulated and clumsy."

Cleo in love? Gwen hoped this King fellow was worthy of her.

"I think he likes me too," Cleo continued as she settled onto a chair at the kitchen table. "But he sure is slow letting me know for sure."

Gwen sat opposite her sister and took hold of her right hand. "I'm sure he will when the time is right."

"I hope so." Cleo inhaled deeply, then gave her head a shake. "But that's not what I'm here for. Let's get down to business. What's our strategy now that Tattersall has withdrawn?"

"No different. My greatest hurdle is the fact that I'm a woman."

Cleo screwed up her mouth. "Hmm." She

tapped the fingers of her left hand on the table. Then her eyes widened. "I know. You write down what you see as the two or three most important issues facing Bethlehem Springs. Then when I go to talk to folks, I can share your own words with them. Afterward, I'll invite them to come to the debate on Saturday. It will give them a chance to see that you can think like a mayor and hold your ground with any man."

"I hope that's what they'll see." Gwen released Cleo's hand. "I'm starting to feel nervous. Maybe I shouldn't have agreed to the debate. Maybe it will convince more people to vote for Mr. McKinley than for me."

"Well, if that's the outcome, I guess we'll have to believe it's God's will. Won't we?"

Strange, the way Cleo's words broke through the worry that had been swirling inside Gwen. Her sister was right. She must leave the results in God's hands. If He wanted her to be the mayor, then it would come about, and if not, then better she lose.

She drew in a deep breath and let it out, then stood. "I'll get some writing paper and prepare my comments for you. And while I'm working on that" — she pointed toward the layer cake on the counter — "why don't you cut yourself a piece of cake? I made it for you."

"Well, if that don't make me as happy as a pup with two tails." Cleo whipped off her hat and hung it on the spindle of her chair, then made a beeline for the triple-layer cake.

Laughing softly — thinking to herself that there was no other woman in the world like Cleopatra Arlington — Gwen went after her writing materials.

NINETEEN

On Tuesday, Morgan found himself frequently checking his watch and the clocks in various rooms in the house. It seemed to him that three o'clock could not get there soon enough.

That morning he'd sent invitations to a number of influential members of the community for a dinner party in his home on the following Friday evening. But at the last minute, he decided that the occasion wouldn't have anything to do with his campaign. And since it wouldn't be campaign related, he could invite anyone he wanted — including Gwen Arlington. Therefore, he had one more invitation in his possession. It was addressed to her. He wanted them to be friends. No, closer than friends.

How much closer?

His mother had longed to see him married. She wouldn't have minded grandchildren either. But after his experience with Yvette Dutetre, the last of a number of unfortunate romantic relationships, Morgan had decided he was a failure when it came to finding the right woman. He had reconciled himself to growing old without a wife or children. His life was full in many other ways. He had good friends, like Fagan Doyle, and he had the kind of wealth that allowed him to do good works, to be of service to others.

Only now, having met Gwen, Morgan was no longer reconciled to bachelorhood. He even thought she might be the reason God had brought him to Bethlehem Springs. New Hope could have been built in at least a half dozen other places in the western states, and yet he'd believed with certainty that this was where it was meant to be. Could Gwen be why?

He wandered into the front parlor and sat on the piano bench. His fingers settled on the keys and he ran through several scales. Then he checked the time again. Almost three o'clock.

He rose and walked to the front door, opening it in time to see Gwen arrive at his gate. "Good afternoon, Miss Arlington." He stepped onto the veranda.

"Good afternoon, Mr. McKinley." She

came down the walk and climbed the steps.

The skirt of her dress was narrow, the hem reaching only to her ankles, the waistline loose in the style of the day. The fabric, a dusty-rose color, complemented her complexion. Her pale hair was parted in the middle and swept up and back. Morgan wondered how she would look if the pins were removed and her hair was allowed to tumble around her shoulders.

Beautiful. That's how she would look. Just as she did now. And unlike too many other young women he'd known, her beauty was more than skin deep.

He realized then that he had been staring at her, and she knew it. Her flushed cheeks told him so.

"I'm looking forward to my lesson." As soon as the words were out of his mouth, he regretted them. He sounded like a schoolboy with a crush on his teacher.

He held the door open and motioned her inside.

She walked without hesitation into the front parlor. At the piano, she set sheet music on the music desk, then turned to face him. "Let's begin with scales."

So that's how it was to be. All business. All right. He hadn't excelled in business by quitting at the first sign of difficulty. He wasn't about to quit in his attempts to win her affections just because she seemed uninterested.

He sat on the bench, placed his fingers on the keys, and began running through the scales, all the while aware of where Gwen stood — behind him and one step to the right. He also heard the tap of her shoe on the hardwood floor, keeping time like a metronome.

Morgan McKinley had elegant hands. Large hands with long, narrow fingers. The hands of a gentleman. Yet Gwen suspected they were also the hands of a man unafraid of physical labor.

She imagined her right hand enfolded in his left, his right hand in the small of her back — gentle but firm, guiding her every step — as they twirled around a ballroom, an orchestra playing a waltz. Oh, how very much she loved to dance.

But it wasn't an orchestra bringing the melody to life. It was Morgan. He'd finished his scales and now played from the sheet music — a basic but recognizable Viennese waltz — she'd left for him a week ago. Thankfully, he wasn't looking at her. Thankfully, he could have no idea where her imagination had taken her.

"That was very good," she said when he finished.

He turned on the bench. "I've practiced every day. I wanted you to know I'm serious about becoming accomplished on the piano."

Think of him as you think of any of your other students. He is just one of your students. Nothing more.

Tell that to her rapidly beating heart. What was it about this man that created such confusion inside of her? Whatever it was, she must put a stop to it.

She walked to the other end of the grand piano and looked at him through the open lid. "I shall have to bring more difficult pieces for you to learn, Mr. McKinley. You have a natural talent."

He rose and stepped to one side. "Would you play something, Miss Arlington?"

"Me?" Her pulse quickened again.

"Please." His voice was warm, almost like a caress. It was also irresistible.

With a nod of acquiescence, she returned to the keyboard and settled onto the bench. The smooth wood was still warm from his body heat.

Concentrate. Concentrate.

She chose to play a more difficult version of the same Viennese waltz, and it wasn't long before she was lost in the melody. The instrument was a wonder, every note so clean and pure. The music swirled around her and filled every corner of the room. When she reached the end of the song, it was hard not to return to the beginning a second time. She was reluctant to stop.

Morgan cried, "Bravo!" and applauded.

Pleasure swept through Gwen. "Thank you."

"You've given me something to aspire to."

"I suspect the day will come when you surpass my playing, if you are diligent with your practice."

"I'll be diligent." He leaned forward, resting his forearms on the side of the piano. "I can be very single minded when I have a goal in mind."

A frisson of expectation shivered along her spine.

Morgan straightened. "Have you something new for me to work on this week?"

Sanity returned, and she reached for the sheet music she'd brought with her. "Yes, I do. I brought several songs for you to learn." She opened the first one and played it for him. Afterward, she rose and offered him the bench. "Now you try it."

It was like an intricate dance, Morgan

thought, the way they moved around each other. One moment Gwen drew near. The next she moved away. One moment she smiled, her eyes filled with warmth. The next her expression was cool and distant.

She beguiled him.

She confused him.

He was almost relieved when Inez Cheevers entered the front parlor. Perhaps he could get his thoughts in order if he had a moment or two away from Gwen.

"I'm sorry, sir, but there's a telegram for you. I thought it might be important or else I would have waited."

"Yes. Of course." He nodded at the housekeeper, then said to Gwen, "I won't be long. Please excuse me."

Morgan had expected the telegram to be from one of his suppliers for New Hope. Instead, he found a message from William Rudyard:

ARRIVING BETHLEHEM SPRINGS THURSDAY. BRINGING TWO FELLOW SENATORS INTERESTED IN YOUR RE-SORT. STAYING UNTIL SUNDAY. WILL FIND WAY TO RESOLVE ISSUES.

BILLY

Morgan chuckled softly. Grass didn't grow

under the feet of William Rudyard. He'd known that. But he hadn't expected such a quick response. Nor had he expected William to come to Bethlehem Springs in person. At least, not this soon.

He glanced toward the parlor.

The three senators would be here for his dinner party. Perfect!

He set the telegram on the table in the center of the entry before returning to the front parlor. Gwen stood at the large windows that overlooked the town. He crossed the room to join her there.

"You can see the roof of my home from here," she said softly.

"Which one is it?" As if he hadn't discovered that on his own. Was his question the same as a lie?

She pointed. "There. The one with the tall weeping willow in the backyard."

"Ah, yes. I see it."

She looked at him, concern in her eyes. "I pray the telegram wasn't bad news."

"No." He shook his head. "Not bad news. In fact, it was good news. I'm to have some visitors from the state capital. Three senators who are coming to see New Hope."

"Word of your health resort is spreading already. That's good."

This seemed the perfect opportunity, and

Morgan took it. "I'm going to have a dinner party on Friday night. I'd like it if you came." To ensure her agreement, he added, "If you become the mayor of Bethlehem Springs, it wouldn't hurt for you to know some of the men in state government."

Gwen Arlington would never make a good poker player, Morgan thought, for he would swear her eyes revealed each and every thought as she weighed his invitation. He knew the precise moment she decided to accept.

But to be on the safe side, he said, "I would be very honored to have you here."

"Thank you. I accept your kind invitation."

Relief flooded through him and he smiled, not trying to disguise how pleased he was.

Gwen smiled too. "You are a rather strange political opponent, Mr. McKinley. Asking me to give you piano lessons. Giving me a private tour of your resort. Inviting me to your dinner parties. Aren't you concerned how I might use the things I learn about you to my own advantage?"

"Miss Arlington, if you should learn something that makes me unworthy or unsuitable to serve as mayor, then it would be your right and your duty to inform the voters of it. I expect nothing else."

Her smile faded as he spoke, replaced by a frown that pinched the skin above the bridge of her nose. "I don't understand you."

Morgan wanted to kiss away the frown, but he wisely took a step backward, out of temptation's reach. "Shall we continue my lesson before our time is up?"

"Yes." Her cheeks grew flushed. "Of course."

He would kiss her. One day he would kiss her. He hoped that day came soon — before the waiting drove him crazy.

TWENTY

When the dust-covered Cadillac rolled into the turn-around in front of the McKinley house on Thursday afternoon, Morgan stepped onto the veranda and waited for the vehicle's passengers to disembark. The household had been in a general uproar for the past two days as guest bedrooms were cleaned and aired and everything made ready for William and his fellow senators. Now they were here.

Senator William Rudyard — Billy to his friends — was a large man, both in height and weight. His complexion was naturally ruddy, but his love for the outdoors made it even more so. Though not yet sixty, his hair was pure white.

"By George! We're here at last, Morgan." William strode toward the front steps. "I hope we haven't come at an inopportune time. I gathered from your message that you want these troublesome matters resolved as quickly as possible." He climbed the steps to where Morgan stood.

"You're welcome in my home anytime, sir. You must know that." Morgan shook the senator's hand.

William turned toward the other two men who now stood at the top of the steps. "Gentlemen, this young man is Morgan McKinley. Morgan, meet Senator Jeremiah Hayes and Senator Clive Austin."

"How do you do?" Morgan shook the men's hands. "Welcome." He motioned toward the front door. "Do come in. I'm sure you'd like something to drink to wash away the dust of your journey. I'll have your luggage brought into the house and put into your rooms."

William put an arm around Morgan's shoulders. "I must say. I was surprised when I learned you'd moved to Idaho. More than once I tried to convince Danielle to marry me and settle here."

"I know."

Softer this time: "I miss your mother."

Morgan nodded.

"She was the finest woman I've ever known or ever expect to know."

"Then you'll understand why New Hope is important to me. It was her dream to see something like this built. I mean to see it happen, despite the problems I've encountered."

William dropped his arm and turned toward the other two men. "Are you up to a tour of the building site today?"

Jeremiah Hayes answered, "Certainly. It's why we're here."

"How far is your resort from Bethlehem Springs?" William asked.

"Not far," Morgan answered. "About half an hour in an automobile."

"Then I say we wet our whistles and be on our way."

Harrison stared out the window of his law office, his gaze resting on the McKinley home on the hillside above him. "You're sure?" he asked his clerk.

"I'm sure. I was talking to Nathan Patterson when Senator Rudyard came in to ask directions to the McKinley home. Heard him introduce himself with my own ears. Heard him clear as day."

William Rudyard was a name Harrison knew well. He was a powerful man and not just in Idaho. He had the ear of men in positions of power in the business and financial worlds as well as in government, both state and national. How did McKinley know him? Why was the senator in Bethlehem

Springs?

"Did he say anything else?"

"No, sir. Just wanted directions, and when he got them, he went on his way. There were two other men in the automobile with him. Can't say who they were."

Harrison continued to stare up at the house. After a minute or two more, his clerk left, closing the door softly behind him.

Harrison didn't like this. He didn't like being left in the dark. If someone like Senator Rudyard was in Bethlehem Springs, he wanted to know why. Elias Spade should have known about this, should have informed him before his clerk stumbled on the information.

"What are you up to, McKinley?"

Perhaps Gwen Arlington knew.

A frown furrowed his forehead. He'd heard that McKinley had attended All Saints last Sunday and sat with Gwen. First piano lessons, then church, and now this. Something had to be done.

Morgan and his three guests had just stepped out of the house when he saw Cleo riding her horse along Skyview Street. He raised an arm and motioned her over. Cleo obliged, hopping down from the saddle. After she tied her horse to the hitching post, she strode toward the veranda with that easy gait of hers.

"Gentlemen," Morgan said when she arrived, "I'd like you to meet Miss Cleo Arlington."

"By George!" William exclaimed. "You're a woman."

Cleo bumped the brim of her hat with the knuckle of her index finger. "So my father told me." She smiled, as if to show she was neither surprised nor bothered by his words.

Morgan finished the introductions, then asked, "What brings you to town?"

"I'm campaigning for Gwen this week. But I don't reckon it would be a good idea to give my little speech to you. Not unless you've decided to drop out like Tattersall." Her voice rose in question.

Morgan chuckled. "I haven't thrown in the towel yet."

"Then I'd best be on my way. More folks to see before the day is done. Gotta make sure they vote for the right candidate." She tugged on the brim of her hat, first to Morgan, then to his guests. "Good day to you." She strode back to her horse, untied him, swung into the saddle, and waved a final good-bye.

"What a strange young woman," Jeremiah Hayes said.

Morgan glanced over his shoulder. "Believe me, Senator, the world would be a far better place with more people like Cleo Arlington and her sister in it."

Gwen was sweeping her front porch when a motorcar pulled to the curb outside her yard. For the briefest of moments, she thought it might be Morgan, and her breath caught in anticipation. But it wasn't his car and it wasn't him. It was Harrison Carter.

Disquiet replaced disappointment. She wished he would go away. She no longer wanted his support in this election. She didn't care for his attitude toward her and, even more, had begun to distrust him, although she couldn't say why. But she had better keep that to herself. If she won the election, she would have to work with him at least some of the time. Better they be friendly acquaintances than unfriendly ones.

She leaned the broom against the side of the house and stepped to the porch railing. "Good afternoon, Mr. Carter."

"Miss Arlington." He opened the gate and came up the walkway. "I trust you are well."

"Quite well, thank you."

"We haven't had an opportunity to visit since the night of the dinner party. I wanted to inquire if there was anything I could do

239

for you. Perhaps I could help in some way in preparation for the debate on Saturday."

"That's kind of you." She motioned toward the chairs on the porch. "But I believe I'm as prepared as I can be."

He sat and removed his hat, setting it on his knee. "Your sister has been campaigning for you, I hear. It might be wise if you made those calls yourself. Your sister is . . . well, unconventional, to say the least."

Gwen's smile was forced. "Cleo is wonderfully unconventional, sir, and I have complete trust in her as my representative."

"Miss Arlington" — he leaned forward — "I am more experienced in these things, and I urge you to consider my advice before discarding it out of hand." He motioned toward her, indicating her attire. "You are nothing like your sister."

She bit back a retort. He was rude and boorish, and she wished he would leave.

"I've also heard that you're giving McKinley piano lessons."

She remained silent.

"Miss Arlington, really. This isn't wise. Trust me, he has an ulterior motive in hiring you. Have you considered that he might try to compromise your reputation? You and he alone in his house . . . ." He shrugged. "How does that look?"

Gwen drew a deep breath to steady herself and let it out slowly before answering. "Mr. McKinley and I are not alone in his house. Mrs. Cheevers is there. We are less alone than you and I are right now."

"It isn't the same thing."

"Isn't it? Well, you needn't worry anyway. Mr. McKinley is not that sort of man."

"You are naive."

"Perhaps." She rose to her feet. "But as long as he wishes to take lessons and is diligent in his practice, I shall continue with his instruction."

"If it is income you need —"

"My income is none of your concern." There was no disguising her anger now. He had to see it in her eyes and the stiffness of her posture.

Harrison stood. "I'm sorry." There was nothing apologetic in either his tone or his expression. "I did not mean to offend."

"I must ask you to excuse me, Mr. Carter. It is time I put dinner in the oven."

"Of course." He set his hat back on his head. "I shall see you on Saturday evening."

She forced herself to say, "Thank you for dropping by."

Now that was a lie if ever she'd spoken one.

TWENTY-ONE

"This was a mistake," Gwen whispered to her reflection in the mirror.

"Balderdash," Cleo said from the bedroom doorway. "You'll turn all the men's heads tonight. Those senators won't know what hit 'em once they lay eyes on you."

Gwen turned to face her sister. "That isn't why I'm going."

"Land sakes, Gwennie. It doesn't hurt to use what you've got. Didn't God make you this way? Both smart *and* pretty. Pretty as sunrise on the prairie, that's what you are, and nothing you do is going to change that."

Gwen swallowed a sigh. Better she drop the subject than argue with Cleo. She would never win. Her sister could be as stubborn as the day was long.

"I'll go hitch the horse to the buggy. You should've accepted Morgan's offer to come for you. Then neither one of us would have to take care of Shakespeare when you get back. It's likely to be mighty late."

"Mr. McKinley has other guests to see to without worrying about me. I've unhitched my horse from the buggy late at night before. I'm not helpless, you know."

"Yep. I know."

As soon as her sister left the room, Gwen sank onto the stool before the dressing table and massaged her temples with the tips of her fingers. Her head was beginning to throb. Perhaps she should send Cleo with her regrets. She could crawl into bed with a cup of tea and a good book and forget about making small talk with strangers.

But of course she couldn't do that. She had an election to win, and that meant being polite and glad-handing one and all.

"At least Mr. Carter won't be there."

Thinking of the man brought a frown. Look how he'd reacted to the piano lessons. Just imagine how upset he would be once he learned she'd attended a dinner party at Morgan McKinley's home. He'd be livid.

Poor Susannah Carter. Gwen didn't doubt that Harrison's wife would bear the brunt of his ill temper. He seemed that type of man. The dictatorial sort who believed women should stay in their place, be seen but not heard, right along with his children.

Which made her wonder why he'd backed

her for mayor.

Harrison Carter was also a good reminder of why she'd chosen to remain unmarried. She would rather enter old age as a spinster than allow herself to be joined to a husband who might treat her as a possession. And maybe as mayor, she would help others realize that women were not second-class citizens, that their thoughts and opinions had value.

Her confidence and resolve restored, she rose from the stool, checked her appearance one last time, then turned and picked up her wrap from the foot of the bed. It was time to leave, lest she be late. Gwen hated to be late.

Morgan saw William Rudyard's eyes widen and heard the older gentleman's intake of breath, and he knew Gwen had arrived. He turned toward the parlor doorway.

There she was, a vision in a pale-blue gown the same shade as her eyes, the bodice and skirt accented with white Venetian lace. Her upswept hair was dressed with pearls to match the simple strand of the same that encircled her throat.

"Excuse me, Senator."

Morgan crossed the room, no doubt smiling like a complete fool. He couldn't help it. The world seemed a brighter and better place when he was near Gwen. He hadn't seen her since his lesson, and the days had dragged by from then until now.

"Good evening, Miss Arlington. I'm glad you could come."

Her smile was polite but slightly guarded. "Good evening."

"Come with me." He offered the crook of his arm. "I want to introduce you to Senator Rudyard and his friends."

"Meeting them is why you invited me, is it not?"

That might be her reason for coming, but it wasn't his reason for inviting her. That had only been his excuse, a way to get her to agree to come, a reason for him to spend an evening with her, to offer her his arm and have her accept it, the way she did now.

He escorted her across the room filled with guests and stopped in front of William. "Senator, may I present Miss Gwen Arlington. Miss Arlington, this is Senator Rudyard."

"It's a pleasure to meet you, sir." Gwen offered her hand.

William took it. "The pleasure is all mine." He studied her with an assessing gaze before releasing her hand. Then he looked at Morgan. "I can see why you're

245

worried about winning the election. This young woman is made of sterner stuff. I can feel it in her handshake and see it in her eyes."

"Indeed," Morgan answered.

"Are you enjoying your stay in Bethlehem Springs?" Gwen asked the senator.

"We are. Morgan here is a fine host. Yesterday we drove up to the site of his new health resort. I had no idea it would be so impressive. I venture to say it will be a boon for your town and for all of Idaho. Have you been up there, Miss Arlington?"

"Yes. Mr. McKinley was kind enough to give me a tour of the building site. Like you, I was surprised and impressed."

William leaned closer to Gwen. "Then I expect you will want to lend your support to its timely completion."

Morgan placed his fingers against the small of Gwen's back. "Billy, you are dangerously close to talking politics before we have dined. I'm going to rescue Miss Arlington. She has yet to meet my other guests."

William winked at Gwen. "We shall talk more of this, my good woman."

As had been the case three weeks earlier at the Carter home, Gwen knew most of the people at the table, including Nathan Patterson and his wife. They had been present at the Carters' dinner party as well, and the commissioner would be as unhappy with them as he would be with her when he learned of their attendance tonight.

"You should visit Yellowstone," William Rudyard — seated on her right — said. "It is unforgettable, I promise you. One need not travel to the interiors of Africa in order to experience the beauty of nature. We have it in abundance in our own backyard."

"You've been to Africa?"

"Indeed. I went with Teddy Roosevelt's hunting party in aught-nine."

"I imagine Africa is quite exotic. Did you shoot any big game yourself?"

"One does not travel to Africa with Teddy and not hunt with him."

The sound of Morgan's laughter drew Gwen's gaze to the head of the table where he sat. His head was thrown back in enjoyment, and Christina and Nathan Patterson were laughing with him.

"Morgan's one of the finest young men I've ever known," the senator said softly.

She felt her cheeks grow warm, wondering what her expression had revealed to the older gentleman. "How long have you known him?"

"Since he was born. I was a friend to his father in our youth, and later, I grew very fond of Morgan's mother. Asked her to marry me the year after she was widowed, but she would have none of it. Her heart always belonged to Alastair McKinley, Morgan's father. Right to her death, she loved him."

It must be wonderful, Gwen thought, to have parents who loved each other, who were devoted to each other until death. Surely, if Elizabeth Arlington had loved Gwen's father enough — or ever — she would have stayed with him while he built his ranch in Idaho.

Her eyes turned once again toward the head of the table. Did Morgan know how blessed he'd been, to have parents who loved each another? Yes. She believed he must know. It was the kind of man he was.

"Dear, is everything all right?"

Harrison looked as his wife, seated in a nearby chair, an open book now lying face down in her lap. "Why do you ask?"

"You've seemed out of sorts for days."

"Have I?" He folded the newspaper and set it aside.

"Is there anything I can do to help? I would like to, if I can."

"No, there is nothing you can do." He rose from the sofa. "I've had business matters on my mind. That's all. Nothing that concerns you."

She looked as if she would say something more, then took up her book and began reading again. A wise choice of action. Nothing irritated Harrison more than when Susannah tried to understand a man's business.

He left the parlor and walked to the library, closing the door behind him to ensure he wouldn't be disturbed again. At the window, he looked across the darkened town to the McKinley home, now ablaze with lights. A dinner party — much the same as the one he'd hosted three weeks earlier — was happening there, a party whose guest list included three Idaho senators.

Why were they in Bethlehem Springs? What was their relationship with Morgan McKinley? How would their presence affect the election? Or would it?

Harrison didn't like that he had no answers to those questions. Lately it seemed that the world was set against him.

He pinched the bridge of his nose between thumb and index finger as he turned from the window. His headache was worsening.

He cursed softly as he sank onto a chair. To the devil with McKinley and his friends. Harrison Carter would achieve his goal. McKinley would give up on completing that resort. Before many more weeks had passed, the fellow would be begging for someone to buy those one hundred acres of land. And Harrison would be more than willing to oblige.

But what will it take to make him sell?

"A wonderful evening," William said, his foot on the bottom step of the staircase. "Superb in every way. I believe you've made a good impression on the folks who were here tonight."

Morgan nodded.

"I'm looking forward to the debate tomorrow evening. Should prove most interesting." He chuckled. "And don't underestimate Miss Arlington."

"Believe me, Billy, I won't."

"Well, good night then." With a wave of his hand, the senator turned and climbed the stairs to his guest room.

Morgan left the entry hall and went into the front parlor. At the piano, he brushed his fingertips along the white keys, then went outside to stand on the veranda. The night air was balmy, a soft breeze rustling the leaves of the trees and shrubbery.

It had been a good evening. The company had been pleasant, the food had been as fine as any served to him in the best restaurants. He would give his compliments to Mrs. Nelson when she arrived in the morning, along with the accolades of his guests.

Gwen had seemed to enjoy herself too. He was glad of that.

He smiled as he leaned against a post. Lately, whenever he thought of Gwen, a smile was his automatic response. He'd never expected his feelings for her to change — never expected he would actually fall in love — but change they had. And because of that change, he had a feeling more changes were in store for him. What that was exactly he couldn't be sure.

Twenty-Two

Gwen awoke Saturday morning with a smile on her lips. She'd been dreaming something wonderful, something happy, but she couldn't recall the details. She wished she could.

Stretching while releasing a soft groan, she opened her eyes. Sunlight filtered through the curtains over her window, and she knew that she'd slept later than was usual. She should get up. A busy day awaited her. Still, she would rather lie in bed and try to recapture her dream.

Only it was thoughts of her evening at Morgan's home that came to her instead.

William Rudyard had been an interesting conversationalist and had offered numerous bits of information about Morgan. Gwen had been careful not to ask too many questions, but the senator hadn't needed her to. He was quite forthright without encouragement from her. Everything he'd said had made her like Morgan a little more than before. Even more than she wanted to like him.

She closed her eyes and pictured her political opponent in his fine black suit and tie. She hadn't seen Morgan in formal dress before. It suited him. She could imagine him walking along a promenade, hands gloved, swinging a cane, a dashing figure in a silk top hat.

Dashing. That was a good description. Morgan was, indeed, dashing.

Gwen covered her face with her hands and groaned a second time. It was most inconvenient to like the opposition in this mayoral race. She never should have accepted his invitation to last night's dinner party. She never should have agreed to give him piano lessons. She should have kept her distance from the start.

A rap sounded on her door. "Hey, sleepyhead," Cleo called to her. "Are you ever getting up?"

"Yes."

The door opened, and her sister looked into the room. "When?"

"Now." Gwen sat up, her back propped against the pillows.

Cleo entered and sat on the foot of the bed. "So tell me about last night. What did you think of the senators?"

"It was a lovely affair. Senator Rudyard sat beside me at dinner, and I found him most entertaining. He and the other two senators were impressed with Mr. McKinley's spa."

"So they should be, from what you've told me. Did much politicking go on?"

"Not a bit."

"That's strange, isn't it?"

Cleo was right. That was odd. Surely politics had been Morgan's reason for hosting the party, and yet he'd said not a word about the election. He'd even warned the senator off of politics early in the evening. Perhaps he hoped to win the race by charm alone. Judging from last night that might be possible.

"Want to go over your opening comments for tonight?" Cleo asked, oblivious to Gwen's thoughts.

She shook her head. "Later. Right now I'd like some breakfast, and then I think I'll go over to All Saints. I feel the need for some solitude."

"I can get out of your hair, if that's what you're needing."

"Oh, Cleo." She reached forward and took her sister's hand. "I didn't mean you were in the way. I just want to be silent before the Lord, to settle my thoughts and hear His voice. The church seems the best place for it."

"I reckon you're right." Cleo slid from the bed. "I'll scramble some eggs. Coffee's all ready for you."

"Thank you. You've been such a help to me this week. I'm going to miss having you here every day."

"Much as I love you, Gwennie, a week of living in town is just about all I can stomach in one stretch. You know that. Just like ranch living didn't suit you when you tried it. You like living in town and being involved with your neighbors and all. I need those wide open spaces to make me happy."

William Rudyard placed the document on Morgan's desk. "You needn't worry about this. Clive and Jeremiah are as thoroughly impressed as I am. We'll make sure that these petty impediments are resolved within the month."

"That soon?"

"That soon. Trust me. The county commissioners can be pressured by the state in this regard. I believe Mr. Carter will see the writing on the wall and acquiesce. I should think you'd have your commitment from the railroad in a few weeks. I know a number of men on the board of directors, and I'll be placing calls to them as soon as I return to Boise."

"Thank you, Billy. This means a lot to me."

"As it would to Danielle. I rather like knowing I'll have a hand in seeing her vision for this spa fulfilled in Idaho. You know how I felt about your mother."

"Yes, I know."

"She would be proud of all you've accomplished."

"I hope so."

"You can know so." The senator paused, then added, "And I believe she would approve of your affection for Miss Arlington, as well."

Morgan's eyes widened.

The senator chuckled. "It *was* rather obvious last night."

"Was it?"

"Good heavens, man. Of course it was. At least to me." William slapped his knee. "And I understand why you feel that way. I think her a good match for you, my boy. Few of the fairer sex are, as yet, ready to serve in public office, but I believe she is. Come to think of it, I'm mighty glad she would rather be mayor of this small town than seek an office at the state level. If she were running against me, it might be the end of my political career."

Gwen was all the things William had said about her. She was beautiful, both inside and out. Last night, she had outshone the most brilliant of lights in the room. It had been hard for Morgan to take his eyes off of her and pay attention to what the guests seated on either side of him were saying.

She wanted to be mayor. Not because she could use her office to accomplish something for her own gain, but because she loved Bethlehem Springs and the people in it. He cared too, but not the way she did. It had been a selfish purpose that spurred him to enter the race. If elected, he would serve with honor. He knew that much about himself. But still . . .

The sanctuary was silent on a Saturday morning, the lighting dim with the doors closed and no candles or lamps burning. Gwen knelt at the rail before the front pew, hands folded, head bowed.

In nine hours, she would be in the basement of another church on the opposite side of town, facing many of the voters of Bethlehem Springs, trying to convince them that she was the better candidate for mayor. Was that true? Would she be able to govern as she should? Would she make a better mayor than Morgan McKinley?

Father, fill me with Your peace.

She wouldn't have agreed to run if she hadn't thought God had told her it was the right thing to do. She wouldn't have run if her father and sister hadn't agreed that she should.

May Your will be done, Lord.

Cleo had worked hard this past week, going from house to house and business to business, sharing what Gwen wanted to accomplish as mayor — improvements to the school, better streets and sidewalks, new equipment for the fire department. Would that information help persuade those who had reservations about a woman holding office?

Which one of us do You mean to be mayor?

Gwen didn't doubt that Morgan was a follower of Christ. She'd observed him enough, listened to him enough, to convince her that his faith was real.

But shouldn't he concentrate on the resort if he believes You brought him here to build it?

Guilt pricked her spirit. That was a selfish prayer.

Help me not to be envious or resentful if he should win the election.

Gwen opened her eyes and stared at the

wooden cross on the wall above the altar. Like a caress, she felt peace brush against her heart. The nervousness she had felt earlier was gone. Whatever happened tonight, she would be all right. Whatever happened in the election, she would be all right. She would trust in the will of the Lord.

Thank You, Father.

She stood, stepped into the center aisle, and walked toward the back of the sanctuary. Moments later, she moved into the bright June sunshine. The day was already warming. She hoped it wouldn't be too hot by the time Owen arrived for his lesson.

Speaking of the boy, wasn't that him riding pell-mell toward her on a bicycle? Kitty must have come up with the money to fix the tire, but how Gwen couldn't imagine.

When Owen saw her, he skidded to a halt. "Hey, Miss Arlington."

She walked up to him. "Good morning, Owen. I see both your knee and your bicycle tire are much improved."

"The tire wasn't fixed. It's a whole new bike!"

"A new bike?"

"Mr. McKinley brought it to me this morning. He had it shipped up from Boise special, just for me."

"He did?"

"Ma tried to tell him we couldn't accept it, but he talked her into it. But she says I'm gonna have to do some chores for him until I've paid him back."

Yes, that sounded like Kitty Goldsmith. She might be poor but she was proud.

Owen's smile was brighter than the sunshine. "I've never had nothin' as nice as this bike. Not ever."

"It's a beautiful bicycle, Owen. Be careful that you don't take another tumble."

The boy laughed. "I won't, Miss Arlington. I'm gonna take real good care of it."

As Owen prepared to ride away, Gwen said, "Don't forget your lesson this afternoon."

"I won't." And away he went.

She wondered if Morgan had any notion what a wonderful thing he'd done for that boy. He was a wealthy man, she knew, and well able to afford the gift he'd given. But had he understood in advance how much it would mean to Owen?

Yes. He must have. And she couldn't help but like him all the more for it.

If she lost the election to him, at least she could take comfort in knowing he was a man with a compassionate heart.

Twenty-Three

The basement of the Bethlehem Springs Methodist Church was filled with chairs and benches, most of them occupied fifteen minutes before the hour. It was an even better turnout than Morgan had expected.

"Mr. McKinley."

He turned toward the sound of Gwen's voice. She stood in the doorway of the small room where he'd been collecting his thoughts. She wore a jacket and skirt, deep rose in color, and a small hat without decoration. Her attire, he was certain, was meant to say, *Take me seriously. I mean business.*

"Owen Goldsmith showed me his new bicycle today," she said.

"He was excited when I delivered it."

There was an unspoken question in her gaze. "It was a wonderful gift."

"I could see how things are for the Goldsmiths. Owen wouldn't have had a new tire for a long while. Maybe not ever." He shrugged. "I wanted to help out. A boy should have a bike."

"Mr. and Mrs. Goldsmith have had a great deal of trouble in recent years. They won't forget your kindness to them."

Could she mean — ? No, surely she didn't mean that. But just to make certain, he said, "I didn't do it to get their votes, if that's what you're thinking."

She looked surprised. "Of course not. I believe I know you better than to think that."

Did she? Did she know him well enough not to suspect his motives? He hoped so. He wanted her to know him well. Well enough to fall in love with him.

Gwen Arlington already owned his heart. He'd sworn he would never again fall victim to a pretty face, and he hadn't. Oh, she was beautiful, but he'd fallen for so much more than that. And if it weren't for the election, he would have made it clear by now that he was courting her. He wouldn't be moving with such care. Maybe he would already have a better idea how she felt about him.

Kenneth Barker, the Methodist minister, opened the door and looked into the antechamber. "Here you both are. It's time we begin. Are you ready?"

"Yes," Gwen answered.

"We're ready," Morgan added.

"Good. I'll introduce you, and then we'll begin with Miss Arlington. There's a good crowd. It's great to see the community so interested." The reverend disappeared from view.

"Well, here we go." Morgan motioned for her to precede him. "Good luck to you."

"I don't believe in luck, Mr. McKinley." She walked toward the door, shoulders straight and head high.

Morgan smiled. *Neither do I.*

Gwen had felt a few flutters of nerves earlier in the evening, but they vanished when she faced the crowd. She didn't have to look at her notes to remind herself what she wanted to say. She knew what concerned her friends and neighbors, because those things concerned her as well.

"As mayor, it would be my goal to encourage new enterprises to do business in Bethlehem Springs. That will become even easier once a railroad spur is brought up our way. Will the railroad come to our town? I have it on good authority" — she sent a fleeting smile toward Senator Rudyard where he stood in the back of the room — "that it will. And once my worthy opponent's health spa opens" — she nodded toward Morgan — "we will see an influx of visitors to our community. That will benefit many of our local businesses and tradesmen."

Her gaze fell upon Harrison Carter, seated in the third row center. There was no misunderstanding the expression on his face. He was displeased with her opening address. Knowing he was against the completion of Morgan's spa, she knew he wasn't happy with her endorsement of the same. She didn't care. Everything she'd said in the past ten minutes had been from her heart.

She brought her comments to a close with some words of thanks to those who had supported and encouraged her in her candidacy, especially her father and sister. Then she returned to the chair beside Morgan and sat down.

"Excellent job," he whispered.

Kenneth Barker stepped to the podium. "And now we will hear from Morgan McKinley."

Morgan rose, and there was some applause. "Thank you. You're very kind." He glanced at his notes, then set them aside on the lectern and began to speak.

Gwen noted his ease as he addressed the audience, most of whom he'd never met.

His voice was pleasant and engaging. He had an air about him that seemed to invite people to be his friend. Magnetism. Charm. Business experience. A knowledge of the world at large. All of these were obvious assets.

He talked about the need for improvements to the school, the firehouse, and other city departments. He talked about the need for more openness in government at the local level. He talked about the need for more businesses, and he talked about the importance of the railroad. In many ways, he seemed to be parroting her comments.

She sat a little straighter. Yes. He *was* parroting her. How could he do that? Was his strategy to say that both candidates wanted the same things, therefore, vote for a man instead of a woman? It made her so angry she wanted to box his ears. It made her so angry that she almost missed his closing statement.

"As you have heard, my positions are almost identical to those taken by Miss Arlington. And so I tell you this. While I will serve the people of Bethlehem Springs with integrity and purpose if elected, I believe Gwen Arlington will be the better mayor. She is your neighbor, and her family has lived here for over three decades. Miss Arlington knows Bethlehem Springs and loves it. Thus, when I go to the voting booth on Election Day, I plan to cast my vote for my worthy opponent. I encourage you to do the same." Morgan turned toward Gwen and gave her a slight bow.

The room was gripped by a stunned silence. Not so much as the creak of a chair or the tap of a foot. Gwen found it hard to breathe. Had he said what she thought he'd said?

The Methodist minister stepped forward and placed a hand on Morgan's shoulder. "Well . . ." He cleared his throat. "I must say that was unexpected. I'm not sure how these two people can debate after that pronouncement." He glanced at Morgan. "Perhaps we should take questions from the audience instead." His gaze moved from Morgan to where Gwen sat.

She nodded, rose to her feet, and moved to stand beside Morgan, hoping she looked more composed than she felt. Her mind was still trying to understand this surprising turn of events. How could she form intelligent answers with her thoughts in such disarray?

But no one posed any questions. Instead, one by one, people began rising to their feet and applauding.

"Vote for Arlington!" someone shouted — it sounded like Cleo — and the chant was picked up by others. "Vote for Arlington!"

Gwen felt a flush of excitement in her cheeks as she raised a hand to wave at the crowd. She was going to win the election. She could feel it in the air.

And I have Morgan to thank for it.

That dampened her pleasure a little. After all, she'd wanted to win because she was qualified, because voters liked her ideas and had confidence in her ability to be a good mayor. Was that the case now? Or would they vote for her because Morgan had told them to?

What are you up to, McKinley? Harrison wondered as he stood with the rest of the crowd, applauding.

A man didn't throw an election to his opponent unless he had something to gain from it. Was Morgan just interested in a pretty skirt or did he have another motive?

Whatever the reason, Harrison didn't like it. He didn't like it one bit. But even more problematic, in his mind, was Gwen Arlington's independent streak. She was proving to be difficult to control, as evidenced by her rejection of the advice he'd tried to give her. He still hadn't decided how he would bring her to heel.

Susannah placed her hand in the crook of his arm. "It's rather exciting to think we will have a woman mayor. How times have changed."

His wife was right. Times had changed. But not always for the better. For instance, it was well and good for women to have the vote — as long as they followed the guidance of their fathers or husbands in how to cast those votes. What he didn't like was the self-reliant streak that was becoming all too common among women in these early years of the twentieth century.

Which brought his thoughts back to Gwen, who was now surrounded by a number of well-wishers, including her father and that outrageous sister of hers.

Yes, we shall have to bring you in hand, Miss Arlington. Indeed, we shall.

"By George!" William Rudyard exclaimed as he slapped Morgan on the shoulder. "You are an unpredictable man, are you not? Whatever made you do that?"

Morgan grinned and shook his head. "I'm not sure, Billy. It wasn't planned. I didn't come here with that in mind. I guess Miss Arlington won me over during her opening remarks." He glanced once more in Gwen's direction, but he could no longer see her in the milling crowd.

"Beautiful women have changed the course of history more than once through the ages. I guess one has done so again." William laughed.

"I didn't do it because she's beautiful."

"Oh, I know that, son. I was joshing with you. You wouldn't have said what you did unless you thought she was the better candidate."

Morgan nodded. He hoped everyone had William's insight, and he hoped everyone understood how remarkable Gwen was. Her remarks had been intelligent, articulate, and right on point. He'd wager even the senator couldn't have given a better speech.

"Shall we return to your home? My friends and I want to get an early start in the morning."

"I'm ready." He stepped off the stage.

The room was beginning to empty out, and he caught a glimpse of Gwen, standing between her father and sister, talking to about a half dozen citizens. Her color was still high, and even from across the room, he could tell there was a look of exhilaration in her eyes.

"Pretty as the day is long," William said.

Prettier, Morgan thought. Much prettier.

And smart. And kind. And caring.

William pointed toward the back of the room. "There's Clive and Jeremiah."

Morgan wasn't surprised to find the two other senators engaged in conversation with Harrison Carter, an attractive woman — presumably his wife — at his side. He had expected the commissioner to try to learn why the senators were in town. This had been the ideal place for him to do so.

Clive Austin grinned at Morgan as he and William approached. "Mr. McKinley, I believe you shocked every last person in the room."

Morgan inclined his head in acknowledgment.

"I'm glad I was here to see this," Jeremiah Hayes said. "Wouldn't have believed it otherwise."

"I merely said what I thought." Morgan turned his gaze on Harrison. "Here is one man who I know agrees with me. He's always thought Miss Arlington the better candidate."

Harrison's eyes narrowed slightly. "Indeed."

Clive said, "I was telling Mr. Carter how impressed I was with your health spa."

That must have thrilled him.

"And I would like to hear more, Senator

Austin," Harrison said, "but it is time my wife and I returned home."

Farewells were exchanged, and then Harrison escorted his still-silent wife out of the basement of the Methodist church.

"You have an enemy there," William said.

"I know, Billy. I just don't know why."

TWENTY-FOUR

Gwen tapped her index finger against her upper lip as she frowned at the paper on her writing desk. A few days ago, she'd had half a dozen ideas for her next newspaper article. Today, each and every one seemed banal, completely uninspired, and overdone.

She could write about her surprise over her opponent's endorsement, but that seemed rather self-serving. Besides, that had been the hot topic of discussion following Sunday services in every church in town. Was it possible anyone who might be interested hadn't heard what happened last Saturday night?

The mantel clock chimed the hour. Two o'clock. Another hour until she was to be at Morgan's house for his lesson. Butterflies erupted in her belly at the thought.

She hadn't seen him since the night of the so-called debate, and she wasn't sure how she felt about seeing him today. With just a few words, he had almost assured her of winning the election. Should she thank him for it? Was there proper etiquette for a situation such as this? If so, she wasn't aware of it.

A sigh escaped her. How much simpler her life had been a month or two ago. She'd gone an entire year without seeing — let alone meeting — Mr. Morgan McKinley. The idea of running for mayor hadn't crossed her mind. She'd been perfectly content, living alone, visiting with her father and sister, writing her articles for the newspaper, and teaching her students. Now look at her. She couldn't concentrate long enough to write a paragraph. And she kept looking at the clock and thinking about her next student.

Morgan.

His wonderful smile. His easy charm. The way he'd touched her hand where it rested in the crook of his arm as he introduced her to his guests at the dinner party last Friday. His long fingers as they traveled over the piano keys during his lessons — almost like a caress.

Heat flooded her cheeks.

Never in her twenty-eight years had thoughts of a man pestered her like this. She found them unacceptable. They must stop. She must make them stop.

She rose from her writing desk and walked to the front porch. It had rained this morning. The air smelled fresher and the lawn looked greener — the colors of her flowers brighter with moisture clinging to blades, leaves, and petals. The sky was still overcast, the temperature cool. It might be wise if she drove her buggy to the McKinley home. But that was such a lot of work, getting her horse into the harness and traces, when she was going such a short distance. The clouds didn't look threatening. No, she would walk and take an umbrella along, just in case.

Gwen checked her watch. Not yet ten minutes after the hour. Oh, how time crawled today.

"Fool," she muttered. "Go and write this instant."

Inhaling a deep breath, she turned and reentered the house, determined to get at least one page written before it was time to leave.

Boston, Massachusetts
June 8, 1915

My dear Morgan,
  I have not had a letter from you in such a very long while, dearest brother, but I

have been a poor correspondent myself, so I cannot scold you too harshly. I hope all is going well for you and that you are pleased with your building project. I know it will be an enormous success. It does seem that the McKinley men have superbly good business acumen. Would that I had inherited some of the same traits, woman or no.

You will not believe this, but I am planning to come for a visit. Our cousin Gertrude is needed to nurse her elderly mother who is in failing health. She has insisted that I find a more enjoyable endeavor with which to occupy my summer, and that is when I thought of you. I have never been west of the Mississippi, and it is high time that I do so. It will be a new and different experience — one I know I shall enjoy.

If all goes according to plan, I should arrive in Bethlehem Springs before the end of June. I cannot tell you in this letter of my precise arrival date as I may wish to stop along the way to visit museums or other sights of interest.

Have you had a telephone installed in your home as of yet? Now that the transcontinental telephone lines connect East to West, it would be ever so convenient if you would do so. Or is Bethlehem Springs too remote for modern conveniences to have reached it?

Do not concern yourself with my travel plans as I will have a companion, the grandson of a friend of our father's. His name is Robert Dudley. I'm sure you remember Marcus Dudley, his grandfather. Robert has agreed to escort me safely to Bethlehem Springs before continuing on to California where he plans to become an actor in motion pictures. (Have you seen The Birth of a Nation?)

If you have a moment, please write to Cousin Gertrude. I'm sure it would lift her spirits to hear from you. I won't tell you to write to me, you wretched correspondent, as I don't know where I shall be by the time you receive this letter. You shall simply have to talk to me in person when I arrive.

Your loving sister,
Daphne

Morgan placed Daphne's letter on the desk and leaned back in his leather chair. He was pleased that his sister was coming for a lengthy stay, and it was nice that it had been her own idea. This letter had been written about the same time he'd penned his to her. She might be reading his even now. He hoped she was as amused as he by their like thinking. And with their parents gone, it would be nice to be closer to his sister — both physically and emotionally.

He heard voices in the entry. That would be Gwen, right on time, as usual. Some women kept men waiting, but that wasn't true of Gwen Arlington. She was punctual — in addition to a host of other attributes he liked about her.

He rose from his desk chair and strode from his study in time to catch a glimpse of her as she and Inez Cheevers entered the front parlor.

"I'll tell Mr. McKinley you're here," he heard the housekeeper say.

Gwen answered, "Thank you."

When he'd caught his last glimpse of her on Saturday night, she had still worn a bemused expression. How would she look now? What would she say to him?

"Ah, you're here, sir," Mrs. Cheevers said as she exited the parlor and saw him in the entry hall. "I was just now coming for you. Miss Arlington has arrived for your lesson."

"Thank you, Mrs. Cheevers."

In the front parlor, Gwen stood beside the piano, facing the doorway. The corners of her mouth curved upward a fraction when she saw him. Not enough to call it a smile, but enough to give him hope.

"Good afternoon, Miss Arlington."

"Mr. McKinley."

"It's dreary out, isn't it?" He tipped his head toward the windows.

"It always smells good after it rains."

He crossed the room to the piano.

"About Saturday night," she said before he could sit down.

He stepped back from the bench, waiting for her to have her say.

"Why did you do it? Why did you say you planned to vote for me?"

"Because I *will* vote for you. Because I believe you would be the better mayor between the two of us."

"Why, if our positions are so much alike?"

A silver-gray light from the windows outlined her head and shoulders and accented the narrow curve of her waist. Sometimes he forgot how petite she was.

"Mr. McKinley?"

He gave himself a mental shake and answered her question. "I would be a good mayor. I would serve honorably and do what I believed was best for the people of Bethlehem Springs. But, Miss Arlington, I came to this town to build a health spa. New Hope is where my greatest passion lies. That's not true of you. You're passionate about serving this town. That's obvious to everyone." He stepped around the bench, drawing closer to her.

She frowned at him. "Don't you believe God called you to run in this election?"

"Yes." He smiled gently. "But maybe He didn't call me to win."

He took another step closer. She didn't move away.

There was a tiny cowlick in the center of her bangs. He hadn't noticed it before. He was tempted to reach out and touch the stubborn strands of hair that refused to lie in the right direction. He was even more tempted to blurt out his feelings for her like some lovesick schoolboy. Fortunately, he was forestalled.

"Did you think I couldn't win without your endorsement?" Gwen asked, her voice low, her stance rigid.

He swallowed a sigh and took a step back. "No, I never thought such a thing."

"I want to win on my own merits, Mr. McKinley."

"And so you shall."

Her gaze turned cloudy, like the darkening skies outside the parlor windows. "But how will I ever know if that's why? You have all but pulled out of the race."

He wished he could reassure her, but he

had the feeling that whatever he said wouldn't be enough — or maybe it would be too much. Her doubts were greater than he'd suspected, and he didn't like that he was the cause of them. That hadn't been his intention. It seemed he was destined to make blunder after blunder when it came to Miss Arlington. Courtship should be easier than this, shouldn't it? He'd better become more adept at the art of wooing and winning this lady's heart. What he'd tried thus far didn't seem to be working.

Gwen cleared her throat, drawing his gaze again. "Perhaps we should get to your lesson, Mr. McKinley."

"Yes. Of course." With that, he slid onto the piano bench and placed his fingers on the keys.

Gwen found her composure again as she listened to Morgan run through his scales. She regretted that she had exposed her lack of confidence to him. He was, after all, still her opponent until the votes were cast. He had told those who came to the debate that if he were elected, he would serve with honor. It wasn't wise to lay bare her less than positive attributes. She wanted Morgan McKinley — and everyone else — to think of her as poised, calm, and self-assured.

And that *was* what she showed him for the remainder of the lesson. She was the instructor. He was the pupil. A good pupil too. When he played the pieces she had assigned to him the week before, she could only listen in wonder. His talent was obvious.

So carried away by the music was she that she didn't notice how dark the room had become. Not until light flashed across the well-polished wood of the grand piano's raised lid. An instant later, a loud crash of thunder shook the room. With a small squeal of surprise, she whirled toward the windows. Another jagged streak of lightning lit the sky and another peal of thunder followed. Then another and another.

Gwen's heart raced as she took a few steps toward the windows.

God, protect us from fire.

That was always her prayer when storms blew through the area. Mountain towns like Bethlehem Springs were especially vulnerable when it came to wildfires. One strategic strike of lightning, one strong gust of wind in the wrong direction, and every wooden building in this town could end up burned to the ground. Thankfully, the weather hadn't turned hot yet. The underbrush in the surrounding hills was still green, the ground moist. Forest fires were more likely to happen in July and August when everything had turned bone dry.

"Quite the show, isn't it?"

She looked to her right where Morgan now stood. "Yes."

He met her gaze. "Are you afraid of lightning storms?"

"Not afraid of the storms. Only of what could follow."

"Fire?"

She nodded, then turned toward the windows again. Light flashed against the panes, almost blinding her with its brightness. "Such a display of power."

" 'For the invisible things of him from the creation of the world are clearly seen, being understood by the things that are made, even his eternal power and Godhead.' "

Gwen felt the skin on her arms prickle as Morgan quoted the familiar verse from Romans. It was the same one that often came to her mind when nature showed her how small she was and how big God was.

Rain began to spatter the windows. Big lazy drops at first, but not for long. The wind rose, driving the rain in sheets as it whistled down the gullies and ravines of the surrounding hills.

"Did you walk here?" he asked.

"Yes."

"You'll need to stay until this blows over. When it lets up, I'll drive you home."

"That's kind of you, Mr. McKinley."

"If it rains like this long enough, you can be my guest for dinner."

"Oh, I —"

"Don't disappoint me, Miss Arlington." His voice was low, made intimate by a room darkened by the storm.

She wasn't quite certain how it happened. She turned, ready to say something — she forgot what. He turned toward her at the same moment. Lightning flashed again and thunder pealed directly overhead. A little gasp escaped her. Then his hands were holding her upper arms and his mouth was lowering toward hers, and it seemed the most natural thing in the world to allow him to kiss her, to tip her head back and let him draw her closer to him as her eyes drifted closed.

His lips were warm upon hers, both gentle and demanding. She surrendered, her thoughts caught in a whirlwind, unexpected emotions careening through her. Her knees weakened, and she leaned into him lest she crumple to the floor.

Gwen had been kissed before but never

like this. Never anything like this. And the storm it ignited inside her was far fiercer than the one that raged outside. By the time the kiss ended, her ability to speak had abandoned her. The same seemed to be true of Morgan, for he said nothing at all. Simply looked at her, his expression serious.

Knees still weak, she turned and moved to the piano bench. She sank onto it and waited for the world to right itself again, waited to recall the reasons she wanted to remain free of romantic entanglements. She knew she had reasons. Good reasons. The same ones she'd had since the day she fled her grandparents' home and her mother's influence and come to Bethlehem Springs.

If only she could remember what those reasons were.

TWENTY-FIVE

"Miss Arlington didn't leave after the lesson as she did last week, sir." Elias Spade sat in one of the large leather chairs in Harrison's library. Water dripped from his wet hair onto the shoulders of his suit coat. "I'd guess she's waiting out the storm. It's still raining mighty hard."

"I'm aware of that," Harrison snapped. "You should have stayed at your post."

"I could see through the windows that the dining room was being set for dinner. Since it appeared she is to dine with him, I thought I would have a bite myself."

Harrison slammed his hand upon the desk. "I don't pay you to eat, Spade. I pay you to keep an eye on McKinley, especially when Gwen Arlington is with him."

"Mr. Carter, I —"

"Go have your dinner." He motioned for Spade to get out.

And the devil take you.

As soon as Spade was gone, Harrison placed his elbows on the table, then cradled his head between his hands and massaged his temples. The pain had been increasing throughout the day, pounding, pounding, pounding until he felt like screaming.

Two of the men who served on the board of county commissioners had dropped by to see him earlier in the day. They were inclined, they'd informed him, to change their opinion — and their votes — as it related to the land use approvals requested by McKinley. Apparently the visit by those three senators had influenced them. Harrison feared he wouldn't be able to change their minds back again. He was losing control over them, and his goal of acquiring the land McKinley owned was facing defeat.

He swore beneath his breath. He didn't like to lose. He wasn't used to losing. He would go to just about any length — short of murder — to win.

Not that Spade wouldn't kill McKinley if that was what Harrison wanted.

Should he consider it? No, even he wouldn't cross that line. Too dangerous. There had to be another way, a setback so huge that McKinley would give up and leave Idaho for good.

■ ■ ■ ■

Opal Nelson, Morgan's cook, had done herself proud once again. The beef was tender and tasty, the vegetables cooked to perfection. However, Gwen didn't seem to notice or appreciate the delicious fare set before her. She ate scarcely a bite, spending far more time moving the food around on her plate with a fork.

Morgan knew he was to blame for her distress. He could tell by the way she kept her eyes downcast. No matter what interesting topic of conversation he introduced, she answered in monosyllables. Every now and again, she would glance toward the window.

The storm continued unabated.

Morgan was both glad and sorry for it. Glad because it gave him time to garner her forgiveness. Sorry because he could tell how anxious she was to leave, to get away from him.

"I'm sorry, Gwen."

The use of her given name drew her gaze when nothing else had.

"I shouldn't have kissed you. Not without gaining your permission first. I have upset you, and that's the last thing I wanted to do."

"Why?"

"Why don't I want you to be upset?"

She shook her head. "Why did you kiss me?"

Her question made him want to kiss her all over again. "Isn't it obvious? I have come to care for you. To deeply care for you."

"That isn't possible. You hardly know me."

"I know more than you might suppose." He pushed aside his plate and leaned forward, forearms on the white tablecloth. "You favor the color pink, but blue is a close second. Your favorite cologne is lilac. You are strong in your Christian faith, firm in your doctrine, and even the love you bear your father and sister could not induce you to leave the Presbyterian church. You love all kinds of flowers and take great pleasure in nurturing your garden and watching it flourish. And music speaks to your soul."

"Mr. McKinley —"

"You love teaching, especially your younger students. Nothing gives you more pleasure than seeing them excel. And although you are always well mannered and ladylike, you have an independent streak and as much strength of will as any businessman of my acquaintance."

Color had returned to her cheeks. She no longer looked wan and distraught.

"Am I wrong so far?"

"Mr. McKinley, I —"

"Am I?"

She slid her chair back from the table. "Please, Mr. McKinley. We should end this discussion. I should have stopped you. When you kissed me, I should have —"

"Why? Are you promised elsewhere?" He knew beyond a shadow of a doubt that she was not.

"No." She stood. "But neither do I want to be promised. Not to any man. If I have given you any other impression, I regret it."

He rose from his chair. "I cannot take back my feelings. They are what they are."

Were those unshed tears he saw in her eyes or was the light in the dining room playing tricks? If they were tears, he had hope.

She turned her back toward him. "Look. The rain has lessened. I had better go home."

"I'll drive you."

"No. It would be better if I walked. I have my umbrella."

"I'll drive you, Miss Arlington."

She must have heard the determination in his voice for she didn't try to argue with him further. "As you wish," she said softly, then walked out of the dining room.

■ ■ ■ ■

If Gwen could turn back time, she would have. But then she would not know what it felt like to be held in Morgan's arms. She would not know the power of his kisses. She wouldn't have heard him express his affections for her.

Neither of them spoke during the brief drive from his home to hers. The only sounds were the puttering of the automobile's engine and the splatter of raindrops upon the car's roof. Upon arrival, Morgan reached across to open the passenger door. The nearness of his arm made her heart palpitate.

"Thank you." She opened her umbrella. "You needn't bother to get out." She stepped to the ground, umbrella in her right hand, sheet music clutched to her chest with her left. "Good evening, Mr. McKinley." She hurried up the walk to her front door, thankful he didn't try to escort her. Better for them both if they were together as little as possible from now on.

Once inside, she leaned her back against the door and listened to the sound of his automobile as it drove away. After the sound faded into the distance, she was engulfed by the silence of her empty home.

Too silent.

Too alone.

But that was ridiculous. She loved her home. She liked her solitude.

Her favorite color *was* pink. All shades of pink. And blue *was* a close second. There was no denying that her favorite cologne was lilac. She wore it always. She *had* considered attending the Methodist church with her father and sister when she first came to Bethlehem Springs, but her heart had pulled her back to her Presbyterian roots.

Tears welled in her eyes, and this time, she allowed them to fall.

She *did* take great joy in nurturing her flowerbeds, and music *did* speak to her soul.

A tiny sob escaped her throat as she slid down the door until she sat upon the floor.

Morgan was right. Nothing made her happier than to see one of her students excel.

"And I *am* independent and stubborn."

How was it that Morgan had come to know her so well? And why did it matter to her so much that he had?

TWENTY-SIX

By Thursday, all signs of the storm had been erased. Clear skies and warming weather had evaporated the puddles and dried the streets of Bethlehem Springs. However, there were still parts of the road to New Hope that were less than desirable. It took Morgan an extra fifteen minutes to reach the spa in his touring car.

"So here you are," Fagan said in greeting. "Sure and I've been wondering when you would return. There's been plenty of talk among the men about your speech last Saturday. Is it true? Have you given your support to Miss Arlington?"

"It's true. She deserves it." With a sweep of his arm, he indicated the buildings in various stages of completion. "This is where I need to be."

"What if you continue to have problems with the county commissioners? We need the railroad spur, and without their cooperation —"

"Billy assured me that the delays will soon be a thing of the past."

"Has he that kind of authority?"

"Billy's opinion does carry a lot of weight in government circles. I imagine the state can apply pressure to make sure certain things happen. Have a little faith, Fagan. Isn't that what you're always telling me?"

His friend grunted.

As they walked toward the lodge, Morgan said, "Looks like we should be able to get telephone lines strung between here and town by midsummer. That will ease communication between you and me. And I've learned that telephone service between Bethlehem Springs and the capital city will be available by autumn."

"Well and good. Does the need for the telephone mean you plan to remain in town even if you don't win the election?"

"For now."

"Plan to help the presumptive new mayor?"

Morgan turned his gaze upward, as if the color of the sky was of the utmost interest. "If she'll let me."

Fagan coughed.

Morgan thought it sounded more like a strangled laugh.

Gaining control, his friend cleared his throat. "Before we go into the lodge, let me show you what's been accomplished on the chapel since you were here with the senators."

"Good idea."

"The men have made real progress on the second staff barrack. You'll want to have a look at it while you're here. But it's time we were about hiring a larger crew, Morgan. The men we've got are spread too thin. We can't keep working them as hard as we are. I'm thinking we've signed on just about every able-bodied man Bethlehem Springs can provide, so it'll be time to cast a wider net."

Morgan nodded. A year ago, he'd hoped that the spa would be in operation by this summer. He knew now that wasn't possible, not with the delays they'd encountered. But if Billy came through on his promises, New Hope should be able to open its doors by late fall or early next spring. Guests would have to travel to Bethlehem Springs via coach or automobile until the railroad brought a spur up this way. Even the good senator couldn't get tracks laid overnight. Especially not in these mountains.

An hour later, Morgan and Fagan returned to the automobile. Morgan had made a mental list of a number of things he must see to as soon as he returned to town. And a trip down to the capital city was probably in order within the next week. There was only so much a man could do with letters and telegrams.

"You and Christopher are doing a fine job, Fagan, managing things up here. I want you to know I appreciate it." He pulled open the door. "Turn the crank for me, will you?"

"Aye."

Morgan slid across the car seat, and when he was ready, he gave Fagan a nod. A minute later, he drove away from the building site, his thoughts churning along with the sound of the engine. And for a few miles, those thoughts were about New Hope and not the pretty piano teacher who'd stolen his heart.

Gwen clucked to Shakespeare, urging the gelding into a faster trot as they neared the bridge. She was anxious to reach the ranch, eager to be with her sister and father for a few hours. Being with them again would put her world aright. They had that effect on her. Perhaps it was because they wanted what was best for her and loved her unconditionally.

Why did he kiss me?

In her memory, she heard his reply, *"Isn't it obvious? I have come to care for you. To deeply care for you."*

Over the years, other men had declared their devotion, but she had turned away every suitor — without a single twinge of regret. Morgan was different. She didn't want to be courted, and yet she couldn't bear the thought of not being with him. She didn't want a serious suitor, had no desire to wed, and yet the idea that he might turn to another woman nearly broke her heart.

A double-minded man is unstable in all his ways, she reminded herself. And her recent thoughts and emotions certainly must be what the Lord meant when He caused James to write that verse. She was definitely of two minds when it came to Morgan.

"Lord, I need Your peace."

As the horse's hooves fell on the wooden surface of the bridge, Gwen remembered the day she'd first seen Morgan. If she closed her eyes, she could picture him still, the top down on his touring car. How could she have guessed what impact he would have on her life from that moment on? No man had ever made her feel this way before.

Feel what way?

Gwen drew back on the reins, stopping

Shakespeare in the middle of the bridge.

Feel what way?

Excited but scared.

Lost and found.

Sad yet happy.

Perplexed.

Befuddled.

Gwen was a person who liked order. She wasn't given to wild flights of fancy. Her feet were planted firmly on the ground.

Well, they used to be.

She slapped the reins against the horse's rump. "Walk on, Shakespeare."

Cleo rested her knuckles on her hips and gave Gwen a hard look. "Gwennie, it's clear as the nose on your face. You're falling in love with him."

Gwen shook her head. "No, it isn't —"

"You may be the pretty one, but I'll be doggone if you aren't the silly one too. Otherwise you'd recognize your feelings and give in to them."

Gwen sank onto one of the feed bins in the barn. "I *can't* be in love."

"Why not? Land sakes! Falling in love isn't a disease. It's the most natural thing in the world." Cleo leaned against a post and crossed her arms over her chest. "So he told you he cares for you and he kissed you.

Didn't you like his kisses?"

"That's beside the point."

"Is it? I may not know much about these things, but I suppose liking a man's kisses must be a good thing if the both of you are falling in love."

"I am *not* falling in love."

Cleo clucked her tongue. "You trying to convince me or yourself, Gwennie?" She leaned forward. "If you could've seen your face last Saturday when McKinley was talking. Land o' Goshen! You were hanging on his every word. Like pearls were dripping from his mouth. And when he said he was going to vote for you come Election Day, there was a second there when I thought you would jump up and give him a hug right there in front of everybody."

"It's not true." Gwen covered her face with her hands. "It's not true, Cleo."

"You know how some say the ostrich down in Africa sticks its head into a bush or the sand. I heard that's just a myth, but it's a good description all the same." She pushed off from the post. "Don't go being an ostrich, Gwennie. My guess is that Morgan is a man among men. One in a million. If he's everything I've observed, you won't have to worry about living under his thumb. My guess is he'll love you so much that pretty soon you'll be thinking he hung the sun, the moon, and the stars in the heavens."

Gwen groaned as she lowered her hands, feeling miserable.

Cleo's expression said she was losing patience fast. "I'd be happier than a fox in the hen house if I was in your shoes. And there you sit, looking like the world's about to end. If you don't beat all." She grunted her disgust. "Maybe the good Lord's got you and me mixed up. I sure wouldn't turn a fine man like Morgan away if he loved me the way Morgan loves you." With that, she spun on her heel and strode out of the barn.

Was Cleo right? Was Gwen falling in love with Morgan?

Oh, it was all so mixed up in her head that she couldn't think straight. And instead of making things better, her visit to the ranch had only made things worse. She was more confused than before, and she couldn't remember a time when Cleo had been this angry with her.

If it weren't for that kiss . . .

Two days later, Roscoe Finch — the gardener and handyman who worked for Morgan — delivered a note to Gwen.

Dear Miss Arlington,

I am afraid I will be unable to have my lesson next Tuesday as I have gone to Boise on matters of business and expect to be away from Bethlehem Springs until week's end. I do, however, look forward to receiving my lesson the following week. I trust you are willing to continue to instruct me since I have heard nothing to the contrary.

Your servant,
Morgan McKinley

"Thank you, Mr. Finch." Gwen looked up from the sheet of paper, composing her expression to reveal none of her conflicting emotions.

"You're welcome, miss. I'm always glad to do whatever Mr. McKinley needs. He's a good soul, giving an old man like me work and a place to live."

"You're not old."

He chuckled. "You're wrong about that. A person can't argue with the passing of time, and I don't mean to try. If you're wise, Miss Arlington, you'll take note of it now while you're young. The years, they go by faster and faster, and you don't want to find yourself at my age, looking back and wishing you'd done things you hadn't or wishing you'd gone places you didn't. You only get one time around on this here earth. You gotta make the most of life while you can."

She acquiesced with a nod.

Roscoe tipped the brim of his hat in her direction. "Well, good day to you, Miss Arlington. I'd best be about my work."

"Good day to you, Mr. Finch." She watched him as he moved toward the gate, a slight limp in his walk.

Loneliness tugged at Gwen's heart as her gaze dropped once more to the note in her hand. She wouldn't see Morgan for another whole week. It already felt like a lifetime.

She groaned at the thought. Only yesterday she'd been determined to tell Morgan she could no longer be his piano teacher. Only yesterday she'd been convinced that putting him from her mind was the best thing to do — for both of them.

Only she couldn't do it. She realized that now. She wanted to see him. If only for half an hour once a week, she wanted to be with him. Because despite all her denials and words to the contrary, she cared for him.

Cleo was right about her. She was a fool with her head stuck in the sand.

TWENTY-SEVEN

Morgan was strolling back to his hotel after a late lunch with William Rudyard at the senator's private club when a female voice stopped him.

"Morgan! Morgan McKinley!"

He turned around.

A young woman with dark hair and eyes hurried toward him, smiling broadly. Who on earth? Was it — ? No, it couldn't be.

"Daphne?" he said aloud.

His sister looked the same as she had following their mother's funeral, and yet she was different too. More of a woman than the girl she'd been. Was it the way she carried herself or the clothes she wore or something else?

Daphne stopped in front of him, rose on tiptoe, and brushed his left cheek with her lips. "Yes, Morgan. Of course it's me. What are you doing in Boise? You are the last person I expected to see here."

Before he could answer, someone joined them on the sidewalk, and Morgan lifted his gaze to see who it was.

His sister looked behind her at the young man. "Morgan, this is my friend Robert Dudley. The one I wrote you about. Bob, this is my brother, Morgan."

Robert doffed his hat. "It's a pleasure to make your acquaintance, Mr. McKinley."

"Likewise."

"Daphne has told me a great deal about you, sir."

"Has she indeed." He looked at his sister. "I'd like to hear that myself. I trust it was entertaining."

Daphne laughed, then asked, "Where are you staying?"

"At the Idanha Hotel."

"That's where Bob and I have taken rooms as well. Are you going there now?"

"Yes."

"Then we shall walk with you, if that's all right."

"Of course it's all right." He offered his arm, and she took hold of it.

Robert fell in behind them on the sidewalk.

"You received my letter?" Daphne asked as they walked. "The one telling you I was coming?"

"Yes, I received it, but I didn't expect you until next week. I thought you were stopping to see the sights. Have you enjoyed your trip west?"

"It's been delightful, although we didn't make as many stops as I'd hoped we would. Bob is anxious to reach California so he hurried us along. He wants to be rid of his obligation to me and be about the business of becoming a well-known figure on the motion picture screen."

"Don't believe her, Mr. McKinley," Robert interjected. "Daphne was the one in a hurry. She was eager to see you."

The idea pleased Morgan — that his sister wanted to be with him. He thought again of Gwen and Cleo, of how close they were despite the many years of separation. Pray God the same would happen between the McKinley siblings.

He patted the back of Daphne's hand where it rested in the crook of his arm. "I'm glad you've come. It's been too long since we were together."

"I feel the same. And to be honest, I was weary of traveling around Europe and just as weary of staying put with Cousin Gertrude. She is a dear woman, truly she is, but I no longer need to be chaperoned as if I were a child. And the way she tries to keep men away from me." Daphne rolled her eyes. "It's positively medieval."

Morgan nodded but made no comment. He knew Gertrude Anderson, an unmarried woman in her forties, had meant to protect the young McKinley heiress from fortune hunters. In fact, that was one of the things he'd charged her with doing when he'd asked her to be Daphne's chaperone. But his sister needn't know that.

"Morgan, you haven't told me why you're in Boise. I know you didn't come to meet me."

"I'm here on business for New Hope. I've got a meeting with men from the railroad later in the week, and in the meantime, I'm hiring more workers and placing orders for materials and furnishings."

"I cannot wait to see what you've accomplished. For that matter, I cannot wait to see where you have settled. Who knows? Maybe I'll decide to stay in Bethlehem Springs too."

Harrison rode his horse down the incline to the water's edge. About a quarter mile north of the wall of trees on the opposite side of Crow's Creek were the pools and the bathhouse of the New Hope Health Spa. Elias Spade had promised him this was the best way to enter the grounds undetected. Maybe the only way, due to the guards now patrolling the area.

It was a risk, of course, for him to be here in the middle of the day, but he'd wanted to see for himself what Spade intended. A stick or two of dynamite, Spade had told him, was all it would take to destroy that section of the resort compound. A spa without pools and bathhouse was no spa at all. Without them, the resort couldn't open. And maybe that would be the final straw for McKinley.

Gwen's article for the *Daily Herald* was due the next day, and she hadn't managed even one sentence. She'd found a dozen other things to do besides write, including baking a cake and two pies and scouring her kitchen. The cake and one of the pies had been taken to the Goldsmiths. She would most likely eat the second pie herself. Every bite of it, unless she threw off this funk.

That was one reason she was now in her buggy, Shakespeare trotting along the road heading north. She hoped the fresh air would rid her of her bad humor and save her from that pie. Her other reason — the more important one — was to see if an idea that had come to her that morning might provide not only tomorrow's piece for the paper but a series of them. She wanted to write articles about some of the men who were building the spa. One article about a carpenter. Another about a stonemason. One about Mr. Doyle, the site overseer. Another about . . . the owner.

Summoned by her thoughts, Morgan's words repeated in her head as they had done often over the past week. *"Isn't it obvious? I have come to care for you. To deeply care for you."* Would he say those words to her again if he were given the chance? Or would he withdraw them for good because of her rejection.

Sounds floated to her through the forest — hammers striking nails and wood, men shouting to one another. She was nearing the building site.

Just as Shakespeare was about to pull the buggy around a bend in the road, Gwen caught sight of a man on horseback down at the creek's edge. She drew back on the reins. If that was Fagan Doyle —

But it wasn't the site overseer. She could see the man's face now as his horse picked its way across the shallow water. It was Harrison Carter. What was he doing down there?

Harrison looked up, saw her, and reined

in, stopping his horse in midstream. After a brief hesitation, he waved to her. "Miss Arlington. Wait there, will you?"

It wasn't a difficult ride from the creek up to the road, and yet Gwen thought Harrison Carter looked as if he'd traveled a mile uphill. There was a sheen of perspiration across his forehead and upper lip, and when his gaze met hers, it skittered away at once. Almost as if he were unnerved by her presence. Which made no sense to her. Harrison Carter was *not* the nervous type, and especially not around women.

"Visiting the resort site?" he asked, glancing toward the bend in the road.

"Yes." She could have told him about her idea for the articles. She chose not to.

"Has Mr. McKinley returned?"

"No, I don't believe that he has."

He looked at her again, then down the road toward town. "Too bad. I wanted to speak with him about some concerns the board has regarding the effect the spa will have on Crow's Creek. Once it joins the river a few miles south of here, it will become our problem."

Gwen almost asked him what those concerns were, but a check in her spirit stopped her from voicing the question aloud. Something told her Harrison was being less than honest.

"Maybe you know when he's to return, Miss Arlington."

"I'm sorry. I don't know for certain."

"He didn't tell you?"

She stiffened. What business was it of his what Morgan said to her? "I didn't see him before he left." True — and she felt no compunction to tell him there had been a note. "You must excuse me, Mr. Carter. I've an article to write and too little time to do it in." She slapped the reins against Shakespeare's rump, and the buggy moved forward, around the bend, and out of Harrison's sight.

Disagreeable man.

Unless the voters of Bethlehem Springs voted for Morgan despite his endorsement of Gwen, she would be the newly elected mayor in a few weeks. She would have to work with Harrison Carter on matters that concerned both town and county. That wasn't a pleasant thought. The longer she knew him, the less she liked him.

The road curved to the right again, then to the left, and once more to the right. The final turn brought the New Hope lodge into view. She imagined herself as a guest arriving for the first time. Surely it would make a guest's heart leap when he or she saw that magnificent building. She was no judge of health spas, having never visited one, but she had to believe this would be as grand as any other.

How many guest rooms would there be in this four-story building? Sixty? Eighty? More? Would a day actually come when all of those rooms would be filled with guests? Morgan must think so or he wouldn't be pouring so much money into its development.

In an area some distance from the lodge was a clearing where several corrals had been built. Each held a number of horses. Nearby were several wagons with horses standing in the traces. She guided Shakespeare in that direction.

By the time she stepped out of her buggy, Fagan Doyle could be seen striding toward her.

"Miss Arlington, sure and it's a pleasure to see you again."

"Good day, Mr. Doyle."

"If it's Morgan you're looking for, you won't find him here."

She nodded. "Actually, it was you I came to see."

"Me? Be still my heart." He placed both of his hands over the left side of his chest.

His grin gave away his jest.

"Perhaps you know that I write articles for the *Daily Herald*."

"Aye, I've read them myself."

"I want to write a number of pieces about you and some of the local men who are employed here. Could I talk to you and a few others? I promise not to keep anyone from their work for too long."

"For you, Miss Arlington, it would be a pleasure." He motioned toward the lodge. "Would you care to see what's been achieved since you were last here?"

"Yes, I would like that. Very much."

Over dinner that evening, Morgan listened to Daphne's animated descriptions of the places and people she and Robert had seen as they came west. Most of their journey had been by rail, although some of their side trips had been by motorcar.

His sister was more articulate than he remembered. More poised as well. He supposed the completion of her education and several trips to Europe had made the difference since the last time they were together. She was pretty too. Not as pretty as Gwen, but —

"Morgan, I just remembered what your last letter said. You're running for mayor?

That's rather unexpected, isn't it? I had no idea you had political aspirations."

"I don't, and I don't expect to win the election. I've stayed in the race, but I've made it known that I plan to vote for my opponent. Miss Arlington would make the better mayor."

Daphne straightened in her chair. "Your opponent is a woman?"

"Yes." He grinned at his sister. "And she isn't a great many years older than you."

"Women have the vote in Idaho?"

Morgan nodded. "Since 1896. Among the first in the nation to grant women full suffrage."

Daphne looked at Robert. "And you said Idaho was a backwater and that I should go with you to California."

Morgan glanced from his sister to Robert and back again. Was something going on between those two? Had Robert Dudley become more to Daphne than was proper, considering they were both young and unmarried and had traveled almost twenty-seven hundred miles together?

He was surprised by the strong surge of emotions that overtook him as the questions formed in his mind. He'd managed not to give his sister too much thought in the years since their mother died. He'd been content to allow their cousin to look after Daphne and to inform him if something was needed. That had changed in an instant.

"Is something wrong, Morgan?" Daphne leaned toward him. "You're wearing the most disagreeable look on your face."

"No. Nothing's wrong."

At least it had better not be, if Robert Dudley knew what was good for him.

TWENTY-EIGHT

On Friday afternoon, Gwen was standing on the sidewalk in front of the *Daily Herald,* visiting about matters both large and small with Christina Patterson and Myrna Evans, when she heard the sound of an approaching automobile. Her heartbeat quickened with hope — the *put-putter-put* of an engine did that to her these days — and her eyes were drawn in the direction of the sound.

Coming up Main Street from the highway was a touring car, top down. She narrowed her eyes. Was that Morgan at the wheel? Yes. Yes, it was. But who was that in the passenger seat? The woman, her hat and face swathed in netting to keep away the road dust, seemed to be looking at the town with great interest, turning her head this way and that.

As the automobile passed the three women, all of them now looking at the car and its occupants, Morgan gave them a nod of greeting, but he didn't slow the vehicle.

Christina said, "Who was that with Mr. McKinley?"

"I don't know," Gwen answered.

"Not anyone from around here," Myrna said. "I'm sure of that." She lowered her voice, as if sharing an intimate secret. "It appears Mr. McKinley had more than business on his mind when he went to Boise."

Gwen felt a sudden chill. Who was that woman and why had Morgan brought her to Bethlehem Springs? Several possible answers to those questions whispered in her head, and none of them brought her comfort.

"Well, I must be getting along home," Christina said, "or Nathan will have nothing to eat for his supper but cold meat and a slice of bread."

Myrna nodded. "I must do likewise." She touched Gwen on the forearm. "And if I don't find Felicity practicing the piano when I get home, that daughter of mine will find herself doing extra chores for a solid month."

Gwen scarcely heard the words her friends spoke. In her mind she saw Morgan and his female companion driving down Main Street. He'd seen her too. Why hadn't he stopped? Why hadn't he taken just a few moments to speak to her?

Because she'd sent him away, that's why. Because she'd told him she couldn't return his feelings, that she didn't welcome his kisses, that she didn't want to be promised to any man.

Was it too late to tell him that was no longer true?

While Mrs. Cheevers showed Daphne to what would be her room for the duration of her stay, Morgan sorted through his accumulated mail and the messages Fagan had left for him. There wasn't anything that needed immediate attention, and he was thankful for that. He was too tired for decision making. What he wanted most was a bath to wash off the road dust, followed by a good meal.

"Mr. McKinley?"

He looked up and watched Mrs. Cheevers descend the stairs.

"I didn't want to say this in front of your sister, sir, but Mrs. Nelson wasn't feeling well and I sent her home. I wasn't expecting you back until tomorrow and there's nothing prepared for your evening meal."

"Don't worry about it, Mrs. Cheevers. Daphne and I will go to the South Fork for dinner."

"I deeply regret these circumstances. It won't happen again."

He placed a hand on the woman's shoulder. "Don't worry. We've been dining out for an entire week. Another night won't hurt us." He dropped the mail onto the entry table. "Anything of interest happen while I was away?"

"No, sir. Not that I've heard. Although Miss Arlington wrote an interesting piece for the paper about one of the local men who works up at New Hope."

Now that *was* news. "What did she write?"

His housekeeper smiled at him. "I believe it would be fair to say that Miss Arlington has given her endorsement to you and New Hope the same as you gave your endorsement to her for mayor."

Pleasure sluiced through him. Perhaps he had reason to hope that she would forgive him for that unexpected kiss. And perhaps she might be willing, in time, to be kissed again.

"If you'll excuse me, sir, I'll see that Mr. Finch brings in the young lady's things. She told me she wants to take a bath." Her gaze skimmed over him, as if to say, *You should do the same.*

He did want a bath — but first he wanted to read Gwen's article. "Are the newspapers in my study?"

"Yes, sir. I left them on your desk."

"Thank you, Mrs. Cheevers."

The woman hurried off to see to Daphne's needs while Morgan headed for his study.

It didn't take long to find what he was looking for.

NEW HOPE FOR
HOWARD SMITH

When the Lucky Johnson Mines ceased operation, Howard Smith found himself out of work for the first time in two decades. For a time, he thought he might have to move his family away from Bethlehem Springs in order to find employment. But for the past year, Mr. Smith has been working at the building site of the New Hope Health Spa as a carpenter.

The article — the first of a series, according to the paper — went on to tell the kind of work Howard Smith had been doing and included numerous quotes by the man himself. Gwen's journalism skills were apparent throughout the piece.

Two other things were also obvious. One, Gwen believed in the benefits New Hope had brought and would bring to Bethlehem

Springs. And two, she cared for Morgan. Not that she said as much, but he sensed it between the lines.

Wishful thinking? Perhaps — but his heart told him otherwise.

Gwen sat on her porch swing, rocking gently back and forth, a glass of tea in her hand. In the summer, this was how she spent many an evening, enjoying the colorful flowers that filled her front yard, soaking in the sounds of Bethlehem Springs as the sun lowered itself behind the mountains, sometimes visiting with a neighbor or two as twilight blanketed the town.

But her thoughts were not restful this evening. The election was only a few days away, and along with the increasing belief that she would be elected had come numerous doubts about her ability to serve the people well. Would she be able to bring about positive change? That was certainly her hope.

Hope . . .

New Hope . . .

Morgan . . .

Oh, how her thoughts betrayed her. She even imagined she could hear him speaking her name —

But it wasn't her imagination. He was

there at her gate, a pretty young woman holding his arm.

Morgan smiled as he swung the gate inward. "I'm glad we found you at home."

Gwen set her glass on the floor, rose from the swing, and stepped toward the railing, all the while pleading with God that she wouldn't make a fool of herself. "I trust your business in Boise was concluded satisfactorily." She forced a smile as her gaze moved to the woman at Morgan's side.

"Miss Arlington, allow me to introduce my sister, Daphne McKinley. She has come to stay with me for the summer."

His sister. Of course. She should have known. Look at them. They had the same color eyes and hair and similar jawlines and noses. There was even something about the way Daphne carried herself that was like her brother. An air of confidence, perhaps.

"It's a pleasure to make your acquaintance, Miss McKinley." Gwen motioned them onto the porch, her smile no longer forced. "Please. Won't you join me?"

"We'd be delighted," Morgan answered.

"Would either of you like some iced tea?"

"Not for me, thanks." He patted his abdomen. "We've just come from dinner at the South Fork, and I'm filled to the gills."

There was not the least bit of doubt

remaining. Gwen was in love. Completely. Totally. Utterly. She wanted to throw herself into his arms and tell him how sorry she was for being an idiot. She *did* want his kisses. She *did* want to be promised to someone. To him!

No one could have been more surprised than Gwen by this storm of emotions roiling inside of her. She had chosen the single life. It hadn't been thrust upon her. She'd chosen to be independent of a husband, to be free to make her own choices, free to come and go as she pleased. She hadn't wanted to hand control of her life to another person.

But freedom no longer felt free.

Gwen realized belatedly that Daphne had answered her about the tea, and she had no idea whether the reply had been yes or no. She hoped the latter for she was loathe to leave the porch even for a few minutes. She wanted to stay right here, near Morgan.

"I'm glad you were at home," he repeated, breaking the silence that had fallen over them. He settled onto a chair next to where his sister now sat. "I wanted Daphne to meet you."

"My brother has had many kind things to say about you, Miss Arlington."

Gwen tried not to let those words thrill

her too much. She failed.

"He knew I was coming for a visit, of course, but he wasn't expecting me to arrive this soon. Imagine my surprise when I saw him walking along the street in Boise."

"No more surprised than I was to see you."

Daphne continued as if her brother hadn't spoken. "I have been eager to meet you from the moment I learned you were running for mayor. I knew right then that you and I should be friends."

"I would like that," Gwen said, meaning it.

"What made you decide to run? Was it something you've always wanted to do?"

Gwen laughed softly. "No. It was my sister's idea. I wouldn't have thought of it on my own, but Cleo is nothing if not a freethinker."

"Oh, yes. Morgan told me that you have a twin sister. I wish I'd had a sister close to my own age." Daphne touched Morgan's forearm and smiled at him. "Not that I don't adore my older brother, but he was scarcely ever around from the time I turned six. I feel like we are just now getting to know one another."

It was strange, the way this information made Gwen feel even closer to Morgan.

Both of them had been separated from their sisters when they were younger. Both of them had been given a second chance to become closer to their siblings once again.

To Daphne, she said, "Then I hope you will remain in Bethlehem Springs for a long time. It's good to reconnect with one's family."

"I hope she'll stay too." Morgan straightened in his chair. "But I think it's time we started for home. It's been a long day, and the hour grows late."

Gwen wasn't ready for them to leave yet, but she could think of no reason for them to remain. However, she *could* think of a reason for them to return. "Would you both come to Sunday dinner? My father and sister will be here. I know they'd like to meet you, Miss McKinley."

Daphne didn't even glance at her brother. "We'd love to come."

"We would, indeed." Morgan stood, then offered his hand to his sister.

Gwen followed them down the steps and along the walk to the gate. It was there that Morgan stopped and turned, so suddenly she almost ran into him.

In a low voice he said, "If it's all right, Miss Arlington, I will call upon you again tomorrow."

TWENTY-NINE

Morgan parked his automobile at the sidewalk near Gwen's front gate and whispered a quick prayer for God's blessing. The last time he'd asked a woman to marry him, it had been a bad decision. Even now, the memory left a nasty taste in his mouth. But Gwen was nothing like Yvette. For that matter, he was a much different man than he'd been before.

Now if only she loved him too. If only she said yes when he asked her. Last night he'd felt as if something had changed between them. Changed in her.

Please, God, let me not be mistaken.

He opened the passenger door and stepped onto the sidewalk. His lungs felt starved for air, and he took a moment to draw a deep breath before opening the gate and striding toward the house. The front door was open, and he could see through to the kitchen where Gwen sat at the table, holding a cup between two hands.

If I've ever wanted anything, Lord, it's her.

He rapped on the doorjamb. Gwen started, as if surprised by the sound, then turned toward the door. Did she look glad or sorry to see him? He couldn't be sure. Her face was hidden in shadows.

"Good morning." He removed his hat. "I hope I haven't come too early in the day."

"No." She rose and came toward him. "It isn't too early."

What if he'd misread her last night? What if she wasn't ready to hear what he had to say? He could destroy any chance he had with her if he spoke too soon.

"Does Owen have a lesson today?" he asked.

"Not today. He's working for the Humphreys at the mercantile for the summer." She pushed open the screen door. "We'll resume his lessons in the fall when school starts up again."

"No summer off for me?" He stepped inside.

She shook her head, voice grave. "Owen is one of my *advanced* students. He can take the summer off without losing ground. You need your lessons."

Morgan couldn't keep from chuckling, loving her all the more for her sense of humor. A slow smile curved her mouth, and the room felt the brighter for it.

Now. Now was the time. Now, while she was smiling at him, teasing him.

"Miss Arlington, I never want to miss another lesson with you. Not any lesson, piano or otherwise, that you want to give me."

Their smiles faded in unison.

"And now, Gwen" — he gently clasped her upper arms with his hands — "I'm going to kiss you."

Gwen found it difficult to breathe and impossible to speak. All she could do was watch as he lowered his mouth toward hers. It was sweet torture, his kiss, his arms now embracing her. Loving Morgan must have been God's purpose for her all along, for surely nothing in her life had felt so right as this.

At long last, he drew back, far enough that she could look into his eyes and see her own swirling emotions mirrored in them.

"I love you, Gwen."

And I love you.

"Marry me."

"Marry you?" she whispered.

"Yes, marry me."

She hadn't wanted marriage. She had

turned her back on it years ago. But now she couldn't remember why. Looking into his dark eyes, she couldn't think of a single reason why she wouldn't want to be his wife.

"Marry me." Another smile began to curve the corners of his mouth, and he nodded, as if to show her how to respond.

Marry him.

Love him.

Cherish him.

Laugh with him.

Grow old with him.

Holding her breath, she nodded in return.

His smile widened a second before he kissed her again, long and warm and sweet. She didn't care if he never stopped. She was willing to stay right there forever, wrapped in his arms, his lips upon hers, their hearts beating in unison.

When he drew back a second time, he surprised her by sweeping her feet off the floor and cradling her in his arms. "You've made me the happiest man in the world, Gwen Arlington. Shall we go tell my sister? Then we can drive out to the ranch to tell your father and Cleo." As if he anticipated what she would say, he continued, "I don't want to wait until tomorrow. I want to tell them now."

She laughed, her joy matching his. "Yes.

Let's go tell them. Let's tell everyone. Let's tell the entire world."

As Morgan's automobile approached the ranch house, a cloud of dust whirling up behind it, Gwen saw Cleo dismount and tie her horse to the corral fence. A moment later, their father appeared from inside the barn. Cleo waved at the passengers in the automobile, then the two of them strode toward the house to await their arrival.

Excitement and nerves erupted in Gwen's stomach. She knew Cleo and their father liked Morgan, but maybe they would think Gwen was rushing things. Maybe they would think she hadn't thought things through. And if they didn't approve? What then?

The touring car rolled to a stop, and Morgan helped Gwen and Daphne out of the automobile.

"Dad, Cleo," Gwen said as the three of them stepped forward, "I'd like you to meet Morgan's sister, Daphne McKinley. Daphne, this is my father, Griff Arlington, and my sister, Cleo."

"How do you do?" Daphne offered her hand to Cleo's father first, then to Cleo. "It's a pleasure to meet you both."

After the group exchanged a few pleasantries, Gwen's father said, "Let's go up on the porch out of the sun."

The five of them trouped up the steps. While the others sat on chairs, Cleo leaned her backside against the porch rail and crossed one booted foot over the other while crossing her arms over her chest. Gwen wondered if her sister had already guessed the reason for their visit. Something about her shrewd expression said she had.

Her father asked Daphne a number of questions about her trip to Idaho and how long she meant to stay and if she'd ever been on a cattle ranch before. Gwen wished he would stop before she exploded with the news of her engagement.

At long last, Morgan cleared his throat and leaned forward on his chair. "Mr. Arlington, I wonder if I might have a word alone with you."

Before their father could answer, Cleo said, "Say no, Dad. I think I'd like to hear this too." She pinned Morgan with a fierce gaze. "I reckon Gwennie and your sister already know what's on your mind, so why should I be left out? Go on. Speak your piece here and now."

Gwen couldn't recall a time she'd seen Morgan when he looked less than confident, but that's how he looked now. He glanced at her, a question in his eyes, and she gave a slight shrug in answer.

"All right." He cleared his throat again. "Mr. Arlington, I've proposed marriage to your daughter, and she has done me the honor of saying yes. So we've come to ask for your blessing."

Cleo let out a whoop as she pushed off the rail. "I knew it!" She grabbed Gwen's hand, pulled her up from her chair, and wrapped her in a tight embrace. With her mouth close to Gwen's ear, Cleo whispered, "I'm so glad you came to your senses, Gwennie. I'm so happy for you and Morgan."

"Morgan," their father said, laughter in his voice, "I believe Cleo has answered for the both of us. You and Gwen have our blessing with our whole hearts."

THIRTY

Although Gwen asked and Morgan agreed that their engagement would be kept a secret until one of them was sworn in as mayor, it didn't escape people's notice that the two candidates spent a great deal of time in each other's company in those days leading up to the Tuesday of the election. Edna Updike, Gwen's next-door neighbor, reportedly said that if Gwen was elected, at least the townsfolk would know she had a competent man behind her, telling her what she needed to know and what she needed to do.

When that comment reached Gwen's ears — passed along on election day by Cleo, who had gone to the municipal building to check on the voting — it nearly sent her through the roof. "As if I need Morgan to tell me what to do for Bethlehem Springs. Doesn't Mrs. Updike know I formed my campaign platform on my own? I didn't even know Morgan when I decided to run for office."

Cleo shook her head. "Edna Updike doesn't think a woman should have an opinion apart from a man's say so. You know that, Gwennie. Don't pay her no mind."

"I don't want anyone thinking I'm a puppet, that's all. You don't suppose Morgan thinks that's what I'll be?" More nervous than she'd expected she'd be on Election Day, Gwen paced the parlor.

Her sister made a sound that was half laugh, half snort. "Nobody who knows you will think that. Especially not Morgan."

Footsteps on the front porch caused Gwen to turn around just as her father and Morgan opened the screen door. "Any more news?" she asked them.

Morgan shook his head. "We were told they'll have the results about nine o'clock. We can go to the municipal building to await the announcement or they can send someone to us with the final tally."

Gwen glanced at the clock. Not yet seven. She might go crazy before the next two hours were up.

"Where's Daphne?" Cleo asked Morgan. "I thought she was coming over with you."

"She said she had some writing to do and wondered if it was okay for her to stay at home. I imagine her correspondence is more important to her than our local politics." He shrugged. "Especially when I told her Gwen was certain to win."

"I wish you would quit saying that."

He put his arm around her shoulders and drew her close. "Stop fussing. The election is yours."

"None of us can know that for sure."

"Sweetheart, I've talked to as many people as I could since the night of the debate. Everyone knows by now that I voted for you today. Maybe I should have pulled my name off the ballot, but —"

"No," she interrupted. "I wouldn't have wanted to win that way."

He gave her an encouraging smile.

Perhaps the election shouldn't mean as much to her now. She and Morgan were engaged and had settled on a date in mid-August for the wedding. After they married, she would move from her little house on Wallula to Morgan's larger home on Skyview. Other women would be content to live the simple life, overseeing their husbands' homes. Why wasn't she like that? Why did she want more?

Gwen swallowed a groan as she drew away from Morgan and walked into the kitchen. She paused briefly, looked around, wondering why she'd come in there, then moved on through and out the back door. She hurried toward the stable that housed Shakespeare. The gelding greeted her with a soft nicker as he thrust his head over the stall door.

"Hello, fella." She stroked his head. "I'm a nervous wreck. Can you feel it?"

Shakespeare bobbed his head.

She pressed her forehead against his neck. "I should be planning my wedding, not hoping to be elected. Why can't I be like other women?"

"Interesting question," Morgan said from behind her. "But I rather like you the way you are."

She sucked in a breath as she turned around. "I didn't know you followed me outside."

"Do you want me to go back to the house? I will if you'd rather be alone."

She nodded, shook her head, nodded again.

He gave her a look that showed great patience as well as tender regard.

She sighed. "You needn't go. I don't want to be alone. I think the waiting is driving me a trifle mad, that's all. Don't you feel the least bit nervous, waiting for the results?"

"No. What will be, will be. We've done all

we can. Now it's in God's hands."

"You won't mind, even a little, if I win?" As soon as the words were out of her mouth, she shook her head and said, "Don't answer that. We've talked about it before."

"What do you say about taking a drive? Just you and me. We'll head down the road and not come back until it's time for the results to be announced."

Was it any wonder she loved him? "No, we'd best stay here with Dad and Cleo. They've been so supportive. I wouldn't want them to feel unwelcome. Is that all right?"

"Of course. Whatever you want, Gwen."

She slipped into his arms and pressed the side of her face against his chest. His heart drummed beneath her ear. *Ba-bump. Ba-bump. Ba-bump.* The sound soothed her. Listening to the steady beat made her feel less frazzled, more grounded.

Morgan was right. What would be, would be. She needed to relax, to trust, to leave it in God's hands.

"Let's go inside." She tipped her head back and looked up at him. Then she smiled to let him know her world had begun to right itself again.

When Morgan and Gwen reentered the

house, they found Cleo and Griff seated at the kitchen table with a deck of cards. Cleo held up the dark red box, *Going to Market* clearly printed on its front. "We thought a game or two might help pass the time. We need at least three players."

Gwen pulled out a chair between her father and sister. "It might help the time go by faster."

Morgan took the seat opposite her.

"It's the latest thing," Cleo said. "Have you played it yet?"

"No."

"It's pretty simple." She showed him a card with the number four in the upper left corner and a drawing in the center with the name of a cereal beneath it. "I'm going to deal all the cards, and the goal is to get all four cards that belong to any set and as many sets as you can. There are thirteen sets in all. So if you got this card that says Postum, you'd want to get the Post Porridge, Grape-nuts, and Post Toasties cards to finish the set."

He nodded to show that he understood.

Cleo quickly explained the rest of the game, shuffled the deck of cards — with the speed and precision of a professional card player, Morgan thought — and began dealing them around the table. When they each had thirteen cards, they picked up their hands and began sorting them into order.

Morgan's paternal grandmother had considered any game that included the use of cards to be the devil's handiwork and his father had forbidden a deck of playing cards under his roof. As a young man away at school, he'd avoided card games — even simple ones like *Going to Market* and *Rook* — out of respect for his grandmother and father. It wasn't that he believed there was intrinsic evil in a deck of cards. It was simply that old habits died hard. Even now he half-expected to feel his grandmother slap his hand.

But that feeling was soon overcome by the enthusiasm of the Arlington family and his own competitive nature. Cleo won the first game and did her share of crowing over his measly three sets. He wasn't about to be trounced a second time.

Before they knew it, the clock chimed nine o'clock. At the sound, everyone laid their cards facedown on the table. There was a quick and wordless exchange of glances before Griff said, "Let's walk down to the municipal building. I can't sit here and wait for them to bring the news to us."

Once out on the sidewalk, Morgan offered Gwen his arm and she took it. "God's in control," he said softly.

"Yes."

When the foursome reached Main Street, they saw that they weren't the only ones who wanted to know the results tonight, as soon as they were announced. Lots of people, most of them in groups of three or four, were walking toward the Bethlehem Springs Municipal Building. The mild evening air was punctuated with their voices and laughter. Some called out to Gwen and Morgan, wishing them luck. Others smiled and waved. No one seemed to consider it odd that the two candidates were walking arm in arm. Morgan had a feeling their secret wasn't much of a secret.

At the municipal building, they found a crowd — about a hundred people, Morgan guessed — gathered at the bottom of the steps. Seeing Morgan and Gwen's approach, the assembly parted like the Red Sea before Moses, allowing them through, Cleo and Griff right behind them.

As everyone settled in again, Morgan caught snippets of conversation: someone wondering if or when the United States would be dragged into the growing war in Europe; a woman expressing horror over the sinking of the RMS *Lusitania* off the coast of Ireland; two men discussing what it took to be a great baseball player.

Morgan and Gwen said nothing. What was there to say now?

Strange, he thought, the importance this election had played in his life over the past weeks. If he'd never declared for office, he wouldn't have come to know Gwen. He probably wouldn't have thought to take piano lessons. They wouldn't be engaged. If he hadn't declared his candidacy, he would still be living in a tent up at New Hope, all of his attention focused on the spa's construction — eating, drinking, and sleeping the completion of the resort.

A murmur passed through the crowd and slowly conversations ceased. Morgan looked toward the top of the steps to see Jackson Jones standing there, a piece of paper in his hand.

"Good evening. The votes from today's election have been tallied, and it is my duty to inform you that Miss Guinevere Arlington, by a margin of twelve votes, has been elected as your new mayor."

Behind them came a couple of shouts of congratulations, some applause, and a few murmurs of dissatisfaction.

Twelve votes. Much closer than he'd expected, but still the victory for Gwen that he'd predicted. But no matter. She'd won.

That's what counted.

Morgan was tempted to gather her into his arms and kiss her in front of everyone. After all, the election was hers. But they'd agreed to wait until after she was sworn into office, and so wait he would.

Dearest Mother,

I have much to share with you. You shall never guess all that has transpired since I last wrote. Remember that I told you I decided to run for mayor in the Bethlehem Springs special election. When I wrote that letter, I was facing two opponents in the race. One of them dropped out several weeks ago. One week after that, the other man and I were to debate each other. Only instead of debating, he told the crowd that he planned to vote for me. It caused quite a stir.

Today was the election, and I won! Not by a great many votes, but I still won. I will be sworn into office in nine days. I wish you could be here, but I'm afraid you won't receive the letter in time for you to arrange to travel here.

But I have another more important reason to ask you to come for a visit. I am to be married in mid-August. Morgan McKinley is my fiancé's name, and he was the opponent who voted for me. A rather strange set of circumstances, I am sure you will agree. But I am also sure the greater surprise for you is that I have chosen to marry at all. I know I told you I wouldn't, but I was wrong. Loving Morgan proved me wrong.

Mother, even though you have said you never want to set eyes on Bethlehem Springs again, I hope you will make an exception for my wedding. Cleo would so very much like to spend some time with you too. Please don't disappoint us.

Morgan's father and mother are both deceased, but he has a younger sister, Daphne, who has come from Boston for the summer. Dad and Cleo both think the world of Morgan and have already made him a member of our family.

Dad is in good health. Cleo is the same as ever. And I am well too.

If you can come, please send me a telegram rather than a letter. It will reach me so much sooner. You can stay with me in my home, which is small, or with Dad and Cleo at the ranch. Or if you would rather, Morgan would make you welcome to stay with him and Daphne.

Please do come.

With much love,
Your daughter, Guinevere

THIRTY-ONE

A half hour after the swearing in ceremony concluded, Morgan leaned his shoulder against the doorjamb and watched as Gwen ran her gloved fingertips over the surface of the large desk.

Didn't most mayors in America have gray beards and round bellies? Obviously the voters of Bethlehem Springs had better taste when choosing who would serve them. Just look at Gwen. She was more beautiful in that rose-colored dress and the matching wide-brimmed hat than he had seen her look before — and that was saying something.

"Well, Madam Mayor. What do you think of your new office?"

She lifted a somewhat bewildered gaze in his direction. "It's a little surreal, isn't it? I keep thinking I'll wake up and find this whole thing has been a dream."

"It's all real, Gwen." He pushed off the

doorjamb, closed the door with his foot, and crossed the room to take her in his arms. "And so is the love I feel for you."

"Good sir." She tilted her head back to look at him. "Are you trying to influence city hall?"

"Indeed, madam, I am." He kissed her, something he'd wanted to do earlier but couldn't with so many people around.

All too soon, she pulled back from his embrace. "I'm expecting Mayor Hopkins any moment. He and I must discuss some matters before he leaves Bethlehem Springs."

"He's leaving town that soon?"

"Yes, for medical treatment at a hospital in Chicago." She removed her hat and placed it on a bookcase beneath one of the windows. "I don't know how long our meeting will last."

"Would you like me to come for you later?"

She shook her head. "It's hard to know when I'll be finished."

"You're sure?"

"I'm sure. Don't worry about me. I'll walk home when I'm through here."

"All right, then." He leaned in to kiss her again. "Don't shake things up too much on your first day in office."

Her laughter stayed with him long after he'd left the municipal building.

It was nearing six in the evening by the time Gwen closed the thick law book on her desk. Her head swam with numbers and laws and rules and expectations and requests. What a day.

Outside the open window in her office, the promise of evening had begun to spread shadows over the town. Music, laughter, and voices could be heard coming from the direction of the High Horse Saloon, located about a block away. If Idaho became a dry state, the High Horse would be forced to close its doors. Gwen had never been involved in the temperance movement, but she had to believe public drunkenness would become a thing of the past if Prohibition was enacted. That would be a relief to everyone.

The air was still and unusually hot, which didn't make for a pleasant walk home. By the time Gwen reached her gate, her dress was clinging to her, sticky with perspiration. What she wanted before dinner was a cool bath and something cold to drink.

She was almost to the steps when she saw a movement out of the corner of her eye. There was someone on her porch. Maybe

Morgan had —

"Guinevere, at last."

Gwen drew in a breath. "Mother?"

"Yes, dear. Believe it or not, I have come."

Gwen hurried up the steps and embraced her mother. "When did you get here? Why didn't you let me know you were coming?"

"I packed my bags the day I got your letter. I couldn't let you plan a wedding without me. It will be difficult enough, living as you do in the middle of nowhere, to have a proper ceremony."

"Bethlehem Springs is not in the middle of nowhere, Mother, and we have churches and ministers who perform wedding ceremonies all the time."

"Mmm."

Gwen felt tension tightening her shoulders. "How long have you been waiting?"

"Only an hour or so."

"If I'd known, I would have left my office and come straight home." She thought longingly of the cool bath she'd planned to take. That would have to wait. "Today was the inauguration. I'm the mayor now."

"So I was told by the nice gentleman who gave me directions to your house."

"Aren't you the littlest bit pleased for me?" Gwen hated the pleading note she heard in her voice.

"I suppose if it's what you want, Guinevere, then I'm glad."

She wished Morgan were with her. She wished she could see him smile at her as he had earlier in the day, could hear him tell her he was proud of her.

"But I want to hear about your intended. How on earth did Morgan McKinley end up here? And now he's engaged to you. There are young women on two continents who wanted to do what you have done."

"Shall we go inside, Mother? There's no need for us to remain standing on the porch. And you must be hungry after your journey."

"No, I do not want to go inside and I am not hungry." Her mother took hold of Gwen's arm and drew her to the chairs on the porch. "Now sit down and answer my question."

There was no use resisting. Elizabeth Arlington could be as stubborn as either of her daughters. Gwen might as well tell her what she wanted to know. "Morgan is building a health resort just north of town. He came to Idaho over a year ago."

"He's been living here all this time? And you never mentioned it once in your letters?"

"I had no reason to mention him. I didn't

know him."

Her mother rolled her eyes. "You should have known I'd be interested. His family is held in esteem on both sides of the Atlantic. In their day, the McKinley family hosted presidents and kings." She shook her head. "And to think you almost settled for that Bryant Hudson fellow."

I almost settled for him? Gwen pressed her lips together, swallowing a retort. Her brief engagement to Bryant was her mother's doing, not hers. How could her mother forget that?

"Oh, my. I can tell you. My friends are green with envy since I told them who you are engaged to marry. What an achievement!"

"It's not an achievement, Mother. I didn't ensnare him or win him. We fell in love."

"Love." Her mother waved a hand, as if brushing away a pesky fly. "A woman is far better served finding a husband who can give her a comfortable life and a secure future. Love can come later, if at all. Women who fall in love first are only asking for heartache. You will regret it if you go into marriage floating on some silly cloud of emotions. You mark my words."

About an hour after they'd eaten dinner

together, Morgan rapped on the door to his sister's room. "Daphne? May I come in?"

"Yes, of course. I'm decent."

He opened the door. "I thought I'd go over to Gwen's for a while. See how her first day in office went. Care to come along?"

"No, thank you." She pointed to the open journal on the small desk. "I'm writing down some thoughts. Besides, you don't need me along. I'm sure you'd like to be alone with your fiancée."

"Gwen and I want you to know you're always welcome, whatever we're doing."

Amusement sparkled in her eyes. "Not always."

He couldn't argue with her. She was right. He would like some time alone with Gwen. He wanted to take her in his arms and kiss her breathless. He wanted —

"And before you ask me if I'm sure, yes, I'm sure. You go on and enjoy the evening. Like I said, I'm busy with my writing. I won't even know you're gone."

"Mother wrote faithfully in her journals all the years that I remember. It's good one of us picked up the habit."

Daphne smiled. "I enjoy it. Writing has become a part of me, I guess." She flicked her fingers at him. "Now go on before I lose my train of thought entirely."

This time Morgan didn't hesitate. With a nod, he backed into the hall, closing the door as he went. Minutes later, he was in his motorcar and driving toward Gwen's home.

He'd thought of Gwen so often since he left her alone in the mayor's office that morning. Had the day gone well for her? Was she loving the work or hating it? Had there been a spare moment in her day when she'd thought of him too?

No matter what, he was certain she'd given her all. That was the way Gwen did everything. At least that was his opinion. Admittedly, he was biased.

He turned onto Wallula and braked to a stop in front of her white fence. He hopped over the side of the car and strode up her walk. The front door was open, probably in hopes a breeze would blow through. Beyond the screen he heard two women's voices. Someone had beaten him here. Whoever it was, Morgan would run her off in a hurry.

He peered through the screen as he rapped on the doorjamb. "Gwen, it's me. I came to hear about your first day in office."

A heartbeat later, Gwen appeared in the doorway to her bedroom. "Morgan," she whispered. She didn't look glad to see him.

"Do you have a visitor?" He stepped

inside, made uncertain by Gwen's expression. "I thought I heard another voice."

"You did." A woman — a stranger to him — appeared in the bedroom doorway, smiling broadly. "I'm Elizabeth Arlington. And you must be Morgan McKinley." She moved toward him, her right arm outstretched. "What a pleasure it is to meet you, dear boy."

Morgan's first impression of Gwen's mother was that she was an undeniably handsome woman. However, he saw little resemblance to her daughters. Elizabeth's hair was auburn rather than blonde, and her eyes were a watery green instead of blue. Perhaps Gwen had the same chin and Cleo the same nose.

He shook hands with his future mother-in-law. "The pleasure is mine, Mrs. Arlington. I assure you."

"I could not believe it when I received Guinevere's letter, telling me of her engagement to you. But Mr. McKinley, I cannot fathom why you chose to move to this god-forsaken town when you have such beautiful family estates in the East. Surely that would be a more appropriate place for you and Guinevere to live and raise a family."

Obviously Elizabeth Arlington knew more than just his name. He'd wager she knew his entire history and the extent of the McKinley fortune as well. That would explain her haste to reach this town she so despised. He wasn't completely surprised. Gwen had given him some warning about her mother. And of course he'd known other women like Elizabeth Arlington.

His gaze returned to Gwen. Her internal conflict was written in her eyes. The Gwen he knew best — the one who wasn't afraid to run for mayor, the one who could stand up to the disapproval of her neighbors and who could live independently — had disappeared from view.

Elizabeth clapped her hands. "But now I am here and we can begin to plan a proper wedding."

Gwen closed her eyes. If only the floor would open up and swallow her whole. She never should have mentioned Morgan's name in her letter. If her mother had thought she was marrying a man of humble means, she might not have come for the wedding at all. But Gwen had wanted her here. Just not like this.

Another knock sounded at the door, and she looked to see who it was, glad for any intrusion.

Fagan Doyle stood on the other side of

the screen. "Morgan, I need to speak with you."

"What is it?" Morgan pushed open the screen door and stepped onto the porch. "Trouble?"

Fagan lowered his voice, but not enough that Gwen couldn't hear him. "One of the guards found dynamite not far from the bathhouse. In the forest just below it."

"Dynamite?"

"I'm thinking someone brought it there with plans to use it. Maybe he got scared away by one of the guards. Maybe it was left there until a better opportunity."

"It's escalating."

"Aye, it is that."

Gwen moved toward the door. "What's escalating?"

"Someone doesn't want the spa to get finished." Morgan looked at her through the screen. "We've had a few cases of vandalism, but until now it hasn't put anyone in danger. It's just cost us time and money." His jaw clenched. "This is different." He faced Fagan again. "Carter's gone too far this time."

"Carter?" Gwen pushed open the screen door. "Harrison Carter?"

"Yes."

She stepped outside. "You think *he* has

something to do with the vandalism. But why?"

"He's made it clear he doesn't think the spa will be good for the town."

"I know that. But it doesn't mean he would destroy property or try to dynamite the spa. That's absurd. Where is your proof? You can't accuse him without proof of some kind."

Morgan's gaze was hard as it met hers. "He's a dangerous man, Gwen."

"Oh, Morgan. I know you don't like him. He isn't my favorite person either. But dangerous?"

"I can't explain it. It's something I feel in my gut. Carter's failed to buy me out or force me out so far, and now he's getting desperate. There's no telling what he might do next." Morgan took hold of her shoulders. "Steer clear of him, Gwen."

"How am I to do that? He and I will be working together on —"

Morgan's fingers tightened on her shoulders. "Stay away from him. Stay home if you must. I have a bad feeling about this."

"I'm the mayor." Anger sparked inside her, and she jerked free of his grasp. "I intend to do my job."

"And I'm telling you it isn't safe. I want you to stay at home until I can make sure you are."

She couldn't believe her ears. She was the mayor. She had duties and obligations. And because he suspected Harrison Carter of some misdeed, Morgan now expected her to ignore those duties — because he said so. What gave him that right? She didn't need his protection. She certainly didn't need him to tell her what she could or could not do.

"I think you and Mr. Doyle should go," she said softly. "It sounds like you have important things to do."

"Gwen —"

"Just go. I need to get Mother settled in for the night. She's exhausted from her journey, and I'm feeling tired myself. It's been a full day."

"All right. We'll go. But promise me you'll —"

"Please go, Morgan. I'm too tired to argue with you."

"I didn't mean for us to argue."

He leaned in to kiss her on the lips, but she turned her cheek to him at the last moment.

"Good night, Morgan."

Gwen was right, of course. Morgan had no proof that Harrison Carter had been behind any of the troubles they'd experienced at New Hope. He'd had his suspicions almost from the start, but without proof, there hadn't been anything to say or do. Besides, he'd thought once Harrison saw the spa succeeding, once he saw it bringing prosperity and progress to the town, he would give up, go away, leave things alone.

He didn't think so anymore. Everything in Morgan said that not only was Carter behind these troubles, but his desperation to force Morgan out had made him dangerous. Why couldn't Gwen see that?

THIRTY-TWO

Gwen arose after a torturous, sleepless night on the cot in her small office, her mind made up. She would break her engagement. They weren't even married and Morgan expected her to obey him. How much worse might it be after they wed? No, breaking the engagement was the only thing she could do. She could take care of herself. She'd lived on her own for more than seven years now. She would be happy to continue living alone in the future.

Happy? Well, perhaps not happy. Maybe content was the better word. She would be content. The ache in her heart would ease with time.

She slipped her arms into the sleeves of her dressing gown and made her way to the kitchen to prepare coffee and was surprised to see that her mother was up and seated at the table.

"Good morning, Mother. I didn't expect

to see you up this early." She filled the coffeepot with water. "Did you sleep well?"

"No, my dear, I did not. Your bed is rather uncomfortable. I'm sure that the beds at the McKinley home are of better quality. Perhaps I should do as you suggested in your letter and go to stay with Mr. McKinley and his sister."

"That wouldn't be a good idea, Mother." She turned to face the table. "I . . . I'm calling off the wedding."

"You're *what?*"

"I'm not going to marry Morgan after all. I thought about it all night long, and I realize I can't go through with it."

"Good heavens, Guinevere! You'll never have an opportunity to marry a man like Morgan McKinley again. You are not exactly in your prime, you know. Do you have any idea what you're throwing away?"

Her heart was shattering into a million pieces. Wasn't that proof enough that she knew what she was throwing away?

"Now you listen to me, young lady. I will not —"

"No, Mother, I won't listen. Not right now. I can't listen to you right now." Tears welled in her eyes, and her throat tightened until she couldn't swallow. Even breathing seemed too great an effort. It would be easier to lie down and die.

She hurried into her temporary bedroom and prepared for the day ahead as quickly as her shaking hands would allow.

Morgan leaned his knuckles against the black surface of Harrison's desk. "Let me make myself clear, Carter. I don't know why you want me gone from here, but you might as well resign yourself to the fact that I'm not leaving. I'm not selling my land. The resort will be finished and it will open. I do mean to discover who has been vandalizing my property. And if you or your lackeys cause harm to even one person, I will see to it that you are in jail for a long, long time."

"Get out." Harrison rolled his chair back from the desk. "You have no business here. Get out or I'll call the police and have you thrown out."

"You want to call for the police?" Straightening, Morgan motioned toward the telephone on Harrison's desk. "Be my guest. Sheriff Winston might also be interested in knowing about the dynamite Mr. Doyle found on New Hope property yesterday. Hidden, as if someone intended to return for it later. And while we're at it, he'd probably like to hear a few of my theories about the vandalism and who might be behind it."

That was fear Morgan read in the other man's eyes. He wanted to take comfort in it, but he couldn't. He wouldn't take comfort until he was sure no one was in danger.

"And, Carter, I'm warning you. Keep away from Miss Arlington."

With that, he turned on his heel and strode from the office. Once outside, he crossed the street to the municipal building and went straight to the mayor's office. He knew he had some apologizing to do. Even though he was sure he'd been right to tell Gwen to avoid Harrison Carter, he hadn't gone about it in the most diplomatic of ways.

The secretary at the desk outside Gwen's office looked up as he entered. "Hello, Mr. McKinley."

The door to the inner office was open, but he couldn't see Gwen.

"If you're looking for Mayor Arlington, she hasn't come in yet."

"Really?" Now that surprised him. He would have wagered a pretty penny that Gwen would ignore his request that she stay at home. Maybe he hadn't left things last night in as bad a place as he'd thought. "Well, please tell her I came by."

"Of course. And Mr. McKinley, may I say congratulations. I understand you and

Mayor Arlington are to be married."

"Yes, we are. Thank you."

Morgan left the municipal building, this time turning toward Gwen's home. Even if she had honored his request, that didn't mean he shouldn't tell her he was sorry for the way he went about it.

A few minutes later, he arrived on her front porch and knocked on the door. When it opened, it was Elizabeth Arlington who stood on the other side of the screen.

Morgan removed his hat. "Good morning, Mrs. Arlington. I was hoping to talk to Gwen."

"She isn't here. She left in her buggy some time ago. I understood she was going to your home."

"We must have crossed paths somewhere along the way."

Elizabeth opened the screen. "So you haven't already seen her this morning?"

"No, ma'am."

"Well, when you do, please talk some sense into her. I certainly couldn't do it. Mark my words. This is because of her father's influence. Filling that girl's head with all kinds of nonsense. Why else would she choose to live all alone in this town when she could have returned to the East and married long before this? And now she wants to throw away the best opportunity of her life. Well, you can imagine how upset I've been."

No, he couldn't understand. She wasn't making a great deal of sense, other than to let him know she was upset with Gwen. Another time he might have stayed and tried to sort it out. But right now all he wanted to do was find Gwen.

Morgan set his hat on his head. "If she returns, please tell her I'm looking for her and to wait for me here."

Shakespeare trotted along the road at a smart clip, and with each stride the horse took Gwen felt the pain in her chest increasing.

"I could be wrong, of course," Mrs. Cheevers had told Gwen a short while before, "but I think Mr. McKinley must have gone to New Hope with his overseer. I understand he and Mr. Doyle were in the study late last evening, and neither one looked too happy when I saw them this morning."

If Morgan was at the resort, Gwen had decided, then that's where she would go. She couldn't accomplish anything in her new office until this matter was settled between them. She must tell Morgan she couldn't marry him. She had to make him understand why.

She loved him. Loved him more than she'd thought possible.

But that wasn't reason enough to marry. Was it?

Perhaps he hadn't meant to come across the way he had.

But if he didn't mean it, he shouldn't have said it.

No, she had to go through with it. She had to break their engagement. She'd known all along it was better that she remain single. She *liked* her life just as it was.

Or at least the way it had been before Morgan came into it.

With a sigh, Gwen refocused her attention to the road ahead. They were nearing New Hope. Less than a mile to go. Her gaze went to the creek off the right side of the road.

"Too bad," she heard Harrison Carter whisper in her memory. *"I wanted to speak with him about some concerns the board has regarding the effect the spa will have on Crow's Creek. Once it joins the river a few miles south of here, it will become our problem."*

Gwen pulled on the reins and brought Shakespeare to a halt. Her gaze lifted to the forest that stood between her and New Hope. The bathhouse and pools had to be due north of where her buggy sat right now.

This time it was Fagan Doyle's voice she heard: *"One of the guards found dynamite not far from the bathhouse. In the forest just below it."*

She was looking at that forest.

What was the real reason Harrison Carter had been down there? Had he told her the truth or had he spoken lies? Was it possible Morgan was right about the commissioner?

She looped the reins around the dash rail and climbed out of the buggy. "I won't be long, Shakespeare," she said, giving the horse a pat on the neck. Then she picked her way down the slope to the creek.

The water was shallow near the bend, slipping and splashing over smooth stones that lined the bottom of the creek. Any other time she would have stopped to remove her shoes and stockings. But now curiosity pushed her across the stream without taking the time to do so. Once on the other side, it didn't take too long to find a narrow trail leading into the forest. She followed it, going from bright light to deep shadows in seconds. A few more steps and she was forced to stop to give her eyes time to adjust.

The air smelled of moss and pine and

blew cool upon her skin. Dried needles crunched beneath her feet as she moved deeper into the woods. Sometimes the trail became indistinct, and Gwen had to guess which way was north.

If Gwen was nowhere in town — and she wasn't; he'd looked everywhere — Morgan realized she must have gone for a drive in her buggy. If she'd only meant to go to his home or to the municipal building, she would have walked instead of hitching her horse to the buggy. Perhaps she'd gone to her father's ranch.

Morgan set out in his automobile to do the same. But when he reached the bridge over the river, something nudged him to head north instead. It made no rational sense, yet the impulse wouldn't be ignored. It was the same sort of feeling that had brought him to Idaho to build New Hope — that belief that God was directing him. Only this time it felt urgent.

He pressed hard on the accelerator with his right hand and drove toward New Hope. Ten minutes later, he saw Gwen's horse and buggy standing on the side of the road, Shakespeare doing his best to find shoots of grass to nibble on. Gwen was nowhere in sight.

Remembering the horse's distrust of automobiles, he braked to a halt while still a good distance away and killed the engine. Then he hopped over the side of the car and hurried forward. Shakespeare was startled by his approach but only tossed his head and took a few steps forward.

"Easy, boy. Easy." He took hold of the reins close to the bit. "Gwen! Where are you?" He heard nothing in reply.

Why would she have left Shakespeare here? Had he pulled up lame? Morgan led the horse forward. No sign of a limp.

"Gwen!"

Silence.

He turned in a circle, and that was when he saw a lady's handkerchief caught in some brush halfway down the slope. He moved toward it and picked it up. The delicate fabric was embroidered with the initials *G. A.*

Gwen.

His eyes searched the area once again and he realized where he was. If a person wanted to reach the New Hope bathhouse without being seen, this would be the way — right through the dense forest in front of him. Gwen must have realized the same thing.

He sprinted the rest of the way down the slope and crossed the creek in a few long jumps, water splashing up to dampen his trouser legs.

Gwen felt something poke her back between the shoulder blades a second before a man said, "Hold it right there."

She caught her breath.

"Lady, what're you doing here?"

This couldn't be one of Morgan's men. Anyone in Morgan's employ wouldn't put a gun to a woman's back. Heart racing, she said, "I . . . I'm here for information."

"What kind of information?"

"For the . . . for the story I'm writing for the newspaper."

The man moved to stand before her, the gun now pointed at her chest. She didn't know him, had never seen him before. He was short in stature and looked more like a banker than someone who would blow up a building. But something in his eyes, even through his spectacles, told her he would not hesitate to use the weapon if provoked.

Fear iced the blood in her veins.

He glanced down the trail in the direction she'd come. "You came here alone?"

"No," she lied. But it wasn't a lie. God was with her. *Help me, Lord.* She stood a bit straighter. "The dynamite isn't there. Your plans have been found out. The authorities are right behind me."

She'd hoped her words would make him retreat. Instead he moved closer, and his expression turned angry.

"Then I guess I'd better keep you close." He pressed the barrel of the gun against her breastbone. "Hadn't I?"

O God. Rescue me!

THIRTY-THREE

Morgan's mouth felt dry, his breathing shallow. Nothing in his life had struck terror in him like the sight of Gwen held captive at the point of a gun. He eased stealthily forward, circling off to the right, away from the trail he'd followed into the forest.

"Let's go," the man with the gun said, motioning with it to let her know the direction they were to take.

"You cannot think you will succeed." Gwen didn't move other than to lift her chin in defiance. "Mr. Carter will see that all the blame falls upon you."

Morgan allowed himself a grim smile. If she was afraid, she didn't show it.

"If you take me with you, I will only slow you down. You had best get away from here as quickly as you can."

The man stepped so close to Gwen that their noses almost touched. "If you don't move now, I'll shoot you where you stand."

Something in his voice told Morgan he might follow through with his threat. Time was running out.

Gwen's captor spun her around and gave her a push. A soft cry of complaint escaped her, and Morgan's response was quick and involuntary. He hurtled forward, tackling the man from behind and sending them to the ground. The gun went off.

God, no! But there was no time to see if the bullet had struck Gwen. First he had to make certain her attacker couldn't fire again.

They rolled across the trail and slammed into the trunk of a tree, Morgan grasping the man's right wrist with both hands, pounding it against the ground time and again until, at last, the gun flew free. The smaller man fought hard, but he didn't have much of a chance against Morgan's fury.

Morgan rose to his feet, dragging the smaller man up with him. Still holding the fellow's shirt with his left hand, he brought up his right fist, catching the assailant under the chin, knocking off his glasses at the same time. He let go of the shirt and followed with two more punches, one to the jaw, the next to his midsection. The other man fell back, his head hitting a tree on the way down. Morgan would have hauled him up again if not for Gwen.

"Stop, Morgan."

Breathing hard, he turned to look at her. There she stood, the gun now held in her trembling hands. He glanced back at the stranger. Out cold. Then he heard her small sob. In an instant he was beside her, taking the gun from her hands, drawing her to him, holding her there, never wanting to release her again.

If he had lost her . . .

She'd thought the man would kill her. For all her bravado, she'd thought she would die. But her silent cry for God to rescue her had been answered. God had sent Morgan. She'd thought she didn't want or need his protection. She'd been wrong.

"Shh," he whispered near her ear. "It's all right. I'm here. The danger is past. The guards at New Hope will have heard the shot. They'll be here soon."

His words proved prophetic almost at once. In the distance, she heard the sound of men's voices and dogs barking.

"Over here!" Morgan called without loosening his tight embrace.

It wouldn't have mattered if he'd released her. She would have stayed right where she was, her forehead pressed against his collarbone, her hands clutching his shirtfront.

"Morgan?"

"We're here, Fagan."

Gwen rolled her head to the side, enough to see Fagan Doyle and three other men — two of them with dogs on leashes — appear through the forest.

"Take this," Morgan said, handing the gun to Fagan. "And our friend on the ground there. He tried to kidnap Gwen and almost shot her. Tell Sheriff Winston that I think with the right incentive, he might tell us who hired him."

"And Miss Arlington? Is she —"

"She's fine. Just scared." Morgan's right hand stroked her hair. "We'll join you in town. My car's back on the road a ways. See that one of the men takes her horse and buggy back to town, will you?"

"Aye, I'll see to it, Morgan." Fagan's voice softened. "Sure and it's good you're all right, miss."

"Thank you, Mr. Doyle," she whispered.

Morgan continued to stroke small circles on her back with the flat of his left hand while rubbing his cheek against the top of her head until long after the other men had left the forest and silence had fallen over them like a comfortable blanket.

At long last Gwen pulled back far enough

that she could look into Morgan's eyes. "I was coming to find you to break our engagement. I didn't want anyone telling me what to do."

"And I was looking for you to apologize for last night." His smile was tender, his gaze understanding. "Forgive me."

"When I faced that man and his gun, I asked God to rescue me, and He sent you." She wondered if he understood the importance of that admission. She wasn't wholly self-sufficient. She needed others. She needed Morgan. And sometimes she even needed to be rescued.

He kissed her, brief touches upon her forehead, the tip of her nose, her lips. " 'And if one prevail against him, two shall withstand him; and a threefold cord is not quickly broken.' Me and you and God. The three of us together will be stronger, no matter the circumstances."

His image blurred as tears welled in her eyes.

"Gwen, I won't ever ask you to change. I fell in love with a woman who had the courage to leave her home in the East and begin a new life in Idaho. I fell in love with a woman who loves to teach music to children and who cares deeply about her neighbors. I fell in love with a woman with enough confidence to become the first woman mayor in Idaho, maybe in the nation. Don't break our engagement. Don't break my heart."

She sniffed and swallowed the lump in her throat.

"Say you'll marry me."

Although she wanted to respond, she couldn't seem to find her voice.

He kissed her again, this time a languid caress that indicated he was willing to stay right there in the forest for as long as it took her to believe him. And when their lips parted, he said, voice husky, "Madam Mayor, how about a vote of confidence for the man who loves you."

A cool breeze whispered through the trees and swirled around them, and as it moved on, she felt the last shred of uncertainty, the last iota of insecurity blow away with it. She believed him. She believed him and she loved him.

She smiled, hoping it would tell him more than would her words. "Yes, my love. I vote yes."

THE DAILY HERALD
Saturday, July 24, 1915

After a thorough investigation by the Crow County Sheriff, the *Daily Herald* has learned of the arrest of Mr. Harrison Carter, Esquire. He is charged with destruction of property and attempted kidnapping as an accessory before the fact. We have also learned that the subject's wife, Susannah Carter, has taken the couple's children and gone to stay with other members of her family in Illinois.

Prior to his arrest, Mr. Carter served on the Board of County Commissioners for four terms and was considered one of the leading members of Bethlehem Springs society.

The trial of Mr. Carter — as well as that of his associate, one Elias Spade — is set to begin in September.

THE DAILY HERALD
Monday, August 16, 1915

On Saturday afternoon, August 14, 1915, Miss Guinevere Arlington, daughter of Mr. Griffin Arlington of Crow County and Mrs. Elizabeth Arlington of New Jersey, was joined in marriage to Mr. Morgan McKinley. The ceremony was held in the Syringa Prayer Chapel on the grounds of the New Hope Health Spa, which is owned by the bridegroom.

The bride wore a delicate tea-length

gown of ivory satin and sheer lace and a tulle veil crowned with roses and beads. Her sister, Miss Cleopatra Arlington, attended the bride, and Mr. Fagan Doyle stood with the groom. Among the guests were the bride's parents; the groom's sister, Miss Daphne McKinley of Massachusetts; and Idaho senator William Rudyard of Boise.

After a honeymoon trip to California where, among other sights, they will visit the Panama-California Exhibition in San Diego, the couple will return to Bethlehem Springs, at which time the new Mrs. McKinley will resume her duties as the town's mayor.

FROM THE AUTHOR

Who says a woman can't be a mayor?

Dear Friends:

I hope you enjoyed meeting Gwen, Morgan, and the other residents of Bethlehem Springs as much as I have and that you will look forward, along with me, to returning to this small Idaho town again.

In *A Vote of Confidence,* Gwen becomes the mayor of Bethlehem Springs in 1915. The first woman mayor in America was, in fact, elected in Idaho, but the year was 1918, three years after my story. The woman's name was Laura Starcher, and she served as mayor of Parma, Idaho.

Here are two more facts that might interest you:

- In 1896, the woman's suffrage amendment to the Idaho Constitution was adopted, giving Idaho women the right to vote.

- Two women ran for the office of president of the United States well before my fictional character ran for mayor. Victoria Woodhull ran for the presidency in 1872 and Belva Lockwood in 1884, and again in 1888. Neither was permitted under the law to vote, but nothing in the law prevented them from running for office. Ironic, isn't it?

As I write this note to my readers, I am busy telling Cleo's story (Who says a woman can't be a wrangler?). Wait until you see who wins her heart! Look for *Fit To Be Tied* in late 2009.

I invite you to drop by my website (www.robinleehatcher.com) and my Write Thinking blog (robinlee.typepad.com) for the latest information available about me and my books.

Until the next time, "May the LORD keep watch between you and me when we are away from each other" (Genesis 31:49 TNIV).

In the grip of His grace,
Robin Lee Hatcher

The employees of Thorndike Press hope you have enjoyed this Large Print book. All our Thorndike, Wheeler, and Kennebec Large Print titles are designed for easy reading, and all our books are made to last. Other Thorndike Press Large Print books are available at your library, through selected bookstores, or directly from us.

For information about titles, please call:
  (800) 223-1244

or visit our Web site at:
  http://gale.cengage.com/thorndike

To share your comments, please write:
  Publisher
  Thorndike Press
  295 Kennedy Memorial Drive
  Waterville, ME 04901